More Than A Number

A Save Five Novel

Janet Vormittag

Janet Vormittag

Cover art by Kristina VanOss.

Author photograph by Lawrence Heibel of Heibel Media
www.heibelmedia.com

Printed in the United States of America.

ISBN: 978-1-939294-31-9

Janet Vormittag
P.O. Box 996
Jenison, MI 49429-0996
www.JanetVormittag.com

www.splatteredinkpress.com

Acknowledgments

I want to thank the members of the two writers groups who have given me support, feedback and encouragement. Neither group has an official name, but I call them the Monday Night Writers and the Sweet Potato Fries.

I'd also like to thank several friends for their help: Leonard Campbell, Melissa Eefsting, Tricia McDonald, Duncan Myers, Pat Pritchard, JoAnn Rachor, Gayle Thompson, Kristina VanOss and Wendy Wamser.

Thanks to Jeanine Buckner for the use of Reuben's Room Cat Rescue for my author photograph. A hug to Oscar who was willing to pose with me.

Dog 281 is the first book in the *Save Five* series.

When her dogs are stolen, Alison Cavera finds herself thrown into an underground world of dog theft and suspicious activities linked to the county animal shelter. Her determination to rescue Blue and Cody gives her the courage to take risks, do things she never knew she was capable of and helps her honor the memory of her son. Along the way, Alison meets Cooper Malecki, a handyman, vegan and animal advocate. As Alison opens herself up to new ways of helping animals, she also finds herself opening her heart.

Dog 281 is a story of redemption, love and rediscovery.

Dog 281
is available at
www.janetvormittag.com
www.amazon.com

Michigan

Lake Michigan

· Ludington

· Muskegon
· Grand Haven
· Grand Rapids

· Manchester
(SASHA Farm)

· Chicago

Chapter One

On days like this, I hate my job. A truck transporting cattle to slaughter overturned on US 10 west of Walhalla. I'll forever be haunted by images of crushed bodies, the smell of fresh blood, and the moans and bellowing of survivors. Several cows died on impact. Most had to be relieved of their pain with a gunshot to the head. At least one lucky cow escaped—two drivers reported seeing a cow trotting across the field into a nearby clump of trees. I was amazed anything had survived the tragedy, let alone be unhurt enough to run.

The dairy farmer who owned the cows sent someone by the name of Bill to catch the animal, but all he did was complain as the temperatures approached 90 degrees and the humidity made it feel like we were hiking through an Amazon jungle instead of the Manistee National Forest, not that I've ever been in an Amazon jungle. Sweat trickled down my face, and my cotton blouse stuck to my back as I trudged through the backcountry of Mason County. Flies buzzed marathon sprints around my face. I tried my best to knock them off course by waving my hands, but never once made contact.

"Call the farm when you find her. I'm outa here," Bill said.

"You're leaving?"

"Alison, I don't get paid enough for this."

"You expect me to keep looking?" Since I work at the county animal shelter, everyone seems to think an escaped cow falls under my jurisdiction. Why would anyone work at an animal shelter if they didn't hope to instill positive change? In the big picture, I hope I'm doing that, but day-to-day, it's tough.

"I don't care," he said.

"Maybe you can come back when it's cooler."

"Depends on what the boss says," he said. The owner of the cow expected the county to catch the wayward animal, but I had insisted they at least help, although Bill wasn't much help. Besides giving up, he insisted the cow wouldn't have gone far from the crash site and was adamant we look only within a half-mile radius of the overturned truck. We didn't find a thing. Not dried blood, fresh tracks, chomped grass or cow dung.

I watched Bill settle into his air-conditioned pickup and drive away. Waving good-bye, I had a gut feeling he wouldn't be back. After a short break that included an apple and a granola bar, I hiked down to the Pere Marquette River. The cow must need a drink, and it was the closest source of water. My reasoning was right. I spotted a cow pie at the water's edge, and it looked fresh: soft and smelly. From the river, her trail led up a slight bank and disappeared under low-hanging branches. Flies kept buzzing my face. My arms swung in constant motion swatting and brushing them from my hair. Trailing the cow was a better workout than a session at the local gym. When she finally left the stream, she headed into a meadow. I was able to follow the tracks for a while, but as the grass thickened I lost them. A tracker I was not!

Scanning the field, I got lucky. The black and white cow was standing in the shade of an oak tree. Not making any sudden movements, I slowly headed in her direction and approached from her backside. I was surprised to see that her tail was short, about a third of the length of a normal cow's tail. The stub swished occasionally, trying to knock bugs off her back. When I was about ten feet away, she turned her head and stared at me with big brown eyes. I could read the number on the yellow tag stapled to her ear—38.

"I'm not going to hurt you," I said in a soothing voice. She didn't appear scared. I had a length of yellow nylon rope and hoped to get it around her neck. When I could almost reach out and touch her hip, she started walking away. Not a fast walk, just fast enough to keep out of reach.

"Come on, honey. Make my life easy, okay? Just let me slip this rope around your neck." She continued to walk, and I picked up my pace. I lunged, tossing the rope at her head. It missed and slid to the ground as she took off at a trot. I grabbed the rope, recoiling it in my hand as I started a slow jog. She started to run. I couldn't keep up. I really needed to get in better shape.

I figured I had spooked her enough for one day. She had water and grass and most likely wouldn't venture far. I'd return with grain in the morning and try to lure her close enough to lasso her. When I made the decision to call it a day, I realized I didn't know which direction was the shortest route back to my car, but I knew one thing: I didn't want to walk back the way I had come. There had to be a shorter way.

I prided myself on my sense of direction and headed east. My goal was to find a road and hitch a ride to my car. As lost as I may have been, I knew four roads boxed me in. The only problem was that the box was a few miles wide, and I wasn't familiar with the terrain.

After hiking for about a half hour, I came across a two-track road. "Yahoo," I said out loud. It had to lead somewhere, plus it made walking much easier.

After ten more minutes of walking, I spotted a chain-link fence ahead of me. There were NO TRESPASSING signs every 25 feet on the fencing and a large sign on a gate that read TRESPASSERS WILL BE PROSECUTED. In the distance I could see a brown pole barn and what looked like doghouses, about a dozen of them. *How odd, out here in the middle of nowhere.* I didn't see anyone or any vehicles. My personal and professional curiosity was piqued. I checked the gate, and while it was locked, the chain holding it closed wasn't wrapped tightly. Skinny me could squeeze through. I continued toward the pole barn with all my senses on high alert.

I had heard rumors of dog fighting in the county but never had proof. Pit bulls, the breed most commonly used for fighting, were seldom brought into the shelter, and when one did come in, there were no scars or other evidence of fighting. Earlier in the year, I had attended a workshop on animal cruelty, and one of the sessions focused on the so-called sport.

They were doghouses—crude, homemade doghouses. The three-sided wooden boxes provided only a fraction of protection from the sun and rain. The stench of dog waste hung heavy in the summer heat. There were twelve shelters. Six of them housed dogs, each animal attached with a ten-foot length of chain. Heavy chains were wrapped around the dogs' necks several times—the weight, I recalled learning, built neck and upper body strength. The circle of ground around each dog, indicating the reach of his tether, was bare dirt littered with piles of dog feces. I expected the dogs to bark as I approached, but they didn't. Four hid in their boxes. One stood with a wide stance, holding its ground and showing no fear. Another growled, a deep warning rumble that convinced me not to go any closer. They were good-sized dogs. Pit bulls. They fit the description of fighting dogs—lean, muscular and scarred. Plus their ears and tails were missing. Cropped, no doubt. In a fight, ears and tails were an easy target, so it's best to get rid of them beforehand. Ears and tails also signaled a dog's mood; without them, body language wasn't easily detected.

Steering clear of the chained dogs, I made my way to the pole barn in search of more evidence, perhaps a fighting ring, equipment or paperwork identifying who was involved.

The structure didn't have windows, which protected the interior from prying eyes, but the top of each wall had a row of translucent plastic panels to allow natural lighting.

There were two doors—front and back. The back door was closest to the chained dogs. I tried the front door, and it was unlocked. Either the owners thought the secluded location and fence provided enough security, or they planned on returning soon.

I slipped inside and gave my eyes a couple of minutes to adjust to the dim light. Sure enough, in the middle of the floor was a blood-splattered, plywood-enclosed fighting area. Folding chairs were in disarray around the place as were a few small tables. There were weight scales, washtubs and buckets—dogs were washed before each fight to ensure nothing had been rubbed on their coats that would sicken the other dog if ingested.

At the far end of the room was a door to another part of the building. I slowly opened it and spotted the door leading to the dogs outside. The room looked like a gym with various pieces of equipment. The only thing I recognized was a treadmill that I knew was used to build endurance. Chicken wire stretched the length of the tread on both sides to keep the dog from hopping off. A cabinet held syringes, vials of drugs, chains and a stack of dog-fighting magazines.

While gazing around at all of this evidence, I heard the sound of an engine. I froze. Car doors opened and closed. I heard voices and the sound of the pole barn's front door opening. *Do I have time to get out the back door? Will there be someone out by the dogs?* I had yet to investigate the loft and sprinted to the narrow staircase leading to the upper area. The upstairs was used for storage and had an office. I squatted behind a file cabinet and tried to calm my nerves with deep breathing. From the sound of the voices, I thought there were at least two men. I strained my ears but couldn't make out what they were saying.

Someone came into the gym room. A few moments later I heard someone else bring in a dog. I heard what I guessed to be the treadmill starting and then a dog whining.

"Shut up," a man growled. Then I heard a slap and the dog was quiet. A door opened and closed, and I wondered if both men had left the room. I could hear the jingle of a leash and the grinding of the treadmill and assumed the dog was getting its workout. I didn't detect any sounds from the men. The quiet calmed me enough to notice my surroundings. It looked like the loft was built only over a portion of the building. A window looked over the lower main room. I stood up, tiptoed to it and looked over. I didn't see anyone. There was a small crack between one of the translucent panels and the siding, so I could see out the front side of the barn. Two men were talking by a dark-blue cargo van. One was white with dark brown hair, slender and young looking. The other man was dark-skinned and wore a baseball cap.

The van was situated so the building blocked the view of the gate I had squeezed through. I quickly climbed down the stairs. The dog turned its head and stared at me, not missing a step in its workout. I slipped outside and ran as quietly as I could to the gate where I had come in and wiggled back through the opening.

"Hey you!" I heard someone yell.

I ran. A vehicle started up and, by the sound of it, was heading in my direction. I veered off the road and ran into the woods. I continued to run, dodging low-hanging branches, jumping downed trees and ignoring the thorny bushes that tore at my clothes and skin. I ran until I could run no more. Stopping, I crashed to the ground and listened. All I heard were my gasps for air.

Chapter Two

It wasn't long before I heard an engine. I assumed it was the cargo van. Doors slammed. Voices shouted. *To run or hide,* that was the question. My pounding heart answered. I couldn't run any farther. Looking around I spotted a downed tree. I scrambled to the rotting trunk and, on the far side, scooped out a trench in the half-rotted leaves and moist soil. I crawled into the shallow trough and stretched out alongside the dead tree as if spooning with Cooper, my boyfriend. I pulled the dirt, leaves and nearby branches over me as best I could. My face was tucked in the crevice where log met earth—if I couldn't see the men, they couldn't see me. Right? I waited.

I heard the crunch of boots on the forest floor and the snapping of branches as at least two pairs of footsteps forged a path in my direction.

"I'm positive she went this way," I heard a male voice say. He was close. I held my breath.

"It was a broad?" another guy asked.

"I'm pretty sure," the first man said.

"Where the hell did she go?"

"I don't know. She ran in this direction."

"Well, she's not here. Now what?"

"Mel's gonna kill us if we don't find her."

"No shit! What do you suggest?"

"Keep looking."

The conversation was followed with a stretch of silence. There was a faint rustling of clothes, and then I smelled cigarette smoke. I strained with my whole being to hear any clue of what the men were doing. I felt like a dog—cocking an ear in their direction to hear better. I imagined them searching in every direction with a focused gaze. I expected a hand to grab me at any moment. I had no choice but to hold my ground—or rather my trench. It reminded me of the time I had hidden in the grass outside Kappies Kennel when the teenage partiers interrupted my midnight visit to the animal dealer. The partiers didn't know I was hiding in the weeds within feet of their moonlit pizza party. But this was more serious. My gut told me these dog guys meant business.

Finally, they retreated, sounding like a herd of elephants trampling through the underbrush. I smiled, they should have sounded like a herd of cows since it was a cow who got me into this predicament. Their woodsy noises grew distant. I waited for their vehicle to start and finally it did. I listened to it drive away. Then came the mind game—did they *both* leave? Or was one still waiting for me to come out? How long should I wait till I dared make a move? I decided an hour. As quietly as I could, I pulled my wrist within eyesight. It was 1:23. I was hungry. Mosquitoes were feasting on my blood. It felt like spiders were crawling on my ankles, exploring the inside of my pants. I imagined grubs and other creepy crawlers wiggling beneath me. My nose filled with the earthy aroma of the forest floor. Then I thought of snakes.

It was 1:24.

Think of something else.

Cooper was my guilty pleasure. Whenever I couldn't sleep, which was often, my thoughts always turned to him. Our story played like a looped video in my head.

I had moved to my grandmother's farm in Pearline, Michigan, after my son died and my marriage disintegrated. Grams had hired someone to help on the farm after Gramps died—a guy named Cooper. Shortly after moving to the farm, my dogs, Cody and Blue, were stolen. I found Cody the night I broke into Kappies Kennel. If not for Cooper, I would have never found Blue—the beagle had been sold to a company that used dogs for research experiments.

Birds started fluttering about—a sign that all was normal in the woods? I didn't dare get up, but the tension eased. Eased enough to notice the moisture of the earth dampening my clothes.

1:43

14

Cooper had traded his freedom for Blue's. While Cooper is in prison in California, Blue sleeps on my bed every night. Cooper was accused of setting fire to a horse slaughterhouse and took a plea bargain instead of standing trial for arson.

Tears filled my eyes at the thought of Cooper in a prison cell. One of the reasons he didn't want a trial was because of what he had done to help me find Blue. He didn't want to answer the questions that would come up if anyone seriously looked into his stay in Michigan. He was a suspect in the break-in that saved Blue, but the cops had no proof.

1:52

The urge to itch my ankles became unbearable. Ants? Spiders? Resist. Resist. Resist. I bit my lower lip hoping pain would divert the desire. When I tasted blood, my ankles ceased to exist ... for a second. I heard dead leaves crinkling, not loudly, and suspected a scurrying chipmunk.

The first time I had seen Cooper, I was getting out of my car at the farm. He walked up from the barn, introduced himself and offered to help unload my car. It was love, maybe lust, at first sight, but I wouldn't admit it to myself let alone anyone else. I was rude, mean and acted immature when he was around.

1:59

Because my involvement in Blue's rescue slid under the radar, Cooper and I don't have direct correspondence. His grandmother became our go-between. I send her letters and she relays information when she visits or receives letters from him. She sends me long letters detailing his prison life and whatever tidbits he tells her on her visits. She also writes a lot about his childhood. My thoughts drifted to our last night together ...

2:19

Five more minutes. Then what? Find my car. Call Cindi—my cell phone was in the car. I vowed it would be the last time I left it in the car. From now on, I would be one of those people who was inseparable from technology.

2:23

I lifted my head and peeked around. I didn't see anyone. I sat up and brushed dirt, spiders and leaves from my hair and clothes. Next, I scrunched down my socks, examined my ankles and gave each a good fingernail scratching. It felt wonderful. I stood. When all remained quiet, I silently crept in the direction opposite from the one the men had taken. After trudging through the woods for an hour, I came to a cornfield. Soon I spotted a house, which I recognized. My car was about a half mile farther.

Back at my car, I called Cindi, my boss at the animal shelter. After listening to my story, she told me to come back to the shelter. In the meantime, she'd call the sheriff and get some help.

Three hours had passed since I first looked at my watch while hiding by the log. Sheriff Marc VanBergen had obtained a search warrant and assembled a team of five—six, including me—to investigate the barn. It seemed impossible that Sheriff VanBergen trusted my judgment--it wasn't that long ago that I sat opposite him at a table while he grilled me about the fire at Kappies. Now I was a county employee whose word carried weight.

"You didn't get the license plate number? Not even a partial?" he asked.

"No. All I saw was the front and side of the van. It didn't have any windows on the side and looked like it had a Ford logo, but I couldn't say for sure. There were two men—one white, the other dark-skinned, but I couldn't tell if he was Hispanic or African American. The white guy had short dark-brown hair and was skinny. He looked young. The dark skinned guy wore a baseball cap that hid his face."

"Was there a logo or name on the cap?"

"I didn't notice."

"What were they wearing?"

"Good question. I don't know ... work clothes? They weren't wearing suits, that I can say."

"Think about it, maybe something will come to you."

"When I was hiding in the woods they did drop a name. One of the guys said something like, 'If we don't find her, Mel is going to kill us.'"

"Mel? Good. At least that's a start."

VanBergen had an aerial photograph, about a year old, of the section of the county where I had been lost. The barn couldn't have been any more secluded—a perfect place for anything illegal. The photo didn't show any doghouses.

16

"You sure this is the place?" VanBergen asked.

I studied the terrain. "This is where I parked my car." I pointed to a place on the map. "I walked through this field until I came to this river," I said, tracing the route with my finger. "I followed it for a bit and came out into this meadow. That's where the cow was. I continued in this direction until I found the two-track—it's not on this map, but it wasn't far from the barn. The fence isn't on this map either."

VanBergen was familiar with the property. He said there used to be an old farmhouse there until it had burned down a few years ago, the result of some kids starting a bonfire too close and it got out of control. As far as he knew, the barn wasn't being used for anything. He had tried to find the owner, but county records revealed the property had been sold to a corporation from Chicago. He hadn't been able to find a phone number for it.

"There's only one road that leads to the barn. We'll take three vehicles. I have help on standby if we need it," he said. "We're just going to take a look around."

We climbed into the vehicles. I rode with Cindi in the shelter's pickup truck. We were the last in the parade—first was the sheriff's SUV, then a county cruiser.

We drove slowly down the dirt driveway. When we got to the barn, the cargo van was gone. The sheriff knocked on the barn door. No one answered. The door was locked.

"Let's check out back," he said.

We walked around to the back of the building. The dog coops were still there, but five of the dogs were gone. The remaining dog was the one that had been hiding in its coop when I had been there earlier. It was still hiding.

"It looks like they left in a hurry," VanBergen said.

"Wonder why they left a dog."

"How many pits can you fit in one van? They probably didn't have room," Cindi said. She walked toward the red-coated dog who cowered in the back of its coop.

"Hey, big boy, how ya doin'?" she cooed. She took a dog biscuit from her pocket and tossed it to him. The dog ignored the peace offering. She moved closer. "Come on, Red. We're your friends."

Red didn't move but growled a warning. Cindi backed off.

"Do you want the catch pole?" I asked. The extendable aluminum rod with its loop on the end to slip over an animal's head was invaluable when working with aggressive dogs.

"Yeah, I do. I don't think I should trust him. Can you get it?"

As I left to get the pole, the sheriff and his men turned their attention to the barn. I saw them enter the back door—apparently someone forgot to lock it.

Cindi deftly got the loop around Red's neck. The dog acted subdued when cornered. She tugged on the pole, and the dog got up and took a few steps.

"It's a female," Cindi said. "Maybe breeding stock."

While Cindi restrained the dog, I sweet-talked her and was able to get close enough to unclasp the chain from a stake in the ground that tethered her in place.

"See if she'll let you get it off her neck too," Cindi suggested.

"Really?" I wasn't so sure about getting that close.

"Fighting dogs aren't usually people-aggressive. They're just taught to hate other animals."

I tried to read the dog's intentions. Her head hung low and her gaze was forward. I could see the ripple of ribs under her dust-covered coat. She had a few scars, none of them open.

"Hey, girl, let us help you." I reached out and touched her back. Red trembled. I ran my hand along her back up to her neck and took a step closer. The chain was triple hung around her neck and clipped in place.

"The loop is in the way. I need to loosen it."

"Be careful."

I gently moved the loop and unclipped the chain. I lifted one end of the chain and gently unwrapped it from around her neck. "That's got to feel better," I whispered. No response.

"There, she's free," I said, stepping back. Cindi tightened the loop. I offered the dog another treat, but she refused it. Cindi tugged on the pole and Red took a few more steps. As she walked Red to the truck, I went inside the barn.

"What's missing from when you were here before?" VanBergen asked.

I walked around. "I didn't have a lot of time to look, but this cabinet had vials of drugs and other medical stuff." The cabinet doors stood open and the shelves were empty. "This area had exercise equipment—it looked homemade." It was gone.

"They did leave this," VanBergen said, kicking a wooden contraption that looked homemade.

"What is it?" I asked. I hadn't noticed it before.

"A rape stand."

"What is *that*?"

"A female dog that's in heat is tied to it so a male can mount her."

"You're kidding me."

"Nope. They muzzle the male dog so he doesn't rip her apart, but I guess the mating urge trumps killing."

In the upstairs office, the drawers of the file cabinets stood open and barren.

"They left in a hurry, but they were thorough," VanBergen said. His crew was searching every inch for clues. "Did you hear them say anything?"

"No, I was too far away."

Not much had been removed from the big room. The fight pit stood in the middle with tables and seating intact.

"Definitely a fighting operation," Cindi said when she saw the blood splattered arena. "Did you find any names? Any leads to who's behind this?"

VanBergen shook his head. "Not yet, but we're still looking."

"I don't understand the mentality of people who get their kicks from watching dogs try to kill each other," she said. "I always thought it was a big-city problem. I can't believe it's made its way here."

Chapter Three

I reflected on the day as I soaked in an Epsom salt bath. It had started with one goal—to catch a cow. Not only had I failed at that, but now a whole new problem existed. My muscles ached from the walking and running and tension. My arms were scratched and itching from mosquito bites. Why hadn't I thought of taking insect repellant? My ankles had exploded into a mass of red welts.

Blue, Cody and Shadow snoozed on the bathroom floor. All three dogs jumped to their feet at the same time and headed into the bedroom. Their behavior made me pause, but then I heard what they heard—Grams' car. A minute later she came into the house.

"I'm up here taking a bath!" I shouted.

"Did you have dinner yet?"

"Yeah, but I could eat again. Give me 15 minutes."

We were unlikely roommates—Grams in her 80s and me close to five decades younger. I grew up in Chicago but spent a lot of time during summer vacation with my grandparents. As a little girl, I often fantasized about living on their farm year round. I never thought that, as an adult, the dream would come true. It wasn't quite how I imagined it though. In my fantasy world, Gramps was alive and teaching me the secrets of farming and how to fix my bike when it broke. In reality, his death was the reason I made the move.

By the time I got downstairs, Grams had made us each a salad.

"I stopped by Frank's Bakery. Look at this," she said as she held out a loaf of bread. I read the label: organic whole-wheat sunflower bread. Grams had gone off the deep end when it came to eating healthy and was determined to pull me in with her.

"Sounds delicious," I said. It did sound tasty, but I would have been happy with sliced white bread at half the price.

We sat at the dining room table. It felt lonely, just the two of us. How long did it take to get over missing someone like Gramps? For a while, Cooper had filled the empty chair and kept us too busy to dwell on our loss.

"How was your day?" Grams asked.

I told her about my failure to catch the cow.

"Wish I were younger. I'd go out and catch her. Take apples and grain next time. That'll bring her around."

I assured her I would do exactly that. "I felt bad, she was missing part of her tail."

"Probably docked," Grams said.

"Docked?"

"Some dairy farmers think the tail is dirty and causes health problems for the cows so they amputate it, but I think it has more to do with the farmer not wanting to get swatted with the tail while they're hooking up the milking machine."

"That's mean. The poor cow was covered with flies and couldn't get rid of them." Then I told her about the pit bulls. "They left one behind. Cindi thinks they didn't have room for it in the van, but who knows."

"Where is it now?"

"At the shelter."

"That's not a good place for a dog who has been taught to fight."

"I know. Right now she's the only dog in the quarantine room. I'm not sure what's going to happen to her. We'll temperament test her tomorrow. If she's too aggressive, we might have to put her down." I couldn't believe my own words. Euthanasia, once so foreign to me, was now routine. Too many animals. When would people *get* it?

"You could bring her here. We have the kennel in the barn where we could isolate her. I bet I could bring her around."

"I bet you could too. I'll see how she does tomorrow and suggest it to Cindi." Grams had a way with animals. "Do you know anyone named Mel?" I asked.

"Mel?"

"I overheard one of the guys at the barn say something about a Mel."

"Let me think. There's Mel Ortiz from church."

"How well do you know him?"

"I met him once, but I really don't know him. I'm in a Bible study class with his wife."

"Think of anyone else?"

"I know Mel Crawford. His wife is in my gardening club. They're summer people—from Chicago I think."

"Either one strike you as the type who would be involved in dog fighting?"

"Not really."

"Between the two, I'd bet on Crawford, only because he's from Chicago. Dog fighting is popular in big cities."

"What are you going to do?" Grams asked.

"We're meeting in the morning with the sheriff to come up with a plan."

I cleared the table and helped Grams wash dishes.

"Did you see you had some mail?" she asked.

"Mail? No, I didn't. I was in a hurry to get out of my clothes." On the table in the hallway sat two letters: one with a return address of Cooper's grandmother and the other from my parents in Chicago. I felt like a schoolgirl getting a note from a boyfriend. "It's from Grandma Lucia," I said. I sat on the couch and ripped it open. "He has a release date," I shouted. "He'll be out in two months, but he'll probably be in a halfway house and then on probation."

"Which means he probably won't be able to leave California," Grams said.

"For how long?"

"I don't know."

"We'll have to go visit him. When was the last time you saw Lucia?" Lucia and Grams were childhood friends.

"I can't even remember," Grams said. "It's been years."

22

The second letter was an invitation.

"I got one, too," Grams said.

My parents were celebrating their 30th wedding anniversary and decided to host a last-minute dinner party at their house on Chicago's north side on Saturday. Mom apologized for the late notice and hoped we could rearrange our schedules to attend.

"You want to go?" I asked.

"Do I have a choice?"

"At least we can go together. We'll have to spend the night. I know Cindi would come over and take care of the animals. I haven't been back for a visit since I moved here."

"Do we have to spend the night?"

"It's too far to drive there and back in one day. Plus, we'll be drinking at the party. They have plenty of room at the house for us ... she even wrote that in the invitation." With that, I said good night and let the dogs out one last time, all five of them. Elvis and Sinatra belonged to Grams. They accepted any newcomer into the pack with only a sniff of a hello. Grams often took care of neighbors' pets while they vacationed, so the singing duo were used to other dogs coming and going.

Up in my room, I smeared calamine lotion on my irritated skin. Grandma Lucia had included a letter that Cooper had mailed to her, which I hadn't read downstairs. Just seeing Cooper's handwriting made me happy. He asked about family and friends and wrote that he missed everyone. He was reading *The World Peace Diet* by Dr. Will Tuttle. I made a mental note to buy the book. Knowing we were reading the same book at the same time made me feel connected to him. Kept us in sync. With Cooper's letter tucked under my pillow and the dogs sleeping on their beds, I turned out the light.

The next morning I arrived at the shelter earlier than usual, but Animal Control Officer Jason Bentley still beat me there. He had the coffee brewing and bagels ready to be toasted. Jason had taken yesterday off and missed all the excitement. I found him in the quarantine room.

"Where did this girl come from?" he asked. The kennel door stood open and the pit stood next to him chewing on a dog biscuit.

Jason always carried a baggie full of treats, making him an instant friend to most canines. As soon as Red saw me, she turned and slinked into the kennel and crouched in the far corner.

"What did you do to her?" Jason asked.

"Nothing. Honest." I filled him in on what he had missed the day before and explained that the pit never showed Cindi or me any sign of friendship. "I can't believe she took a treat from you." I tried to coax the dog to come to me, but she wouldn't budge. I'm a dog person, dogs are supposed to like me.

"Why don't you leave the room? I'll see if she comes back out when you're gone," Jason suggested.

I went and got a cup of coffee. The quarantine room had a window so I quietly returned and peered in. Sure enough, Red was out of the kennel and next to Jason. I heard Cindi come in, and I put my finger to my lips to shush her. I pointed to the window and mouthed the word watch.

She looked in, turned and gave me an inquisitive look. I shrugged my shoulders, opened the door and went back in. Once again the dog retreated into her kennel. This time Jason clipped the kennel door closed, and we went into the hallway.

"What's up with that?" I asked him. "You'd think she'd be scared of men, not women."

"Maybe she's never been around a woman."

"Maybe. I've never seen a dog scared of me and not you." I felt a little miffed. Dogs liked me. Why didn't this one?

"She needs to be temperament tested. Can you do it?" Cindi asked Jason.

I left him alone with Red and got started cleaning, feeding and watering everyone. I saw Jason walk Red on a leash into the kennel area to see how she reacted to other dogs.

A half hour later he gave us a report. "She's not food aggressive, and she prefers to avoid other dogs rather then pick a fight, which is good. I still don't know what to think of her not liking either of you. She likes me."

"After her quarantine, do you think she could be in a kennel in Ward B?" Cindi asked. Ward B was where strays were held for the state-required four to seven days.

"I think so. We can try."

"Are we going to try and rehabilitate her for adoption? Or should we try and place her in a sanctuary? Grams offered to bring her to the farm and work with her."

"It's too early to make a decision. She can stay where she is for now. Jason, you take care of her, since she likes you," Cindi said.

When we finished the morning chores, I left to check on the wayward cow once again. Armed with a backpack filled with cow snacks—apples and grain—and a cow halter and lead rope, I set off. This time I doused myself with bug repellant and put my cell phone in my pants' pocket.

The walk to the stream where I had last seen Cow 38 gave me time to think about the men with the pit bulls. The only real leads were the blue van and the name Mel. I brainstormed ideas: search for the van, track down guys with the name Mel, maybe try to sell a pit bull and see who was interested, contact veterinarians in the area and ask if they have clients with pit bulls, check the local pet supply store and see if anyone had bought large quantities of dog food. None of the options sounded real promising.

There was fresh cow dung by the creek in the same place that I had found it the day before. It seemed that cows were creatures of habit. I headed toward the meadow taking the path of least resistance, avoiding thickets of prickly bushes and swampy areas. I spotted the cow lying in the shade of a tree chewing her cud, contented as could be. She stood as I approached. I got the snacks out of my backpack.

"Look what I brought for you," I cooed. Coming from a dairy farm, I wondered if she'd ever had snacks before. She stared as I slowly walked in her direction. Flies swarmed her. Her stub of a tail was in constant motion trying to swish them away. Occasionally she'd stomp a foot to knock the irritating buggers off. At least I hoped her foot-stomping was due to the bugs and not a signal for me to back off.

I tossed her an apple. My aim was off and it landed about two feet in front of her. I tossed another. It hit the first one and bounced a little closer. I felt like I was playing bocce ball, a horseshoe-like game. She ignored both pieces of fruit. I opened the plastic bag of grain, grabbed a handful of it, and let it sift through my fingers and fall back into the bag. Maybe the sound or the sweet smell of oats and molasses would get her attention. Did cows have a good sense of smell? I didn't know. I backed off a few feet and squatted down on my heels. Maybe she needed some space. After a couple minutes, her head lowered, and she took three steps and snatched up the first apple. She chewed so delicately that I could almost taste the sweet juices of the red delicious apple in my own mouth. She must have liked it, because she took another step to reach the second apple.

"Do you want more?" I stood up and tossed her another one, this time intentionally making it a short throw. She took another step forward to retrieve it. She liked apples. Too bad I'd only brought six. With the fourth apple in my outstretched hand, I walked toward her slowly, but deliberately. She read my bluff, turned and walked away.

"Damn it," I said in a cheery voice so she couldn't read my frustration. She continued to walk, and I trailed at a distance. She followed the tree line, staying in the shade. She occasionally stopped, turned her head and looked at me.

"I'm still here," I told her. "Want some grain?" Apparently not. It took about ten minutes for me to realize that I wasn't going to catch her by trailing behind her. I didn't want to push her too far from her home base by the creek, so I decided to call it a day.

Since I was close to the barn where the dogs had been, I decided to continue on and see if anyone was there. A slight breeze was coming from the west and as I got close to the two-track, the faint odor of decaying flesh—a putrid smell that's instantly recognizable—penetrated the fresh scent of morning air.. Like a hound dog, I put my nose to the wind. The smell came from the opposite direction of the barn. It warranted investigation. It didn't take long to discover the reason for the odor: dogs. Some of the bodies had been buried, but had been unearthed by wildlife looking for a meal. Others were tossed in a heap, a mangled mound of decaying carcasses.

The stench got the better of me. My eyes watered, and my stomach twisted in turmoil. I leaned against a tree and heaved up breakfast. After I collected myself, I covered my nose and mouth with my shirt to keep out the disgusting odor. There were at least twenty corpses—an accurate count was impossible. Not all were pit bulls. Some had long hair like a collie or golden retriever. There were also what looked to be cats. I saw tails, paws and sunken-in heads.

I pulled out my phone and took photos. I sent one to Cindi and then called her.

"Did you see the photo? It's a damn graveyard, about a mile from the barn. The two-track ends here."

She said she'd send Jason and for me to meet him by the barn. She recommended that we document the scene and then bury the animals—this time in deeper graves.

The task was gruesome. Jason brought masks and offered me a jar of Vicks VapoRub.

"Put some under your nose. It'll help with the smell." Jason took a couple dozen photos and a video of the scene.

"Too bad you can't record the stench," I said.

When I got home later, I peeled off my clothes in the laundry room, poured extra detergent and some bleach in the washing machine, and set the dial for the longest possible wash cycle. I took a long hot shower and scrubbed and scrubbed my skin. I could still smell death, but at least it was fainter. I used a sea-salt solution in a neti pot to rinse my nostrils of the last remnants of the stench.

With a change of clothes and wet hair, I headed to the Farmer's Co-op. It was the least expensive place to buy pet food. After introducing myself to the young man behind the counter, I asked about any special orders for dog food or any large purchases.

"I don't handle orders. You'll have to talk to my boss and he ain't in right now. I can leave him a note, if ya want."

"Sure, do that. What's his name?"

"Melvin. Melvin Sumpter."

The name caught me by surprise. "On second thought, don't leave a note. I'll stop by later. When do you expect him?"

"He had a family emergency in Kalamazoo. He'll be back Monday morning."

Chapter Four

Two things popped into my head when I heard the name Melvin Sumpter and that he was out-of-town until Monday. First, his absence was an invitation to pay a visit to his house. Second, my friend Erica who lives in Kalamazoo could check out Sumpter, if need be.

Back at home, I looked up addresses for the three Mels: Melvin Sumpter, Mel Ortiz from Grams' church, and Mel Crawford whose wife was in Grams' gardening club. Tomorrow would be a Mel day.

I needed to clear my head, and the best way to do that was a horseback ride. I went to the barn and whistled, and Dappy came running along with Chester and MaryLu, my grandparents' horses. I slipped the bridle on Dappy's head and led him from the pasture. Using the fence as a ladder, I slid onto his back. I loved riding bareback. I loved the feel of oneness that comes with the intimate connection of soft, warm muscles. A nudge of the heels and a "let's go" was all it took. The entire pack of five dogs joined us for the run.

The long days of summer were shortening. There was a crispness to the air. Crows cawed. It was time to just be. A time to block the negatives of the day and dwell on the now.

Grams was feeding the barn cats when I returned. I gave Dappy a rubdown and put him back in the pasture. The first thing he did was get down on his front knees and gently roll onto his back. He wiggled his body back and forth, massaging it on the earth. Then he stood and sauntered to the water trough.

"How was the ride?" Grams asked.

"Perfect. Exactly what I needed. It's been a day."

"I worried about you taking the job at the shelter. It's not easy work, and it never ends."

"I know, but Cindi needed help. I didn't think it would be this bad. Some days are worse that others."

Evenings had become routine for Grams and me. We cooked together, ate together and usually stayed in for the night. We filled the time with conversation, card or board games, television, old movies and books. Tonight was no exception.

The next morning I helped Cindi with the shelter chores and then went on the hunt for Mel. Mel Crawford was first on my list. His wife was definitely into gardening. Instead of grass, their yard was ablaze with black-eyed Susans, purple coneflowers, hibiscus and petunias. A grove of sunflowers towered at least six feet tall. A trumpet vine, with its orange trumpet-shaped flowers calling out to hummingbirds, entwined a split-rail trellis. The yard was a butterfly and bird haven. None of the plants looked trampled or peed on by dogs. I knocked on the door, and a tall thin man answered.

"Hi, I'm Alison. Are you Mel?"

"I am."

"Is your wife home? My grandmother is in her gardening club, and I have a favor to ask her."

"She's out back. Come in." The house was spotless. Mel did not fit my stereotype of someone who fought dogs. He was articulate, well-dressed and lived in a pristine home in a good neighborhood. He led me through the house and opened a sliding glass door for me to go outside.

"Susan, there's someone to see you."

My pretense was asking advice on what type of bulbs to buy Grams for fall planting. After talking bulbs, I steered the conversation to pets. Susan said they had never been pet people.

"Mel has allergies. I don't even bring cut flowers in the house," she said.

She asked me about Chicago—we had that in common. But neither of us had truly lived in the Windy City. We were both suburbanites. I knew dog fighting was popular among city gangs and more organized crime syndicates, but as far as I knew, it hadn't found its way to the well-to-do residential neighborhoods.

I crossed Mel Crawford off my list.

Next was Mel Ortiz, who lived in downtown Ludington. When I knocked on his door, a woman answered. After I introduced myself as Grams' granddaughter, she introduced herself as Mel's wife, Mildred. Mel wasn't home. She offered me coffee, which I accepted. My gut said her husband wasn't the Mel I was looking for either. Loving husband, father of four, and grandfather of ten. He didn't fit the profile. He was no longer a high priority, but I wouldn't cross him off my list until I met him face-to-face.

Next up was Melvin Sumpter. He lived south of Ludington in a rural area, which made him a better suspect. There were no signs of life when I pulled into his driveway. I knocked on the door. I heard a dog barking, but it didn't sound like it came from within the house, more like out back. When my knock went unanswered, I walked around the house to the backyard and saw a detached garage and a red pole barn. The dog, a German shepherd, was in an outside run with a large doghouse painted white with green trim—it matched Mel's house. The dog continued to bark, but calmed down when I approached and asked how he was doing. His water bowl was clean and filled with water. The kennel was spotless.

"Someone's taking good care of you," I said. He tilted his head, trying to understand what I said.

The pole barn had a paddock with electric fencing. I didn't see any horses, but from the smell, which I loved, I knew that's what the barn housed.

Disappointment settled in. I really thought Sumpter was my guy, but I sure didn't see any evidence.

When I returned to the shelter, Cindi gave me the names and addresses of two people who called about feral cats. Two months ago we had implemented a new policy of not accepting feral cats. Bringing them to the shelter was a death sentence. No one adopts unsocialized cats, and we were tired of killing healthy animals whose only crime was being born outside and not kissing up to

30

people. By law, the county shelter had to take in stray dogs, but it didn't have to do anything with cats.

When we quit accepting ferals, we started a trap-neuter-return program. The goal was to let the feral cats live out their lives, but to stop them from reproducing—cats are prolific breeders.

Volunteers made the TNR program possible. They live-trapped the cats and took them to a veterinarian we contracted with to give them a quick health exam before performing the spay/neuter surgery. While anesthetized, the vet cut a quarter-inch off the tip of the cat's left ear. Ear tipping was the universal sign of a sterilized feral cat.

The cats were kept a couple days after their surgery and then returned to where they had been caught. Most people resisted the idea at first. It was my job to educate and convince them that TNR was the right thing to do.

"One of the women sounded open to TNR. She was feeding several cats, but the numbers were getting out of control. An older tabby was limping, which prompted the call," Cindi said.

"And the other caller?"

"She has a stray cat killing birds at her feeder. It might not be feral. She wants it out of her yard."

It didn't take long to convince the first woman to let volunteers set traps in her backyard to catch the cats. I explained the vacuum effect—if you remove the cats, sooner or later the empty habitat attracts cats from neighboring areas.

"If there's shelter and food, more cats will come," I said. She had an old barn, trees and open fields, perfect environments for mice, chipmunks and birds. Plus, she felt sorry for the homeless felines and didn't mind feeding them.

"On any given night there's at least 14 coming to feed," she said. "If I sit on the picnic table with a can of food, two of the kittens will come to me and eat out of my hand."

"If we get them fixed, would you want to take the kittens in the house?"

She hesitated for a second and then said maybe. "My husband never allowed me to have animals in the house, but he passed last year," she said.

I considered a "maybe" as good as a "yes" when it came to cute, irresistible fluff balls. "I'm sorry to hear about your loss. My Dad was like that, too. Luckily, I had grandparents who loved animals and had a house full. Kittens are wonderful companions. They'll keep you entertained. We can get them fixed and vaccinated."

"That sounds wonderful."

"Cindi mentioned one of the cats is hurt?"

"There's a big orange tabby who is limping on a back leg."

"We'll take care of him. Probably a wound from a fight. Once they're fixed, the males won't be fighting over the ladies, so it should be quieter."

I left a message with Carol, our volunteer who loved trapping cats, telling her that we had a project for her. Carol's mission in life was to "fix" every feral cat in the county.

The second woman, Linda Levecca, lived in the country. Her driveway wrapped around the house and led me between the back of the house and a big red barn. She had three bird feeders and a birdbath in the backyard. She came marching out of the house before I even got out of the truck.

"Are you here for the cat?"

"I am."

"Someone must have dropped it off. They're always dumping animals here. Usually my daughter takes care of them for me, but she's not here. I want it gone. It slinks under the bushes and waits for the mourning doves to feed on the ground. I can't stand to watch another dove be killed."

"Is there just the one cat?"

"One too many."

"Can you get close to it?"

"I never tried."

"I'll set a live trap near the feeders with some cat food in it. Call me when the cat's caught. I'll leave a sheet that you can use to cover the trap after the cat's inside. He'll calm down if he's covered. Can you do that?"

"I suppose so."

She watched as I baited the trap with a can of shredded chicken in gravy. I heard a noise in the bushes off to my side and spotted a black and white cat with odd markings. He was mostly black but had white feet and a white head. The black on his face gave the impression that he was sporting a Groucho Marx mustache.

"Here, kitty, kitty," I cooed as I got up. Groucho took off in the opposite direction. "Was that him?" I asked.

Linda hadn't seen the cat, but did say the one she wanted gone was black and white. I gave her the sheet and a business card with my name and number.

"He's interested in the food. I think we'll catch him soon. Call as soon as he's inside, even if it's late. We don't want him sitting in the trap too long. That's my cell number so call anytime."

She assured me she would.

Back at the shelter I checked on Red. She still cowered at the sight of me. I tried winning her over with a can of savory beef tips, but meat didn't convince her to come out. I gave her the food anyway hoping it would soften her fears.

"I'm not giving up on you," I said.

I reviewed two adoption applications and called their references. Both applications checked out good. Two more dogs were going to new homes.

Before heading home, the kennels needed to be spot cleaned, litter boxes scooped and water and food bowls filled. Sometimes we were lucky enough to have volunteers help with the manual labor. Not today. Cindi and I worked together on the cleaning and feeding, which made for the perfect time to talk about the day. We were almost done when we heard the buzzer indicating that someone had come into the lobby. Before we could react, the door to the kennel opened.

"It's just me," Sheriff VanBergen said.

Cindi gave me a look. I shrugged my shoulders and nodded my head in agreement. VanBergen seldom came to the shelter. While he portrayed the big tough cop on the outside, on the inside his heart was a marshmallow—soft, tender and sweet. He couldn't handle seeing the homeless animals.

"Can you wait ten minutes? We're almost done," Cindi said.

"No problem. I'll wait in your office, if that's okay."

"Sure. There's pop in the refrigerator. Help yourself."

We stepped up our pace and finished in five minutes. VanBergen was drinking a Coke when we came in the office.

"Does this involve me or can I leave?" I asked.

"Stay. I think you'll want to hear this."

I took a seat next to him and Cindi sat at her desk.

"We got a call this morning from a hiker in the Manistee National Forest, a few miles from the farm where you found the dogs. He said there was a burned out van and it looked like there was a body inside." VanBergen took a sip of his Coke.

"Was it the blue van?" I asked. It had to be. Why else would he be telling us?

"Yup. And there wasn't a body inside. There were *two* bodies inside. Both had been shot before the van was torched."

"Have they been identified?" Cindi asked.

"Not yet. Whoever set the fire didn't do a very good job. The bodies were still recognizable, and they fit the description of the two men you saw at the barn."

"Really? That's crazy. They said Mel would kill them, but I thought it was just a figure of speech," I said.

"We're trying to figure out who they are, and we're still looking for Mel."

"I've been looking too."

"What do you mean you've been looking?" VanBergen shifted in his chair and faced me.

"Grams gave me the full names of two men she knows named Melvin, and I found another one—he manages the Farmers Co-op. I checked them all out but don't think any is our guy."

"*Our* guy?" VanBergen slammed the Coke can down on Cindi's desk as he stood up and turned to me. "You are not authorized to do police work. You stick to animals. Do you understand?"

Usually, the sheriff kept his emotions tucked inside his head, but my foray into his arena uncorked his bottle. "There are dogs involved," I said. My excuse sounded weak. I had overstepped my boundaries, and I knew it.

"No. These guys are serious. Dead serious. They're not playing around. If they're willing to kill their own, who knows what else they'll do. I don't want you anywhere near them."

"I agree," Cindi said.

"Okay, okay," I said. I agreed not to look for Mel, but the name was on my radar screen. I'd keep my ears and eyes open.

Chapter Five

On my drive to the shelter Friday morning, I realized that Linda Levecca hadn't called regarding the stray cat. The thought of the cat sitting in a trap overnight made me livid. I turned around in the next driveway and made a detour to her house. The trap was gone. I knocked on the door. No answer. Why couldn't people follow simple instructions? Why hadn't she call me?

Jason and Cindi were both at the shelter when I arrived. "Did anyone bring in a live trap with a cat this morning?" I asked.

"There was a trap by the door when I came in, but it was empty. It's in the hall," Jason said.

Our traps were numbered. The trap in the hall was the one I had left at Linda's.

"Is there a problem?" Cindi asked.

"I don't know. The woman I left the trap with was supposed to call when the cat was caught. I gave her my cell number and told her to call any time. She never called. I went there this morning and the trap was gone and no one answered the door. Now I find she's returned the trap, but without a cat."

"Maybe she found the owner."

"Maybe. I'll call and ask her."

Linda didn't answer the phone, so I left a voice message asking her to call me. My goal for today was to catch Cow 38. Grams and I were leaving for Chicago tonight. A search on the Internet led me to a rescue group in the Windy City that focused on rehabilitating fighting dogs. Friends Not Fighters was founded and managed by a guy named Rocky Pahn. I had emailed him asking if we could meet, and we set up an appointment for Saturday morning. I was looking forward to hearing about his group.

Next I called Clover Dairy, with the hope that Bill could come out and help catch the cow. The woman who answered the phone said he wasn't available.

"Can I talk to the owner?" I asked.

It took several minutes for Aaron Baker to come to the phone. The wait left me irritated, especially since I had to listen to a recording of facts about milk. *From probiotics to vitamin D to milk's nine essential nutrients, people need to know that as part of a healthy lifestyle, dairy foods may help reduce the risk of osteoporosis and hypertension, achieve and maintain a healthy body weight, and have a beneficial role in cardiovascular disease, type 2 diabetes and the metabolic syndrome.*

"This is Aaron."

"Hi, Aaron. This is Alison from the county animal shelter. I've been out twice trying to catch your cow and can't get close to her. I need some help."

"What cow?"

"The one who escaped from the truck during the accident on Tuesday."

"I thought Bill got her."

"No, he didn't. He gave up and told me to call when I caught her. I'm spending too much time trying to get her. I need help."

"Bill's not in today. Maybe he can help next week."

"Are you suggesting we just let her run loose?"

"Is there a problem with that?"

"Well, part of the time she's on private property. I haven't had any complaints yet, but I will if she starts eating crops. The other part of the time she's in the national forest, and she shouldn't be on public land either."

"I'll have Bill call next week," he said and hung up. I stared at the phone, thankful it was Friday.

I went to the break room and poured myself a cup of coffee. Jason was sitting at the table with his laptop.

"Do you have plans for the day?" I asked.

"Nothing pressing. You need help?"

"I do. I need help catching a cow."

36

He laughed. "Sounds better than the last time you needed help. I can still smell those carcasses."

"No kidding. I still owe you for that one. You have any experience with cows?"

"I drink milk."

"That's it?"

"To be honest, I've never even touched a cow. But I'm willing to learn," he said as he closed the computer and stood up. "Let's go lasso us a dogie."

Jason was a bright spot in a day that had been growing dim.

I explained my plan to Jason on the drive. Grams' idea was to wrap a rope around some trees to create a makeshift corral. We drove by the dog-fighting barn, which was still deserted, and down the two-track lane. If the cow was still in the same area, the two-track was the closest road to her. We doused ourselves with bug spray. I carried a bag of apples, and Jason had the coil of rope slung over his shoulder.

"She's docile, but she stays out of my reach," I said.

"Maybe she knows what's in store for her. Being out here beats going to the slaughterhouse."

"Yeah ... why am I doing all this work just to send this poor creature to slaughter?" I asked.

"So I can have a burger for lunch?"

"Right." We walked in silence for a while. Why was I so intent on catching this cow destined for slaughter? All of a sudden, I wasn't quite so eager to catch her.

The first place we looked for Cow 38 was where I had previously fed her the apples. She wasn't there, but from the trampled grass and cow pies it looked as if she had been. We walked to the river and still didn't spot her.

"If you were a cow, where would you go?" I asked.

"You're asking me? Oh, I don't know. Some place without bugs? Some place cool? Some place with other cows?"

"Where are the nearest cows?"

"I have no idea."

I put two fingers to my lips and whistled.

"Are they like dogs? Do they come running when you whistle?"

"Who knows? Our horses do. I don't remember my grandpa ever calling the cows. They had a routine. They knew when it was time to come to the barn for feeding."

We walked along the river, taking the easiest route available, following a path most likely made by deer and other wildlife. Jason spotted the renegade grazing in a clearing.

"Hey, Bessie. Remember me?" I said. "I have more apples for you." The name Bessie slid off my tongue without thought. The name belonged to one of Gramps' cows from years past.

She looked up and then went right back to eating.

"What's the plan?" Jason asked.

"Let's calmly walk toward her and see what she does."

Bessie appeared to ignore us, but I could tell by her cocked ears that she heard every noise we made. When we got too close, she started walking away, still chewing the last tuft of grass.

"This is what she does," I said.

"Let's tie the rope between those trees," Jason said, pointing to a grove of saplings. "Then we'll walk around to the other side and herd her into our trap."

When we quit following her, Bessie stopped and resumed eating. We tied one of the ropes to a tree, wrapped it around a second tree about ten feet away and then secured the other end to a third tree. The rope sagged, but it was worth a try. With the flimsy corral in place, we backed off and circled around until we were in front of Bessie. Then we started walking toward her. She began walking toward the roped area. Jason and I quietly high-fived each other. When Bessie got close to the corral, she veered to the left and walked right past the enclosure.

"Darn," I said.

"She's not dumb," Jason said. "I think the idea was good, but our execution sucked."

As we talked, Bessie listened. She had stopped walking and was staring at us. I tossed her an apple. She didn't hesitate to eat the sweet fruit. She waited for another.

"At least she's getting used to me," I said as I tossed her a second apple.

"That's good. Next time we need more rope for a bigger corral. I think we're on the right track."

"It'll have to be next week. I'm gone this weekend."

I fed Bessie the rest of the apples while Jason took down the rope. She seemed content. Juice from the apples oozed from her mouth. Her pink tongue swished, and she slurped with what looked like enjoyment.

By the time we got back to the shelter, it was time to clean the kennels and feed the animals. I watched as Jason took Red for a walk. When I approached them, the pit hid behind Jason's legs.

"She's not good for the ego," I said.

"She's a good girl, except when you're around. Or Cindi."

I leaned over and offered the scared pit a biscuit. "Come on, baby. I'm okay, really I am." She refused to take the treat from my hand, but when I tossed it on the ground at her feet she gobbled it up. Between her and the cow I was feeling like a failure.

I gave Cindi last minute instructions on taking care of all the critters at Grams' farm and handed her a key.

"We're leaving all the dogs at home. It'll make my folks happier," I said.

"Cats, dogs and horses, that's it?"

"You got it. We'll be back Sunday night." I didn't tell her about my appointment with the group in Chicago. I wasn't sure what I expected from our meeting. I just needed to know more about the type of people we were dealing with.

Chapter Six

I felt bad leaving Grams alone with my parents. But what the heck? My mother was her daughter; they should be able to spend a morning together without me refereeing.

The meeting with Rocky was at ten o'clock. I left early enough to stop at the cemetery to visit Thomas's grave. I hadn't been there since the funeral 19 months ago, but I was ready. My son, Thomas Cavera, who was named after his grandfather, died from leukemia when he was only nine years old.

I had to go to the cemetery's website to find the location of the grave. The funeral had been a blur, mostly because my doctor had given me drugs—I don't even know what kind they were. But they got me through the days when I didn't want to live.

Even with a map, I had difficulty finding the grave. To my surprise, there was a fresh bouquet of daises next to the headstone. The black granite stone had an etched black and white picture of Thomas and Blue. Tears welled in my eyes, and I crumpled to the ground. I traced the etching with my fingers. It was real. My boy was dead.

"Alison?"

I didn't have to look to see who called my name. It was a voice I would forever recognize—Rob's. I couldn't answer.

"What a surprise," he said.

All I could do was nod my head. He kneeled next to me and put an arm around my shoulder. I didn't resist his touch.

"Are you okay?"

I nodded.

"Is this your first time here?"

Again I nodded.

"I come every week," he said.

His admission came as a surprise. During the months that Thomas had been sick, I felt alone, like Rob didn't care. Looking back, I realized that we both had been absorbed in our own agony and had lost touch with one another.

We sat on the grass. Beneath us was a concrete vault, an oak casket with a blue satin lining and a little boy whose body had wasted away.

"I'm sorry for everything. I hope you don't hate me. Please don't hate me," Rob whispered.

"I did for a while but not anymore."

"How are you doing?"

And just like that, the burden of what had happened between us lifted. I could physically feel my shoulders lighten. "I'm good. Living with Grams in Michigan."

"How is she?"

"She's the same. Feisty. Independent. How are you?"

"Okay. I'm doing okay. I'm still busy at work, but it's good."

"You bring daisies?"

"Not all the time."

"That's sweet."

"Do you want to get a cup of coffee or something?"

The question zapped me back to reality. I looked at my watch, and realized I needed to hustle. "I have a meeting I need to get to. But maybe another time? I'm here for my parents' anniversary party. It's tonight, at the house. Why don't you stop by? I'm sure they'd like to see you." As soon as the invitation left my lips, I regretted it.

"You think?"

"Sure, why not?" We hugged goodbye. I left him standing by the grave and hustled to my car.

I was never more thankful for my GPS. I wouldn't have made it to my meeting navigating these streets alone. The south side of Chicago was not an area I normally visited. The neighborhood had boarded-up buildings, and the businesses that were open had bars on the windows. People stopped walking and stared at my car, obviously recognizing me as someone who didn't belong. When the GPS's electronic voice announced the arrival at my destination, I spotted a man sitting with a leashed, black pit bull on the stoop of a redbrick building. He waved and directed me to pull into the alley next to the building. In my side-view mirror, I could see him follow me down the narrow drive. He waited as I disconnected the GPS, shoved it under the seat, and grabbed my purse, notebook and pen.

"Hi, I'm Rocky," he said, holding out his hand. The dog sniffed my shoes and legs. "And this is Bina."

"Thanks so much for meeting with me," I said as I shook his hand. Then I held my hand out to Bina, who took a step forward and sniffed it. She was antsy with excitement, her tail wagging so hard it almost knocked her off balance. "She's a sweetie," I said.

"She was confiscated in a raid by Animal Care and Control and turned over to us when she passed their temperament test. We think she was a breeder, but she's fixed now."

"Lucky dog."

"Definitely. Would you like a tour?"

"I would."

I guessed Rocky to be about 30 years old. His dark brown hair was clean but shaggy—he needed a haircut, but it matched his untrimmed beard. He wore tired blue jeans and a black T-shirt with FRIENDS NOT FIGHTERS silk-screened on the back.

Rocky, with Bina at his side, led me to the front stoop where he had been sitting. The building had numerous small windows, and black metal bars protected each one. The metal front door was painted a matching black and had a lock in the handle and two deadbolts. Rocky opened the door and held it open for me to go through first. Inside was a small lobby with a door leading to a conference room that doubled as an office. There was a computer and filing cabinets. The space had a musty smell that someone had tried to cover up with a plug-in air freshener. Photos of pit bull-type dogs plastered the walls.

"These are some of the dogs we've saved," Rocky said, holding out his right arm to present them to me.

"How many have you rescued?" I studied the photographs. The animals were a variety of colors: black, white, shades of brown, brindled and spotted. All had short fur, broad heads, muscular neck and shoulders, and stocky bodies.

"When we started, we didn't do a good job of keeping track, but I'm guessing close to 600."

"Impressive. Are things getting better?"

"No. I keep hoping we're having an impact, but I don't see it yet," he said.

"That's depressing."

"It is. They're good dogs. They deserve better. Pit bulls are hard to adopt out and are the first dogs to be euthanized in shelters when they run out of space."

Leaving the conference room, we entered a hallway with doors leading to a bathroom, storage room and small kitchen. From the kitchen, we exited a door leading to a kennel. As soon as the dogs heard the door open, they started barking. The smell changed from musty to dog, but dog in a good way. Someone had spent more time cleaning the kennels than they had the offices.

"Quiet," Rocky said in a loud, deep voice. The dogs instantly settled down. He walked down the corridor giving each one a treat. Bina stayed right with him.

"These are the guys we're working with," Rocky said. There were about a dozen chain-link dog runs. Some of the fencing had plastic slats inserted in the links to help separate the dogs. Each dog had toys, blankets, water and food bowls.

One of the kennels had a cot with a pillow and rumpled blanket, a dog bed and a backpack. An orange extension cord ran from an outlet in the hall to the cozy sleeping quarters.

"The dogs never spend the night alone. One of the volunteers always spends the night, and the dogs take turns sleeping with the volunteer. Last night was my turn."

"Why?"

"To help socialize the dogs. Plus, we worry someone might break in and try to steal them. There are a few people who don't appreciate what we do."

"That surprises me."

"Does it? Dog fighting is business. Big business. We're stepping on toes. We must be doing something right because they feel threatened."

"Why do you say that?" I asked.

"We get phone messages and e-mails telling us to back off. Unflattering graffiti shows up on the building."

I was distracted by one of the dogs, a muscular tan animal stood at attention staring at us. His ears had been cropped flush with his head, and his taut body was rippled with scars. I said a mental thank-you for the wire mesh fencing that separated us.

Rocky noticed my fixation. "That's Benny. We're trying to find him a place at a sanctuary. Some place away from the public with only experienced caretakers. He's come a long way, but he's as scarred emotionally as he is physically."

"He's a handsome boy, but intimidating."

"That he is."

Rocky introduced me to the rest of the dogs. Each had a story, and Rocky had high hopes for every one of them. In the far back of the building, an attached garage had been converted to a training arena. "We let the dogs run loose in here to stretch their legs and, when they're ready, to socialize with other dogs."

"Do you have outdoor space for them?"

"Not here. We try to keep a low profile. One of our volunteers has a van and we do take the dogs, one at a time, to a park, but only when they're ready. Training is different for every dog and can take months."

"You must have some dedicated volunteers."

"We do. Let's head back to the office, and you can tell me why you're here."

Back at the office Rocky offered me a cup of coffee, which I readily accepted. He pointed to a chair at the conference table and, as I sat down, he set the cup in front of me. The aroma alone oozed strength. One sip and I felt jolted. The strong brew was in a travel mug bearing the group's logo, telephone number, e-mail address and website.

"You can keep it," he said, pointing to the mug. He took a seat across from me. Bina lay down by his chair.

"Thanks," I said as I took another sip. "You're not worried about the threats?"

"Yes and no. There are different levels of dog fighting. Young kids who think it's cool to try and get their dogs to fight. Street gangs—basically the young kids a bit older, who are more serious about it. Then there are the professionals. If they viewed us as a threat, they wouldn't mess around with warnings."

"So you think the threats are from the gangs?"

"I do. They're dangerous, but we keep our guard up. Some of them are reachable."

"How so?"

"We try to get them to see their dogs as friends. Hence our name, Friends Not Fighters. Our mission is to educate the youth and rescue and rehabilitate the dogs. We leave the professionals alone. We let the police and the big organizations, like the Humane Society of the United States, deal with them. If we come across something out of our league, we pass the information to the right authorities."

"Are they really that bad?"

"They are. Wherever there's dog fighting, there are drugs, gambling and guns. We're not equipped to deal with any of it."

"Understandable."

"So what's happening in Michigan?"

"I'm not sure. I work at an animal shelter in northern Michigan and recently came across an isolated barn with a half-dozen pit bulls chained outside. Inside I found what I think was a fight ring with bloodstains. There was a treadmill for dogs and magazines and books about dog fighting. I almost got caught. When I came back later with the sheriff, the place was pretty much emptied out. They did leave one dog behind, and we have her at the shelter. Then later we found a burial ground with what we think were bait animals and some of the losing dogs."

"Was that the first sign of organized fighting you'd seen in the area?"

"It was. I just happened to be coming to Chicago for my parents' anniversary party this weekend so I thought I'd look for someone to talk to about it. I'm not sure what I'm looking for, maybe just more information. I associate dog fighting with big cities, so I was surprised to find it near us."

"It's everywhere. Urban. Rural. It doesn't matter. It crosses the whole economic spectrum. It's a poor man's sport *and* a rich man's sport. There've been lawyers and doctors busted. And don't forget Michael Vick. It doesn't surprise me that it's creeping into rural Michigan. That's where Chicago folks vacation."

Rocky got up as he was talking and picked up some brochures from the top of a filing cabinet. He put them in front of me. "Reading material for later," he said.

I told Rocky about the two men who chased me and how they mentioned a Mel. The name didn't mean anything to him. When I told him about the two men being found dead, he reacted.

"They're not playing around. It's time to step back and let the sheriff do his work," he said.

"The sheriff is looking into it. I just can't seem to shake it. I see those poor dogs in my head and want to rescue them."

"It's not worth your life. If they've killed two of their own, I have no doubt they would not hesitate to kill you."

"Maybe that's what I needed to hear. I think I'll let the sheriff do his job." I stood up and thanked Rocky for his time.

"If you have any other questions, don't hesitate to call or e-mail. Our contact info is all there," he said, pointing to the coffee mug. Rocky and Bina walked me to my car. "It's not the best neighborhood, but it's where we're needed."

"I appreciate the work you do." We shook hands, I petted Bina on the head and then headed back to my parents' house.

Back at the house, party preparations were in full swing. Caterers were setting up shop in the kitchen. Florists were placing arrangements wherever my mother pointed her finger. I found Grams reading in the library.

"How was your morning?" she asked, closing her book and placing it on her lap.

I took a seat in Dad's chair behind his desk. "I ran into Rob at the cemetery. He puts flowers on Thomas's grave every week."

"And you thought he didn't care."

"I did. I don't know what to think now."

"Everyone handles death and grief differently. Too bad it came between you two."

"It was good to see him, but there's no going back. Oh, and I did a stupid thing."

"What's that?"

"I invited him to the party."

"You what?" Grams sat up.

"I knew it was a mistake as I was saying it, but it was too late. I doubt he'll come." Just the thought of Rob coming to the party felt like a betrayal to Cooper who was sitting in prison, partially because of me, and here I was hanging out with my ex-husband.

I couldn't have been more wrong. Not only did Rob show up, he came as the man I had fallen in love with years ago—handsome, confident and always with a smile. He wore a dark gray suit, which complimented his black hair, a white linen dress shirt, and a silk tie with purple and gray diagonal stripes. His choice of clothes always made me aware of my down-to-earth style.

He greeted me with a hug and kiss on the cheek. As soon as Mom saw him, she made a beeline in our direction.

"Rob, what a delightful surprise," she said, greeting him with a hug.

"I hope you don't mind my stopping by. I saw Alison earlier today and she invited me."

"Of course we don't mind. You'll always be family."

Out of the corner of my eye, I watched Dad excuse himself from the circle of well-wishers he was talking with. He did a speed walk to us and greeted Rob with a half hug and handshake.

"Good to see you, son," he said. "How've you been?"

Son? This is your ex-son-in-law. Don't you remember?

"It's good to see you, too. Fine, I'm doing fine."

Looking for a reason to get away from the syrupy talk, I spotted Sara and Ryan Hartwick and excused myself to greet them. Sara, a childhood friend and longtime confidant, lived in Grand Haven, a small city on the Michigan coast of Lake Michigan.

"Sara, thank God you're here. You, too, Ryan. I need friendly faces, but I'm surprised you're here."

"We were flattered your mother sent us an invitation. Since you moved to Michigan, we never see your parents, so we decided to come to town for the weekend," Sara said. A waiter stopped by with a tray of glasses filled with wine. All three of us took one. I could have used a bottle.

"I don't see my parents very often either," I said.

"Is Grams here?"

"She is, but she won't be at the party for long. She said it's one of the few times she appreciates being old—she can use it as an excuse to leave early." Sara and Ryan laughed.

"I'm shocked you talked her into coming," Ryan said.

"It wasn't hard. She's in the garden if you want to see her."

The stream of arriving guests was slowing and the noise level rising. Sara and Ryan nodded yes to my suggestion and followed me through the maze of people to the French doors leading to the garden behind the house. Rope lighting was entwined in some trees and strung along the porch railing. It competed with the setting sun in lighting the redbrick walkways and flowerbeds. Wrought iron benches and mosaic-topped tables with chairs peppered the garden and provided comfortable seating for intimate talks. We found Grams seated at one such table with a glass of wine. She was chatting with one of the food servers who excused herself when we approached.

"It doesn't take much sweet talking to get a bigger one," Grams said, holding up her wine glass, which looked to be twice the size of my empty glass. She stood and greeted Sara and Ryan with hugs. "Good to see familiar faces ... let me help you with that." Grams reached behind her chair and pulled out a bottle of wine. "Not only did Marie bring me a proper size glass, she brought me this." She re-filled our glasses. I preferred this size of party: four people sitting outside on a warm evening with a bottle of red wine. But my contentment didn't last long.

"There you are," I heard Rob say.

"Here I am."

"Grams, Sara, Ryan. It's good to see you." Rob greeted Ryan with a handshake. Awkward small talk and silences replaced the camaraderie. No one had seen Rob since the funeral. The divorce soon followed and split the marriage-based relationships. Sad. After two glasses of wine on an empty stomach, I found myself inside my head spending more time trying to think of what to say and making mental judgments rather than joining the conversation. It didn't take Rob long to realize he should move on, but he couldn't leave me alone just yet.

"Can I talk to you alone for a minute?" he asked

Against my intuition to decline the invitation, I said yes. I got up, told Grams and the Hartwicks that I'd be back, and followed Rob. He led me off the path to a place I had introduced him to when we first dated. My favorite place in the garden: a tree house in a century old oak. *My* tree house. We climbed the stairs, ducked through the entrance door and sat on a large branch that served as both support and seating. Twilight didn't provide much light, but it wasn't needed. Every inch of the space was engraved in my memory. I preferred the dark. I didn't want to hear whatever Rob had to say. After what seemed like forever, he talked.

"First, I want to thank you for coming with me. I didn't think you would." I nodded in agreement, which he probably couldn't see. More silence.

"I want to apologize for not being there for you when you needed me, when Thomas was sick. I should have been better at expressing how I felt. What I was going through. But I couldn't. Instead, I shut down and left you burdened with everything. I'm sorry. I need you to know I am so very sorry."

I did my best to keep the tears from seeping from my eyes and dribbling down my face, but I failed. Then there were the sniffles. Rob reached out and hugged me. I melted into his chest. When I could talk, I pulled away.

"Thank you for the apology. I probably could have handled things better too. It was a tough situation." We sat side by side in the dark, not touching. In the distance, I could hear the muffled sounds of the party: music, laughter, talk. I could hear Rob breathing. I could smell his aftershave.

Before I could react, he reached his arm around me, pulled me close and kissed me. A strong, passionate kiss. I responded for a moment but came to my senses and pulled back. "We're not doing this," I said.

"I love you. Always have and always will. Can't you give us a second chance?"

"Really? I don't hear from you in months and now this? You love me?"

"I've been in counseling. I needed time to get my head together. But I know now that you're the love of my life. I want us to be together."

"I've moved on," I said. I got up and started down the steps. I heard Rob follow. Once on the path, he grabbed my arm and pulled me to a stop.

"Can't you at least think about it? I know the idea is new, but please, just think about it."

"Okay, I'll think about it, but don't get your hopes up. Like I said, I've moved on. There's someone else." In the dim light of the rope lighting, I watched as all emotion left his face. Without a word he walked past me, and I didn't see him again that night.

Chapter Seven

Grams and I decided the best thing about the party was leaving Chicago.

"If I never come back, I'm good with it," Grams said as we cruised down 294, bypassing downtown Chicago. The visit was an excellent reminder of why we lived in the country: fewer people, less traffic, better smelling air. Give me farm-fresh manure over smog any day. We had been itching to leave as soon as we got up, but mother wouldn't hear of it. Her persuasive powers made us feel guilty enough to stay for brunch. We left just after eating. Michigan welcomed us back with a big blue sign, but it wasn't until we got off I-94 and onto I-196 that I truly felt we were back in my home state. I-94 is a multi-lane expressway that runs from Chicago to Detroit and is overrun with 18-wheelers. We made a stop in Holland for gas and a quick snack.

We arrived home shortly before six. When we went in the house, the dogs barked and jumped around like little kids with Fourth of July sparklers. We let them outside and watched as they raced around the yard. We walked to the barn and checked the horses and cats. Everyone looked content. I bridled Dappy and went for a bareback ride to the river. Afterward, Grams and I had a relaxing evening. I savored the quiet and was not quite looking forward to another week at the shelter.

Cindi was working at her desk when I arrived. "Ready to meet?" I asked. We met every Monday morning to plan the week. Seldom did a week go according to plan, but at least we had direction.

"I am. Come in," she said as she shuffled the papers on her desk into a stack. "How was the trip?"

I put my cup of coffee on her desk and took a seat across from her. "Let's just say this: It's good to be back."

"That bad, huh?"

"I don't like the city. I don't care for parties. I saw my ex. That about sums it up. How were things here? Everyone looked good at home."

"No problems at the farm. Here was a different story."

"What happened?"

"Remember the lab puppy who was reported stolen last month? Well, it was found by a hiker. It was torn up pretty bad. Dr. Johnson said it looked like the work of a bigger dog. Some of the wounds were partially healed and others fresh. She thinks there's a possibility it was used as bait."

"You're kidding."

"No, I'm not, and it means we most likely have a dog-fighting operation in our county."

"What does the sheriff say?"

"He's made his deputies aware of it. They'll be on the lookout for anything suspicious."

"Should we talk to people who've reported their pets missing, find out if there's a possibility they were stolen?" I asked.

"I don't think so, but why don't you go through the lost-and-found logbook and see if any were reported stolen."

"I can do that. Should we contact the media?"

"Not yet. Let's see what the sheriff comes up with first."

"Okay, but something on the news would alert pet owners to keep closer tabs on their pets."

"Let's give it a week. I'd rather catch the bastards than scare them out of the area. What do you have going on this week?"

"I still have a cow to catch. I'm finalizing plans to have the Spay Neuter Express come to town, since so many folks have asked about their low-cost surgeries. Was there something you want me to work on?"

"What's up with the cow?"

"Well, I called her owner, but he doesn't seem too concerned. He said he might send someone out this week, but I wouldn't bet on it. I think Jason and I'll be able to get her today. What do you think of sending the dairy a bill for my time?"

Cindi shook her head and laughed. "I don't see why not. If they pay without complaining, we're that much ahead." She handed me an envelope. "Look at this, and let me know what you think." Her telephone rang and I excused myself.

The return address on the envelope showed Jackson Biological Supply Company. Inside was a letter explaining that the company provided institutes of higher education with cats for dissection. They were interested in purchasing euthanized cats for $5 each. They would supply the shipping material.

The letter brought back memories of biology class. In grade school, we dissected cow eyes. In high school, it was frogs and fetal pigs. In college, we dissected cats. I never gave much thought to where the animals came from. I did recall the cat assigned to me had been black. Actually, several of the cats in the classroom had been black. It made sense to me now. The hardest cats to find homes for were the black ones. People loved calicos, Siamese, black and white tuxedos, and tabbies. Black cats, no matter how sweet, were often overlooked. Was it the superstition revolving around black cats or just the plainness of the color? I didn't know, but being born with black fur was definitely bad luck. Rescue groups experienced the same thing and seldom said yes to taking black cats from shelters.

I turned on my computer and looked up Jackson's website. They offered a variety of cats: skinned, pregnant and plain. The cats were preserved with formalin. I had to Google formalin: *a 40 percent solution of formaldehyde in water, used as a disinfectant, preservative for biological specimens.*

Buyers on the site had a choice: they could purchase cats whose arteries had been injected with red latex, or cats whose veins had been injected with blue latex, or cats whose hepatic systems were injected with yellow latex, or any combination of the color injections. Prices ranged from $40 to $74. Pregnant cats brought the highest price. A picture showed a black and white cat on its back, legs stretched out to four corners. I felt a knot forming in my gut. I tried to remember what had I had learned from dissecting a cat. Mostly what I remembered was being horrified by the experience. I loved our barn cats at the farm. I didn't have empathy for the frogs or unborn pigs, but the cats got to me.

I barged into Cindi's office. "Do you have a minute?" She was off the phone, and I didn't give her time to answer. "Are we so hard up for money that you want to do this?" I held the letter in my hand and waved it toward her face.

"Wait a minute. I didn't say I wanted to do it. I just wanted to see what you thought," she said.

"I think it's better to cremate the animals we have to kill and not exploit them for five bucks!"

"Me, too."

"Dissecting animals teaches the wrong thing. It teaches that animals are mere objects. No wonder cats are disrespected. Students can learn body parts from a computer program."

Cindi stood up and put her hands on her hips. "Calm down. You're right. I was never in favor of supplying them with cats. I just wanted to see what you thought. I wondered if I was being too sentimental, that maybe we could use the extra money."

I took a breath. "Well, now you know."

"I'm glad we're on the same page."

"Me, too."

When the morning chores were done for another day, I called Jason. He was available after lunch to go cow catching and would meet me at the shelter. I finalized arrangements for the spay/neuter day and called the newspaper to see if they would run a preview story alerting county residents of the service. They offered to send a reporter out in the morning. I checked the lost-and-found logbook and discovered two notations of possible dog thefts. I wrote myself a note to contact the owners.

Since the shelter was almost full, one priority was to call animal rescue groups in the state asking if they had room for any cats or dogs. We had a list of 42 approved shelters and rescues that we released animals to with minimal paperwork and no fees. Transferring animals was less expensive than sheltering them indefinitely or euthanizing them. After a few phone calls, I was able to find places for three dogs and two cats. The rescues even had volunteers willing to pick up the animals, a timesaver for me.

Working with rescue groups was a change that Cindi had implemented when she took over the management of the shelter. The previous director had been chummy with a USDA Class B animal dealer, and dogs and cats routinely disappeared from the shelter before their owners could reclaim them or new homes could be found. The dealer sold the animals to research laboratories and universities. My own dogs had been stolen. I had found one at the dealer's kennels, and the other one had already been sold.

I called the owners of the missing dogs recorded in the logbook. The first woman, Mary Hill, had no doubt that her Cairn terrier had been stolen. She spoke quickly with animation.

"My husband and I just got home from church and I'd let Teddy out the front to do his business and while we were discussing what we wanted for lunch we saw a red car pull up and a woman got out of the passenger door and called Teddy over to her and it looked like she had a fast-food wrapper—Teddy loves burgers— and he trotted over to her and she picked him up and got back in the car. It happened so fast. We just stood there and watched and by the time we realized what happened and got in our truck to follow, they were gone. I called the police, but they didn't even send someone out. I reported him missing the next day."

"Did you get a license plate number?"

"No. Like I said. It happened so fast. Have you found him?"

"No. I'm just following up." If Teddy was stolen for bait, she was better off not knowing. There was the possibility he would be sold as a pet. Cairn terriers, made popular by Toto in the *Wizard of Oz*, were great little dogs.

"Do you know what kind of car it was?"

"I don't, but I can ask my husband if he knows. He's not here right now."

I gave her my telephone number. She then told me that Teddy was microchipped.

"If he ever gets to a shelter or rescue where they scan for chips, you'll get a call," I said. "That may be his ticket home."

The second number I called was a man named Kevin who was missing his cat.

"Groucho never leaves the yard," he said. "Someone had to steal him."

"Groucho?"

"Yeah, he has a white face with a black mustache. Looks like Groucho Marx."

"Where do you live?"

Kevin didn't live far from Linda Levecca, which was where I had tried to live-trap the black and white cat I nicknamed Groucho. Coincidence? Could there be two cats in the county with mustaches? I didn't tell him I had spotted a cat similar to his. I didn't want to get his hopes up.

"This is just a follow-up call," I explained. "We'll keep a watch for him, and if he comes home give us a call."

This time when Jason and I headed out to catch the cow, we were equipped with two dozen apples, a bag of grain and enough rope to build a proper corral. On our drive, we discussed the possibility of someone stealing pets to be used as bait.

"Why would they run the risk of getting caught stealing when all they have to do is answer a free-to-good-home ad on Craigslist or in the paper?" Jason asked.

"I don't know. Makes me wonder where those animals came from that we re-buried. Maybe we should have scanned them for microchips."

"Maybe, but I'm not going to dig them up to scan them. Don't even ask," he said.

"If just one of them had a chip, it might give us a lead."

"Do you want to dig them up?

"Not really. I'm just saying maybe we should."

Neither one of us relished the idea of reliving the grizzly job of dealing with rotting corpses, but both knew it was something that needed to be done.

We found Bessie close to where we had left her. She looked content grazing in the field.

"Let's ignore her and string up the rope," I suggested.

Jason agreed. It took us close to 30 minutes to get our makeshift corral built. It was another hot sweaty day. Deer flies buzzed my head. There weren't many things I hated, but bugs that buzzed my head were close to the top of the list. I piled apples and grain in the center of the roped area. We walked back and circled around to Bessie's other side. Jason stayed behind me while I tried sweet-talking the wayward cow.

"Look what I have for you," I said, holding out an apple. She stared at me. Her big brown eyes with black lashes were exquisite. She blinked.

Staring into her eyes transported me back to grade school. My teacher had us gather around a table for a science project. She lifted a plastic sheet and underneath it, on a white glass platter, sat an eyeball. I remember the eye seemed to be staring directly at me. The teacher said it came from a cow that had been slaughtered.

My first reaction had been to run, and I did. The principal found me crying in the bathroom. I spent the next hour in her office reading a book. She gave me a sucker. I don't know what they did with the eye. What was a grade-schooler supposed to learn from a cow's eye? The eye was never discussed. I don't think my parents even knew about it. Seeing Bessie's eyes brought back the haunting picture etched in my memory of the eye staring at me.

Bessie didn't come closer, but she didn't walk away either. "It's okay," I said, as I took a step toward her. I felt like a traitor. It wasn't okay. Bessie was going to end up as hamburgers, and what would become of her eyes? She stared at me, and for a moment I felt she read my mind.

And just like that, I decided she wasn't going to end up on a dinner table. I called to her, and she walked up to me and accepted the apple from my hand.

Chapter Eight

"I'm impressed. What did you say to her?" Jason asked.

I was impressed, too. More like dumbfounded. I hadn't expected Bessie to actually come to me when I called. "I don't think it was what I said. I think it was what I was thinking," I said.

"Huh?"

"She knew I decided she wasn't going to a slaughterhouse. I was thinking about taking her home."

"Says who?"

"Says me. If Mr. Baker wants her back, he's going to pay the county for the time we've spent out here trying to catch her. I already cleared it with Cindi. I'm betting when he sees the bill, he'll squawk, refuse to pay, and she'll become county property."

"Then what?"

"I don't know. Maybe I'll buy her. Meanwhile, I'll call Doug, Grams' neighbor. He has a cattle truck, and maybe I can arrange for him to transport Bessie."

While Jason held Bessie, I called Doug and was in luck. Although he was on his way out, he would swing by and pick up the cow first and take her to the farm. Then I called Grams to see if it would be okay to bring Bessie home.

"Of course," Grams said. "I'll have a stall ready for her."

"We're in luck," I told Jason. "Doug will swing by and pick her up, and I've found a place for her."

"Let me guess where you're taking her."

We both laughed. "Grams will have a stall ready for her at the farm. Do you have any other suggestions? She won't fit in a kennel back at the shelter."

Jason didn't have any better ideas and approved of my taking Bessie to Grams' farm.

I tied Bessie to a tree while we disassembled the corral. She seemed content to munch on the snacks we brought. Jason and I both complained about the waste of time and energy we had spent on the project. The midday sun baked our skin and once again the flies were annoying. Knowing our work added to the bill Mr. Baker would be receiving made it a little more endurable.

"This old corral would have worked. I'm sure of it," Jason said. "Too bad we didn't get to try it."

"She's one smart cow. I think she knew we had her, and that's why she gave up so easily," I said.

"I'd say more like one lucky cow."

I made a makeshift rope halter and fitted it to Bessie's face, but she wasn't used to being led. Jason had to walk behind and slap her on the rump to keep her walking. She ambled along like she was on a scenic tour. She'd stop, grab a clump of grass with her teeth and walk while she chewed. After she swallowed, she'd stop and grab another mouthful. As we approached the parking spot, I could see Doug's truck parked alongside Jason's. He leaned against the cab. The trailer door was open and a ramp in place.

"Sorry," I said. "She's a slow walker. Funny how fast she moved when I was trying to catch her. Then she could really move."

"Cows can have a mind of their own," Doug said.

Bessie refused to walk up the ramp. I regretted letting her eat all the apples and grain. I had nothing to entice her with but my voice, and that wasn't working.

"I'm not surprised she's a little gun-shy considering the accident she was in," Doug said. He suggested we blindfold her, place a rope behind her backside and persuade her to move forward by tugging on the rope. It eventually worked, but it took longer to load her than it did to catch her.

She unloaded much easier. She strutted down the ramp like a model on a catwalk. The first thing she did when she reached the ground was lower her head in search of grass. Grams came from the house just as Doug was putting the ramp back in the trailer.

"She's pregnant," Grams announced as soon as she saw Bessie. She walked over and patted the cow on her shoulder.

"She don't look pregnant to me," Doug said. "She looks a little bony."

"I'll bet you a hundred bucks."

Grams was a gambler, but only when she knew it was a sure bet. She sounded positive.

"I'm not dumb enough to bet against you," Doug said.

Grams ran her hand along Bessie's back, touched her docked tail, and walked behind her and patted her on the rump. "Looks like she's about used up. I bet they didn't think she was pregnant and culled her."

"What's that mean?" I asked.

"If an older cow doesn't get pregnant first try, they don't waste time trying it again. They're sent to slaughter and replaced with a younger one. We had dairy cows for years. But we had a bull. Now-a-days they use artificial insemination. It's all about the bottom line. No time to wait for a cow that won't take."

Grams grasped the rope halter and gave it a tug. "Come on, dearie, you'll like it here," she said as she led Bessie towards the barn. "It'll be good to have a cow around the place again." Bessie walked alongside Grams like she had been halter trained her entire life.

Doug left, and then Jason and I helped get Bessie settled. Afterwards, he gave me a ride back to the shelter to get my car. The work day was over, but on the way home I decided to stop at Linda Levecca's home and ask about Groucho and why the live trap had been returned empty. Linda surprised me when she answered the door when I knocked.

"Just doing a follow up," I said. "You returned the trap, but what happened to the cat?"

Linda stepped outside, the door closing behind her. "Oh, my daughter came home early. She saw the cat in the trap and said she'd take care of it. I told her you wanted the trap back."

"Where's the cat?"

"I don't know what Missy did with it. I'm sure she found it a good home."

"Is she here? Can I talk to her?"

"No, she went out for the night. I can have her call if you want me to."

I gave her another business card and said I'd expect a call the next day. *Found it a good home?* Linda's answer struck me as odd. You don't find a cat a good home in one night.

Grams had a garden club meeting so I was on my own for the evening. After chores and a grilled-cheese sandwich and salad, I decided to read. I had ordered the book Cooper was reading, *The World Peace Diet*, from Amazon. I sat in Gramps' favorite after-dinner chair—a recliner in the living room—and checked out the book's table of contents. Chapter Seven caught my eye: *The Domination of the Feminine*. The first heading under it was *The Dairy Nightmare*. I flipped to Chapter Seven which started with three quotes. The middle one hit home.

> Milk was destined to feed the animal's offspring and not that man should take it with force for himself. The kid has the right to enjoy its mother's milk and its mother's love, but hard-hearted man, influenced by his materialistic and shallow outlook, changes and perverts those true functions. Thus the gentle kid is unable to partake of its mother's love and rejoice in the splendor of life. – Rabbi Abraham Kook, Chief Rabbi of Israel, 1865-1935

Horrified best described how I felt after reading the 16 pages devoted to the dairy industry. A nightmare, indeed. One paragraph in particular struck a nerve. It revealed that pregnant cows were sometimes sent to slaughter because the skin of the fetal calves produced soft leather that fetched a high price. Was that why Bessie was on her way to the slaughterhouse? I'd have to pad the invoice I sent to Mr. Baker.

After scanning through the rest of the book, I put it aside. It would be a slow read, not something to be rushed. Restless, I went to the barn to check on Bessie one more time before bed. She was lying on straw in the corner of the stall, chewing her cud. My presence didn't seem to concern her.

"Is this different from what you're used to?" I asked her. She continued chewing. I had a hard time believing what I had read about the dairy industry. *Were cows mistreated? Were they really artificially inseminated? Did the cows cry when their babies were taken away? Did they only live four years?* There was only one way to find out. I would pay a visit to Clover Dairy.

After my morning routine at home and then the shelter, I put together an invoice for Mr. Baker. The bill was about $4,200, which included my time, Jason's time, transportation and feed. We didn't work cheap!

I then assumed a winning attitude and drove to Clover Dairy to relieve Mr. Baker of a cow. As I neared the farm, I noted the landscape was dotted with large tracts of cornfields and fields of hay. I assumed the crops were part of the milk business.

I drove by the farm twice to get a feel for its layout. A white farmhouse with a red roof stood near the road. There were several red pole barns behind it. Off to one side of the house stood two rows of what looked like white igloos. In the back were black and white cows.

The summer heat greeted me as I stepped from my air-conditioned car onto the driveway. The shade of a huge oak provided some relief from the sweltering temperature. The house was landscaped with flowerbeds of black-eyed Susans, petunias, marigolds and more. I strode up the gray brick sidewalk and knocked at the door. A woman answered. When I asked for Mr. Baker, she informed me she that was his wife, Joanne, and that Aaron, her husband, wasn't in. I introduced myself and gave her the invoice, which she readily accepted.

"I've never been on a dairy farm. Is it possible to have a tour?" I asked. I was curious to see how a large-scale dairy operation worked. I preferred to judge the industry for myself rather than from what I read in a book.

Joanne stepped outside. She wore a sleeveless, knee-length pink dress and brown leather sandals. I guessed her to be about 50, but I could have been off ten years in either direction. Her shoulder-length hair was colored a sandy blond, which probably made her look younger.

"No one is available right now. I was about to leave, but I could give you a five-cent tour or ... you can come back another time."

"The five-cent version sounds perfect, if you don't mind going in the barns all dressed up."

She laughed. A sweet chuckle like she knew an inside joke. "Sometimes the barns are cleaner than my house," she said. "We'll just look and not get involved."

She led me to an office in the closest barn where she gave me blue disposable booties to slip over my shoes. "We don't want anything brought onto the property," she explained. "We have to keep our girls healthy."

Next to the office was the milk-tank room with its huge stainless steel tanks.

"The milk truck picks up every day," she explained. "We milk twice a day and it's cooled to 40 degrees here." The coolness of the milk-tank room felt refreshing. The stainless steel tanks glistened with cleanliness. "Our milk is sold as a premium product. It's also used to make butter, cheese and ice cream."

From there she led me to the milking parlor. "You just missed the morning milking. The ladies are brought in here. Their udders are washed and dried before the automated milking machine is hooked up."

She explained that this was a herringbone milking parlor and the cows stood side-by-side, angled toward the operator's pit. It allowed milking from the side of the udder rather than from behind. The milking stations and equipment gave the barn an industrial feel. There was a worker cleaning the floor.

"He'll sanitize everything and ready it for the evening milking," Joanne said.

Outside the barn, a herd of cows milled around. Some were feeding at a trough that ran along the fence line. Another worker drove a tractor with a scoop and was filling the trough.

"We grow our own hay and corn. The corn is used for silage. A cow that is milking eats about 100 pounds of feed each day. We feed a combination of hay, grain, silage and soy-meal protein, which is enriched with vitamins and minerals. It's a balanced and nutritious diet. Fresh, clean water is also important."

"You sound like an expert."

"I've been on this farm my entire married life. This place is what Aaron lives for. To marry him was to marry the farm."

In another barn, Joanne showed me the calving pens. "The cows are brought here when they are about to deliver so we can keep a close eye on them. They have a nine-month pregnancy, just like us." There was fresh straw on the ground.

"It looks very comfortable."

"We pamper our ladies."

Several pens had cows in them. They turned and stared at us as we stood by the fencing looking at them.

"What happens to the calves?"

"They have their own area. We'll go there next." She led me outside, and we headed for the igloo-like structures that I had seen from the road.

"How do the cows react to their babies being taken away?"

"The calves are removed before a bond is formed. With no bond, the cow is fine. Same for the calf. We take excellent care of them. After all, they are our livelihood. This is the calf nursery," she said as we approached the first row of pens.

Close up, I could see that the hutches were constructed of a hard plastic. The calves came out and watched as we approached. Each had a numbered ear tag. Each hutch had a small fenced enclosure so the animal could also be outside. Clean straw blanketed the ground.

"The calves are vulnerable to disease so each has its own space," Joanne said. "They're bottle fed until they're ready for grains and hay."

"Then what?"

"We keep a few of the females to replenish our herd. The rest go to market."

Joanne looked at her watch and then apologized for needing to leave. "If you want to learn more about the farm, come back when Aaron is here. He loves showing the place off. He's the third generation of his family to farm here."

She walked me to my car and again apologized for being short of time. I was checking my phone for voice messages when I saw Joanne leave. I waved and held up the phone. She smiled and nodded. I had driven about a mile down the road when an empty cattle-hauling truck passed me. On a whim I turned around and followed it. Of course, it turned into Clover Dairy. It drove behind the barns. I parked where I had been parked before. I still had my blue booties on so I walked, following the route the truck had taken.

The truck was still maneuvering into position when I spotted it again. The driver had backed up to a pen holding a couple dozen calves. I stayed close to the barn, not really hiding, but sort of, behind a tractor. I watched as the driver pulled out a ramp and lowered it to the ground. He then jockeyed the fencing into place along the ramp. One of the workers I had seen earlier opened a gate and walked behind the calves, slapping them on their rumps and shouting to get them to move. The calves stuck close together and crowded their way up the ramp. The driver went inside the truck, I assumed he was closing an inside gate to keep the calves corralled. My attention was diverted from the truck when I heard laughter. Another guy was using an electric cattle prod on a cow. He was laughing as the cow flinched in pain. She seemed to have a hard time walking and kept stopping and lifting her head to the sky, bellowing. He would prod her and the electrical zap would startle her into taking a few more steps.

"We have one more for you," I heard him yell to the driver.

"I don't have all day," the driver shouted. "Get her moving."

The guy jolted the cow repeatedly, and she limped along a little faster. It took her ten minutes to maneuver up the ramp. Both men were behind her yelling, slapping and jolting her with the prod. When finally she was inside, the driver lowered the door with a rope and slid the ramp back in place. I could still hear her deep guttural cries.

I hid as the truck pulled out, then made my way back to my car. As I approached the house, I could hear a calf mooing, actually it was more of a drawn-out wail, coming from the nursery area. It made sense—the cow had been calling to her baby as she was forced onto the truck. The baby would never know her momma—so much for not forming a mother-baby bond. I was thankful Bessie wouldn't be coming back here. At least I hoped she wouldn't be.

When I got back to the shelter, I called Jason and asked if he had given any consideration to digging up the dead dogs so we could scan them for microchips.

65

"I think it's an excellent idea, but I don't want to do it," he said.

"I can't do it alone. There's no one else. Come on. I'll take you out for pizza."

"Really? Do you think you can bribe me? Especially with food? I won't be hungry for a week if we have to go back out there."

In the end, Jason agreed to a morning rendezvous.

"It'll be cooler in the morning. I'll bring the scanner."

I fed the dogs and cats and cleaned the kennels and cages. It was an endless job, but it provided me with the time to get to know each animal. I seldom had the time to walk the dogs; thankfully, volunteers came in regularly to help.

The confiscated pit bull was still in quarantine. I made a point to stop and talk to her, but a friendship remained elusive. She watched my every move and still refused to take a treat from my hand.

"Someday, baby. Someday you'll know I'm a friend," I said to her as she cowered in the back of the kennel.

I checked for messages before I left and realized I hadn't received a call from Linda's daughter regarding the cat. I wrote myself a note to call her tomorrow.

I hoped a letter from Cooper would be waiting for me when I got home, but there wasn't one. A note from Grams said she was out to dinner with friends. The disappointment led me to the refrigerator. I poured myself a glass of wine, let the dogs out and sat on the porch swing. Despite the lateness of the day, it was still hot. Always sensitive to my emotions, Blue left the pack and made his way to my feet. He sat in expectation of attention. His blindness slowed him down but didn't stop him. I picked him up and sat him next to me. He gave me kisses before settling down with his head in my lap.

"What a day it's been," I said. I stopped myself from reliving the day and focused on the now. Watching Blue brought back memories of Thomas and how Blue had never left his side during those final days. More memories I didn't need to relive.

Before a second glass of wine, I went to the barn. Summertime chores were easy: fresh water for everyone, oats for the horses, canned food for the friendly kitties and dry food for the feral cats.

Bessie was in a grassy fenced-in area with access to a stall inside the barn. I filled her water bucket and gave her some oats. She could see the horses in the pasture, but we were keeping her separate until she was used to her surroundings.

"Hey, Bessie, remember me?" I fed her an apple from the palm of my hand. "I went to your old home today. It's much nicer here," I told her. She didn't pay much attention to me; food seemed a higher priority. I felt a connection to her. The days spent in the woods trying to catch her had created a bond. "You're safe here."

She kept right on eating. With all the critters accounted for, fed and content, I went back to the house and poured myself that second glass of wine.

I wished there had been a letter.

Chapter Nine

I called Cindi and told her I wouldn't be in first thing in the morning. She admitted she'd rather clean the shelter alone than help Jason and me with our project.

"You need to have Dr. Johnson come out and inspect the bodies," she said.

"I hadn't thought of that. I hope she's available today." I called the doctor's cell phone. She had office hours all morning, but could come out at noon. I gave her directions and told her we'd be waiting for her.

Jason was prompt and arrived wearing faded jeans with a hole in one knee. His T-shirt matched—faded and holey.

"I'm guessing that outfit will go in the trash when we're done," I said.

"You got that right. But we don't look like we're going to the same place. You aren't sending me solo, are you?"

I wore a gray pair of slacks I'd always disliked and a pink girly blouse my mother had given me for Christmas. Neither was my style. "These are my trash clothes. Unlike you, I save my old jeans and tees for relaxing at home." He laughed.

I told him that Cindi wanted Dr. Johnson to exam the bodies, but she wouldn't get there until just after noon.

"So much for an early start," he said. "We'll probably have to wait for her."

We drove as close to the burial site as we could. We drove separately knowing we'd each be in a hurry to get home afterward to shower.

Jason brought shovels, facemasks and rubber gloves. He also brought a box of extra-large, heavy-duty garbage bags.

"Why garbage bags?" I asked as he unloaded the supplies.

"In case we find one with a chip. We'll want to take the body."

"I hadn't thought of that. Maybe the owners would want to bury them. I would."

"Me, too. So what's the goal? Do we have to dig them all up or will you be happy if we find just one chip?" he asked.

"I have no goal. Let's just see what we find."

The ground was dry—there hadn't been any rain in the past few days. But since we were digging ground we had just worked, the process wasn't too hard. *Gruesome* is the best word to describe the sight, and the stench wasn't any better the second time around. I switched to autopilot and did the work without thought. I refused to acknowledge the smell or sights. It took close to three hours, but I think we unearthed all the carcasses and scanned each one. We found two chips: one in a small dog we guessed was a terrier, and the other in a medium-sized, mixed-breed shepherd.

"I hope it's not Mary Hill's dog. She said Teddy was chipped," I said.

"We'll find out soon enough," Jason said.

I took more photos, close-ups of individual animals in case we could match them to lost dog reports.

"I wonder how many of these were 'free to good home' dogs."

"There's no way of telling, but I would bet on the high side," Jason said.

We took our time knowing we had to wait for Dr. Johnson. She arrived at 12:45.

"Sorry I'm late. I had a small emergency," she said. She wore scrubs and a rubber apron and had brought a facemask and rubber gloves. One by one she examined the bodies. She asked if I could take notes for her and gave me a clipboard with a pad of paper. She gave a short description of each animal and then a list of wounds. She gave Jason a camera and pointed out what she wanted photographed.

Dr. Johnson was methodical and disconnected emotionally. When we finished, we had an exact count. There were 33 dogs and 11 cats. Twelve of the dogs were pit bulls.

"Not what I had planned for my afternoon off work," she said, as she stood and stretched in a backward arch.

"Sorry," I said.

"Don't be. It's not your fault."

"I know. So what do you think?"

"I suspect most of these animals died from wounds inflicted by dogs. Three of them also had neck lacerations. My guess is they were beyond help and someone finished them off by slitting their throats."

"Disgusting," I said.

"A gunshot would be too noisy. Sometimes people hang dogs they want dead. A slow suffocation is worse than a slit throat. Either way isn't pleasant."

"What a choice. The lesser of two evils."

"Do you need me for anything else?"

We didn't. We thanked her for her time and hoped the rest of her afternoon was spent on something a little more fun. Reburying the bodies went much faster than unearthing them. We double bagged the two bodies we were taking with us and put them in the back of Jason's truck. When we finished, the smell lingered in the air and clung to us.

"It's in my hair and on my clothes," I whined, as we walked back to where we parked.

"I know. It's bad," Jason said. "I feel like I can taste it."

"I hate to get in the car. I brought newspapers to sit on. Do you need some?"

"Not a bad idea."

I handed him a couple sections of the local paper. "I'll see you back at the shelter in a couple hours."

"Sounds good."

I drove with all the windows down, but the smell still made me gag. At home, I stuffed the newspapers and clothes into a garbage bag. I hated to do it, but my comfy old shoes went in the bag too.

"What have you been doing?" Grams asked, as I stripped to my underwear on the porch.

"Digging up the dead dog bodies we had buried so we could scan them for microchips."

"My word, you smell atrocious," she said, as she plugged her nose and stepped to the far side of the porch.

"I know. That's why I'm here. To change and take a shower."

"Did you find any?"

"Two."

"Well, that makes it worthwhile."

"That's what we were hoping. I'll see you in a little while," I said as I tiptoed into the house and hustled up the stairs.

A regular shower was not enough to remove the smell of decaying flesh. I triple-washed my hair, rinsing with vinegar between each wash. I scoured my entire body with hot water and a Japanese cherry-blossom scrub, its delicate scent slowly winning the battle with the morning's nasal assault.

Mouthwash helped remove the taste sensation of the odor. I turned down lunch with Grams, as food had lost its appeal. Soon I was back at the shelter smelling as fresh as a cherry blossom.

The first order of business was calling 24PetWatch to get the contact information for the owners of the two dogs who had microchips. Unfortunately, as I'd feared, the first number was registered to Mary Hill. The second to a Bob Hudson.

Jason came in while I was still on the phone. I pushed the pad of paper over to him so he could read it. I thanked the woman who gave me the information and hung up.

"So it is Teddy. Do you want me to call her?" he asked.

It was tempting, but I felt an obligation. "I'll do it."

"We need to find out if they want the bodies. We could offer to have them cremated."

"I'll suggest that."

Mary answered when I called. She cried when she heard that we had Teddy's body. She got angry when she learned the details.

"We're doing all we can to find out who's behind this," I said.

"I'd love to get my hands on them," she said.

"Me too, but the sheriff's on it."

I then offered to have Teddy cremated and the ashes returned to her. "The body is partially decomposed. It's not pretty and the smell is horrendous," I said.

Mary insisted we bring her the remains. She wanted Teddy buried in her backyard. "I want him home," she said as she wept.

I told her we'd be over with Teddy within the hour.

Next I called Bob Hudson. He, too, answered the phone. After introducing myself, I asked if he was missing a dog.

"You found Buster?" He sounded relieved. I could tell he assumed we had his dog and that he was alive.

"The news isn't good," I said.

"What's that mean?"

"We found his body while investigating a dog fighting ring."

"What's that mean?" he asked again.

I hated to tell the truth, but I also didn't want to lie. "We suspect he was used to train the fighters how to kill."

For a moment there was silence. Then sobs.

"I'm so sorry," I said. "We're doing our best to find out who is behind this. If you want, we can have Buster cremated and bring you the ashes." But like Mary, Bob wanted his dog buried at home. I told him we'd be there in a couple of hours.

Jason went with me to make the deliveries. Mary already had a hole dug. Tears streamed down her face as we unloaded the garbage bag containing Teddy's remains. She insisted we take him out of the bag. She wanted him placed on his dog bed and covered with his favorite blanket.

"Are you sure?" Jason asked.

"He's not going to be buried in a garbage bag like a piece of trash!" she exclaimed, hurt and anger raging in her voice.

"We can take care of it for you. You don't really want to see Teddy this way," I said.

Mary allowed us to do the work but insisted on watching. She cried even harder when she saw his body gaunt from decay, fur infused with dirt, and open wounds on his face. She held her hand over her nose and then turned her back to us as we laid him on the bed and lowered it into the ground.

"Are you sure it's him?" she asked.

"It was his microchip. There couldn't be a mistake there."

"I'll bury him," she said, as she picked up the shovel. "You can leave. I prefer to do it alone."

"We're so sorry, but I thought you would want to know rather than always be wondering what happened to him."

"Just promise me you'll catch the scum who did this."

"We will."

We had to drive nine miles to get to Bob Hudson's home. We made the drive in silence. Like Mary, he already had a grave dug. He insisted on taking Buster out of the bag. We helped wrap the remains in a blanket before lowering him into the hole. All three of us hid our emotions and acted as if the smell didn't exist. He had two shovels, so Jason helped fill the hole with dirt.

"I have a few questions," Bob said after he stomped down the dirt on the grave.

"Sure, go ahead," I said.

"First of all, tell me where you found him."

I gave a brief version of finding the pit bulls in the barn and then stumbling across the graves of the dogs.

"Later we realized we should have scanned the animals to see if any were microchipped, so we went back out this morning."

"You dug them up?" He was leaning on the shovel as he asked. It was as if he couldn't bare the weight of the information standing on his own feet.

"We did. We were hoping if we found an owner we could get a lead on how the dog went missing. And maybe that would help lead us to whoever did this. Can you tell us how you lost Buster?"

"How many dogs did you find with chips?" he asked instead of answering my question.

"Two, the other one was a smaller dog whose owner watched it being stolen from her yard."

"As you can see, I have a fenced yard," Bob said, sweeping his arm around his yard. "We have a doggie door installed in the sliding glass door so Buster could go in and out when he wanted. Two weeks ago, he disappeared. The gate was open and he was gone. We've been looking for him ever since. I knew someone took him. He wasn't the type of dog to wander off."

"We're so sorry."

"Don't get me wrong. I'm not blaming you. I just want some assurance that whoever took him is going to pay. What are you doing to find the worthless scum?"

"It's out of our hands. The sheriff is working on it," I said.

"Maybe I'll give him a call."

"Do that. It can't hurt. If I hear anything, I'll give you a call."

He thanked us for bringing Buster back. "I'm not sure if it's better to know what happened or not, but at least we can quit looking for him."

"I'd want to know, if it were my dog. That's why we went back and dug them up," I said, as we started to leave. Bob thanked us again and we left.

I felt like I needed another shower, but it would have to wait. When we got back to the shelter, we informed Cindi of the day's events. She was just finishing up in the cat room. The litter boxes were clean and the water and food bowls filled. There were only two empty cages. I would focus on placements for cats tomorrow.

"You smell pretty bad," she said. This from someone who just spent an hour cleaning dog kennels and cat cages.

"This is just a fraction of what it was before. You should have smelled me before I showered."

"No thanks."

"I have one call to make before I'm done," I said. "I've been trying to get in touch with Linda who returned the live trap without a cat."

"She probably had a change of heart."

"I don't know. The odd thing is, there's a cat missing from her neighborhood that fits his description: a tuxedo cat with a black mustache. What are the odds of two black and white cats with black face markings resembling a moustache?"

"Maybe they're from the same litter," she said.

"Maybe, but I'll call."

"Oh, I had a call from Mr. Baker today. He wasn't too happy. You need to call him. He said he'd be available in the morning and would be waiting for your call."

"What'd he say?"

"Let's just say he was surprised by the invoice. I don't think he'll pay it."

"Do you think he'll surrender ownership?"

"I don't know. I told him you were handling the case."

"I'll call him in the morning."

I went to my office and called Linda's number. I was surprised when the ringing phone was answered. Even more surprised when the woman who answered sounded young, not the older voice of

74

Linda. When I asked for Linda, the woman introduced herself as Linda's daughter, Missy.

I introduced myself and explained that I was calling about the cat and the live trap. "Your mom said you took care of the cat. The black and white one that was hunting birds under her feeder. I wondered what you did with it."

She laughed. "Mom loves watching the birds and gets so angry when she sees a cat stalking them. I just shooed the cat away. I'm sure it's still around. I can call you if it shows up again."

"Please do," I said. I scratched "Call Linda" off my to-do list, but something didn't feel right. My gut told me there was more to the story than she was telling me. While it was off the list, the incident was tucked and saved in the back of my brain.

When I got home, Grams was talking on the telephone. She motioned for me to come over to her and then handed the phone to me.

"Who is it," I whispered. She shook her head and smiled.

"Hello," I said. I almost fainted when I heard Cooper's voice.

Chapter Ten

"Cooper? What are you doing calling me?"

"I'm out," he said.

"Out? How can that be?"

"Good behavior and overcrowding. You have to love California's justice system."

Grams looked at me with a big smile and plugged her nose.

"You're out? For good?" I nodded to Grams, walked outside and sat on the porch swing. Blue followed and lay by my feet. The shower would wait.

"Only if I behave. I'm on supervised probation for three years. I had to register with the adult probation department and have to meet with a probation officer every week, which might get switched to monthly down the road."

"That's it?"

"Well, there are a few conditions. I can't have a gun or drink or do drugs. I can't leave the state unless I ask permission, but there's no guarantee it'll be granted. If I break probation, I'll end up back in prison and have to finish my sentence."

"That sounds better than sitting in prison."

"I agree. So can you come for a visit? I'd love to see you."

"I'll have to check with Cindi to see if I can get the time off work. I'll check tomorrow. Where are you staying?"

"At my folks. After I find a job, I'll find my own place."

"You're out. I still can't believe it."

"Me either. I didn't have any warning. Yesterday my lawyer came to see me and asked if I was interested in probation. I said yes! This morning, a guard came to my cell and told me to gather my things. After some paperwork, I was out. My mother was waiting, and she drove me home."

He asked how work was going. I told him about digging up the bodies, visiting the dairy farm and wanting to keep Bessie. Before I knew it, the phone was beeping, signaling a low battery. I looked at my watch. We had been talking for 90 minutes. We had a lot of catching up to do. I could have talked all night.

"I hate to say goodbye, but the battery in this phone is about to die. I'll see if I can get time off work and let you know. Can you call tomorrow?"

"You bet. I love you."

"I love you, too."

"I can't wait to see you."

I sat on the swing for a few moments digesting what just had happened. Cooper was out of prison, but he couldn't leave California. Grams came outside and sat on a chair instead of sitting next to me on the swing.

"I still smell?"

"Not as bad as before, but bad enough. What a surprise about Cooper," she said.

"He told you?"

"I figured you'd be home shortly so we talked while waiting for you."

"He's out, but stuck in California for three years. Probation."

"What will you do?"

"I don't know. First, I'm going to see if I can get time off work so I can go visit him. After that ... I don't know. I'm still in shock."

"Whatever you decide is fine by me. If you want to move out there, you should. Don't let me stand in your way."

"Oh, Grams, I can't move away from here." As the words spilled from my mouth, I questioned their validity. Was moving to California an option?

"Yes, you could. Don't let an old lady keep you from living your life."

"We're jumping to conclusions," I said. "I've never been out West. I don't even know if I'd want to move there. I haven't seen Cooper in forever, so I don't know where our relationship stands. Plus, I like it here. I have a life here. But I want to go visit."

"Take a shower. I'll fix something for dinner."

"Deal," I said. I repeated the morning's ritual, but this time the clothes went in the washing machine instead of in the garbage. I set the water temperature to hot, turned the dial to the longest possible wash cycle and poured in extra detergent. I also repeated the shower routine, scrubbing until the vile smell of rotting flesh disappeared down the drain. All the time my brain worked overtime. *Cooper is out of prison. Cooper is out of prison. What will I do?*

Grams waited for me at the dining room table, which had a salad and sandwich at each setting. I took a seat. An opened bottle of Merlot sat on the table, two glasses already filled with the red wine.

"To good news and whatever the future holds," Grams said, holding her glass up for a toast.

"To good news," I repeated, as we clinked our glasses together. "And to the future."

August was winding down and so was summer. The days were getting shorter and the air had an autumnal feel, sort of dry and earthy. After dinner, Grams and I fed the horses, cats and the newest ward, Bessie. Earlier in the day, Grams had let Bessie in the pasture with the horses.

"I knew the horses would be okay with Bessie, but I was a little worried about how she would react to the horses, but she was fine."

Twilight settled upon us as we stood by the fence watching Bessie and the horses standing side-by-side munching their evening meal. "That's good. Should we leave them together for the night?"

"Bessie will be okay with the horses. I called Doc, and he's coming over to see her tomorrow. Just a check-up."

Dr. Jack Livingston was the veterinarian my grandparents had used for as long as I could remember. "He's still around? I thought he would be retired by now."

"Retired? And do what? He says he wants to die doing what he loves and that's being a vet."

"Do you think Bessie has a problem?"

"No, but I figured it wouldn't hurt to see what Doc says. He works with dairy cows, so he'll be familiar with whatever she might be facing. The milk production expected from cows these days is hard on their bodies. She might need supplements."

"Cindi said Mr. Baker called today about the invoice I'd left him. Sounds like he's mad."

"Let him be mad. It'll do him some good."

"Why's that?"

"I've been to the sales where his calves and spent cows have been auctioned off. He should be ashamed of himself for the way he treats his animals."

"His wife gave me a tour of their farm. She said they treat their 'ladies' good."

"Good for their pocketbook. Not good if you're a cow. Dairy farming has changed. Now it's big business. It's all about money. It's all about the numbers. If a cow's production falls off, she's gone. It's the reason I gave up eating dairy. That, plus it's not good for you. Not to mention the calves being slaughtered for veal. It's all barbaric."

I cringed at the thought of giving up dairy. I could easily substitute soymilk for cow's milk, but I loved cheese in every form. Grilled cheese sandwiches, pizza, lasagna, chips and cheese, cheese and crackers, and burritos. Grams didn't keep cheese in the house, but I satisfied my cravings for it when eating out at lunchtime.

We strolled to the house and sat on the porch swing. Fireflies glowed in the dark and a soft breeze flittered through the leaves. The delicate aroma of fresh cut hay drifted in from the neighboring field.

"It's a beautiful night," Grams said. "I can never get enough of 'em."

All five dogs were snoozing on the porch. I urged them to "go potty" one more time. They trotted off into the grass to give it their best try. After they returned, Grams and I said our goodnights. Her two dogs followed her to bed, and Cody, Blue and Shadow trailed behind me. As usual, they went to their beds on the floor, but I knew by morning all three would be on my bed with me.

Sleep avoided me despite the wine. I couldn't get comfortable and kept readjusting in hopes of finding that just-right spot where I could relax. Cooper's call excited me, but I hated the problem it posed. He couldn't come here, and I knew I wouldn't leave Grams to move to California. Could we survive a three-year, long-distance relationship? Maybe Grams would move to California too. No, she wouldn't leave Michigan. Round and round went my thoughts.

I got out of bed and turned on my computer. I checked travel sites for airline tickets. I couldn't book anything yet, but I was curious to see prices and availability. A flight wouldn't be cheap, but there were seats available just about every day.

Then I decided to check the lost and found on Craigslist. Sometimes I could match lost dogs and cats with the strays that animal control brought into the shelter. The conversation with Jason about "free to good home" ads came to mind. On a whim, I checked under pets and winced at the number of such ads. Without any thought of the sheriff's warning to not get involved, I posted my own ad.

> *Free to a good home. Spayed cocker spaniel mix needs new home. Current on vaccines. Good with children, cats and other dogs. Moving and in a hurry.*

Maybe whoever was collecting animals would e-mail me.

Chapter Eleven

Not only was Cindi my boss at the animal shelter, she was also a friend, a kindred spirit. She knew just about everything about me, but she didn't know I had a boyfriend named Cooper. She didn't know the real story of how I'd gotten Blue back after he had been stolen. I'm positive Cindi wondered about such things, but she was friend enough not to ask.

Cooper had come to Michigan to hide when he discovered he was wanted for questioning in an arson case at a horse slaughterhouse in California. His grandmother, Lucia Malecki, was a childhood friend of Grams, and the two women remained pen pals over the years. Grams knew about Cooper's past and offered him a place to stay for a while. Then I barged in. I thought I was doing Grams a favor after Gramps died. Truth be told, she did me a favor by letting me escape the death of my son and the divorce.

Because of his unsavory background, Cooper kept a low profile while at the farm. He stayed out of sight when we had visitors and seldom went into town.

I rehearsed the conversation with Cindi in my head on the drive to the shelter and went straight to her office when I arrived. My thoughts continued to race with the news of Cooper being a free man, but I did my best to contain my composure. I needed to remain calm while relaying the urgency of my getting time off work to take this trip.

Cindi sat at her desk working on the never-ending pile of paperwork. "I have a huge favor to ask," I said.

"What's that?"

"A friend called last night and asked me to come to California. Is it possible to get time off? I know I haven't been here long enough to get vacation time, but can I have time off without pay?"

"It's that important?" she asked, looking me straight in the eyes and making me feel even more nervous.

"It is. I'll ask the volunteers if they can put in some extra hours and help with cleaning while I'm gone. Carol could probably help with adoptions."

"When do you want to leave?"

"As soon as possible. Maybe this weekend and be gone all next week?"

"If you can get someone to help with cleaning and adoptions, I don't have a problem with it."

"Wonderful. I'll let you know what I arrange. I appreciate it." Again, she didn't ask questions.

After the morning cleaning and feeding, I left a message for Carol asking if she could put in some extra time at the shelter next week. I went home for lunch so I could book a flight. Grams was on her hands and knees weeding the flowers by the side of the house. I parked the car and went over to tell her my plans.

"Grams, why don't you come with me? When was the last time you saw Lucia?"

"It's been years, probably decades. I can't remember the last time I saw her. But I'm not interested in getting on an airplane."

"I'd be with you. Come on, think about it."

"No, you go. I'll take care of things here. I'd rather be here."

Pleading wouldn't help. Once Grams had her mind set, I knew I couldn't change it. I left her tending the flowers and went inside. I found a flight leaving Grand Rapids Saturday morning and bought a roundtrip ticket that returned the following Saturday.

"Do you want me to ask Cindi to come over and help with the chores?" I asked Grams. I felt a twinge of guilt leaving her alone, especially since I kept adding to the number of animals and the work load on the farm.

Before the shelter started its barn-cat program, I had brought home several feral cats who had been live-trapped and slated for euthanasia. I saw no sense in killing healthy, beautiful cats whose only sin was not being socialized to people. They just needed a place to hang out, shelter, food and water. I had them fixed and vaccinated and brought them home. After two weeks of being locked in the barn to get used to new surroundings, they were set free. They never strayed far once they learned where the food was served.

And now there was Bessie.

"No, I can handle it. Chores aren't so bad in the summer. Gives me something to do."

When I went back to the shelter, I called Mr. Baker. His message said he would be available in the morning, so I was hoping that meant he would be gone in the afternoon. A game of phone-tag might give him time to cool down. Just when I thought the call would go to voicemail, he answered.

"Aaron here," he said.

"Hi, this is Alison from the shelter."

He cut me off as soon as he realized who was calling. "I pay taxes in this county! Do you really think I'm going to pay this damn bill? You couldn't have spent that much time catching one damn cow! Who approved this? Who do you think you are?"

I listened. When he finally stopped ranting, I tried to reason with him. "Your guy Bill gave up looking for your cow after an hour. I called you asking for help and you brushed me off. I'm accountable to the taxpayers of this county, and I shouldn't have to spend my time chasing your cow that was running loose on public and private property. We're a shelter for cats and dogs, not cows. You don't have to pay the bill, but if you don't, you're not getting the cow back."

"That cow ain't worth a fraction of what you're charging me! Keep the worthless piece of meat!" he shouted, and the phone went dead.

I took a deep breath. I hated confrontation, but I thought it had gone perfectly. I went to Cindi's office.

"We own a cow," I said.

"Really? What did he say?"

"After a few choice words, he said we could keep the 'worthless piece of meat.'"

"So now what?" she asked.

"I don't know. Put her up for adoption? Put her up for sale? If we sell her, odds are she'll end up at the slaughterhouse. I hate to see that happen after all she's been through."

"I'll talk to the county's attorney. We might be setting a precedent with this. A farm animal falls under different regulations than wildlife or dogs and cats."

"Is it any different from a rabbit or potbellied pig? They're surrendered here, and we put them up for adoption."

"True. Let's sit on it a bit and see if we hear from Mr. Baker again. If we don't, we can put her up for adoption. There's a farm sanctuary near Detroit that might take her."

"Really. I didn't know that. I was really hoping to keep her. She fits right in at the farm, but a sanctuary might be a better place for her. I'll check it out."

Back in my office I Googled "farm sanctuary" and found SASHA Farm in Manchester, a small town southwest of Detroit. It was billed as "Midwest's largest farm animal sanctuary." SASHA is an acronym for Sanctuary And Safe Haven for Animals.

According to the website, the sanctuary has more than 200 animals—cows, horses, mules, pigs, goats, sheep, chickens and turkeys. The website showed the cutest photograph of a pink baby pig named Precious. She looked to be the size of a small dog. The write-up about her said the sanctuary's vet guessed her to be about three weeks old. A motorist on I-94 had found her. I was familiar with the east-west interstate, which connected the Windy City to the Motor City and was home to a constant parade of semi-trucks—I traveled part of this route whenever I drove to Chicago. They speculated the piglet fell off a truck transporting pigs from one farm to another or to a livestock market. How else would a youngster end up in the middle of a busy freeway? What a lucky pig!

The website described how staff and volunteers provided compassionate care and nourishment to heal the animals' bodies. Members of an animal's own species helped new-comers develop a sense of security and belonging that healed their spirit.

The sanctuary held events where visitors could meet the residents. It sounded like a place I should visit. Maybe it would be the ideal place for Bessie, a place where she could be with other cows. When I headed to Cindi's office to discuss the sanctuary, I ran into Sheriff VanBergen in the hallway.

"Hey, Sheriff, how you doing? What brings you here?"

"I had a phone call from Bob Hudson. Why didn't I know about your digging expedition?"

"Oops. I'm sorry. It totally slipped my mind. Of course, I should have called you. Didn't Jason keep you updated?"

"Only after I asked him after Mr. Hudson called. I thought you agreed to leave the investigation to our department."

"I did. I really didn't think finding closure for some of the pet owners whose dogs were used as bait was a big deal."

"Let's talk to Cindi about it."

I followed VanBergen to Cindi's office, fuming all the way. If the sheriff did his job, I wouldn't have to get involved. But once again, I felt like a child being reprimanded.

"Cindi knows we dug up the animals," I said to his back.

Without breaking stride, he barked, "Well, one of you should have informed *me!*"

After being seated in Cindi's office, it took several apologizes to calm the sheriff. He had every right to be indignant. I told him about Mary Hill seeing someone snatch her dog and gave him her telephone number. "There has to be a connection between the two dogs. I can also try and match lost dogs to the remains we found. I took photographs of them all."

Sheriff VanBergen turned and stared at me. "What happened to your promise of letting us do our job?"

"I'm not looking for the people involved. I'm just dealing with the animals. That's what we do here. Are you any closer to finding who's responsible for killing and burying the dogs in the first place?"

"We're working on it."

"That's all you can tell us?"

"Yes, at the moment."

I didn't dare mention the ad I'd placed on Craigslist. I made a mental note to remove it when I got home. I'd let the sheriff handle it. I had plenty to keep me busy, especially since Cooper was waiting for me.

After the sheriff left, I told Cindi about SASHA Farm. She agreed it might be the perfect solution for Bessie.

"That way it won't look like you sent the invoice just so you could get the cow."

"Would I do that?" We both laughed.

I spent the rest of the afternoon preparing for my soon-to-be absence. Carol happened to come in, and I asked if she could help with cleaning and adoptions while I was gone.

"I don't have a lot of time, but I'll do what I can," she said.

I explained the process and showed her my notebook with the list of approved rescue groups. Each had a contact name and telephone number. "Only the person listed is authorized to pull animals. If we get full and there's a chance we have to euthanize for space, start calling. Sometimes the group can handle transport. Sometimes you'll have to arrange for it." Then I showed her my list of volunteer transporters.

"It's a lot of phone work, but it beats the alternative," I said.

I also showed her the list of lost and found animals from Craigslist that I had printed the night before. "This sometimes works. It's just a matter of matching the ads with the animals we're holding. I read the lost-and-found from local newspapers too."

"Sounds like I can do some of this stuff at home," Carol said.

"Definitely. Whatever works best for you."

"Maybe I could even recruit my son to help. Let him be productive while on the computer instead of playing games."

"Perfect."

I hurried home in anticipation of Cooper's call. He didn't disappoint. He was thrilled to hear I had already bought plane tickets and would be arriving Saturday. I was thrilled that he was thrilled. We talked for an hour before I begged off to help Grams with the evening chores.

As we fed the horses and Bessie their dinner, Grams filled me in on Dr. Livingston's visit.

"Turns out he's the vet for Clover Dairy so he recognized Bessie. He said her milk production was down and, given her age, they'd decided to sell her for meat."

"How old is she?"

"Four. Doc said that was the life expectancy of a dairy cow. They had her impregnated and hoped to keep her one more season, but the numbers played out against her."

"Simple as that," I said.

"He did say she looks healthy. That fresh air and foraging for food was good for her. He asked when she was going to be returned to Mr. Baker."

"She's not going back. He refused to pay the bill for my time and said the county could keep her. Cindi suggested finding a farm sanctuary for her. I found one near Detroit, SASHA Farm. Their website is impressive. I think I'll take a trip down there and check out the place. Maybe talk to them about taking her."

"Now there's a trip I'd be interested in taking."

"Let's do it. When I get back, we'll make a day of it."

Just before bed I remembered to remove the ad from Craigslist. I was surprised to see the ad already had three responses. The first was from a woman looking for a dog for her son. The second was from another woman interested in a dog for her family. The third was from a woman named Lissa telling me to be careful who I give my dog to. She warned me about unscrupulous people who took free-to-good-home animals and sold them for research. She was involved in a rescue that could find a loving "fur-ever" home for my dog. Memories of Blue being sold into research popped into my head. I sent notes to the first two women telling them the dog had already been placed.

I sent a note to Lissa thanking her for her concern and asking about her rescue. If her rescue was one I was not familiar with, maybe I could add it to the shelter's list of approved rescues.

Chapter Twelve

My plan for Friday was to work in the shelter the entire day. I took photographs of the latest cats and dogs available for adoption and posted them on Petfinder.com. I called two nearby rescues and asked if they had room for any animals. We weren't full, but I'd feel better about leaving if I knew we had additional empty cat cages and dog kennels. A rescue group in Muskegon offered to take three cats, and Muskegon Humane Society said they could take two small dogs. We had a 6-year-old, owner-surrendered Chihuahua, as well as a stray beagle who we'd held for the state-required four days. No one had claimed him so he was available for adoption.

Neither group could provide transportation, so my shelter day turned into a transport day. But it was worth it to place five animals in the hands of people who had reputations for finding perfect homes for the pets in their care.

I loaded the cats and Chihuahua into carriers and squeezed them into my car's back seat. The beagle went into a larger crate I wedged into the passenger seat. I informed Cindi of my plans and hit the road. The drive from Ludington to Muskegon was a straight shot down U.S. 31 and took less than an hour. It couldn't have been a better day for a road trip. Clouds drifting in from the west kept the grueling sun from solar heating the car. There was a slight possibility of rain, which would be a welcomed relief from the summer furnace.

I dropped the cats off first and then headed to the humane society. A shelter worker and I walked the dogs around the fenced yard so they could potty and sniff their new surroundings. I asked if they took in many pit bulls.

"We don't here, but they do at the county shelter. We only take owner surrendered dogs. The county shelter takes the strays. Most pit bulls come in as strays, but occasionally we'll get one."

"Is there a problem with dog fighting around here?" I asked.

"There's an area not too far from the shelter where injured pits are dropped off. One of the animal control officers makes a point of driving by there every morning. Usually the dogs are dead or beyond help and have to be put down."

"Can't they catch whoever's dropping them off?"

"Nobody cares about dogs. This city has bigger problems. Drugs, guns, gangs. A rescue group took over management of the county shelter a couple years ago, and they're slowly improving things. Slowly."

After we completed the paperwork on the two dogs, I asked for directions to the county shelter. It was less than two miles away and wasn't hard to find.

When I pulled open the metal entrance door, the first thing that struck me was the noise. The sound of barking dogs filled the air. I found myself in a wide hall. The floor was concrete and the walls built of cement blocks. Doors with windows led to aisles with kennels, which looked more like dungeons—vertical iron bars, concrete floors and gray paint. There was nothing to absorb the barking.

The smell surprised me. Maybe I should say, the lack of smell surprised me. The odor of dog was minimal, which told me the dogs were well taken care of.

At the check-in counter, I introduced myself and asked if there was someone I could talk to about dog fighting in the county. Within seconds, the shelter director came to the lobby, introduced herself as Mary Ellen, and invited me to her office.

Mary Ellen was a mature woman, maybe in her 60s. Her gray hair, cut short and curled, looked good on her. She wore baggy blue jeans and a dark green sweatshirt. Her office matched the rest of the building: antiquated and clean.

I told her I had dropped off some cats and dogs at local rescues and had a few questions to ask while in town. "We're starting to see signs of organized dog fighting up by us and wondered if you see any evidence of fighting here."

"It's here. Walk through our shelter. The majority of the dogs are pit mixes. It's sad. We euthanize most of them. Some come in scarred or bleeding, definite victims of organized fights. Animal control knows of a couple dumping grounds. We see some horrible things."

"Isn't there anything that can be done?"

"We're working with city officials, but dogs are a low priority. They have bigger problems to deal with."

"Don't they know it's all related? Dog fighting, drugs, gambling, guns."

"Education is a process. Government moves slowly. We do offer free spay/neuter surgery for pit bulls and pit bull mixes. We don't have many takers though. Pit puppies sell for hundreds of dollars on the street, and it's not illegal to sell them. It would take major undercover work to get to the main players, and the city doesn't have the resources ... or the desire. Between you and me, I think some of the cops are scared of the situation. We once got a tip about a dogfight in progress. The cops responded to it with their sirens wailing. Gave everyone time to escape. It's frustrating."

"No kidding. Do you have problems with pets being stolen and used for bait?"

"I'm sure it happens, but it's hard to prove."

"We have two cases of dogs being stolen and found buried in a mass grave. They were identified through microchips. We also found bodies of pit bulls."

Mary Ellen shook her head with disgust. "They don't bother to bury them here. I wonder if the same people are involved up your way."

There was no way of knowing. We exchanged business cards and agreed to share information. Mary Ellen walked me to the door. As we said our goodbyes, I confided in her that the county sheriff was handling the investigation and had ordered me to leave it alone. "But I hate dog fighting, and I can't leave it alone."

I stopped for a quick lunch at a local restaurant on Apple Avenue in Muskegon. Reading the menu, I found myself dismayed at the meat offerings. A month ago I wouldn't have noticed. Where did all this meat come from? Even the salads came with chicken. Angus burgers, mushroom burgers, cheese burgers, bacon burgers. The last offering was a vegan Boca burger. When the waitress came for my order, I found myself ordering the meatless burger. Cooper and Grams' eating habits were starting to rub off.

The drive back to Ludington was peaceful, neither meowing kitties nor barking dogs interrupted my thoughts. The drive gave me time to think about what I needed to get done at the shelter before I left. One priority was to talk to Jason. I needed to apologize for getting him in trouble with his boss. When I pulled into the shelter's parking lot, I was happy to see Jason's truck. I found him in the shelter sitting on the floor with the quarantined pit bull. I watched the two of them interact through the door window. They looked like best buddies. I knocked on the door. The knock sent the dog into her kennel. Jason motioned for me to come in.

"How's she doing?" I asked.

"Good. I think there's hope for her."

"She still won't come to me."

"You should spend more time with her. Pull up a seat," he said, motioning to the floor. "Ignore her. Let her get used to you being in the room."

I sat down, legs crossed and ignored the hiding dog. "VanBergen stopped by yesterday. He wasn't too happy about our digging expedition," I said.

"I know. He called me after Mr. Hudson called him. I'd meant to tell him, but he was off for a couple days visiting his parents down in Whitehall. It's no big deal."

"He made it sound like a big deal to me. He made it clear that I'm not to be involved with anything related to the case, but he doesn't seem to be making any headway on it."

"He did find out who the two dead guys were."

"He did? He didn't tell me."

"You really expect him to?" While we talked Jason enticed Red with dog treats to come back out of her kennel. I ignored her, but watched out of the corner of my eye.

"I don't see why he wouldn't tell me. Who were they? Or is it a big secret?"

"It's no secret. One of them owned the van. That's how they tracked him down. I forget his name, but he was from Muskegon."

"Muskegon?"

"Yup. The other one was an illegal, but he had family in the Muskegon area."

"What a coincidence. I just came from there. I transported three cats to a rescue and two dogs to the humane society."

"That's good."

"I'm taking next week off and wanted to free up some space."

Red couldn't resist the treats any longer. She moved slowly, keeping an eye on me the whole time. She gingerly picked up the morsel Jason had sitting on the floor next to him. He handed her another one. "Where are you going?" he asked.

"To visit friends out West. Carol is putting in extra hours while I'm gone."

Red sat down by Jason, but her eyes stayed on me.

"Ignore her," Jason said. He stroked her back and gave her another treat.

"I asked the director of the Muskegon animal shelter if they had a problem with dog fighting. She said it was a big problem. They get a lot of pit mixes in the shelter and find dead and injured dogs in different areas. I asked why they don't have surveillance in those areas. She said dog fighting wasn't a top priority."

"I guess I'm not surprised they have fighting down there. For some reason, it's becoming popular, which I don't understand."

"Me, neither. I would think they could put a camera out where dogs are being discarded. Heck, a trail cam would probably work. You know, the ones hunters use?"

"I know what a trail cam is. I'm sure there's a reason they aren't doing it. It's not our business."

"I know. I know. I'm just saying." Red heard the irritability in my voice and slunk back to her kennel.

Jason gave me a look of see what you did. "It's okay, Red," he cooed. "She's not mad at you."

"I have stuff I need to get done. I'll leave you two alone," I said. I stood up to leave.

"I don't know what her problem is, but she is getting better," Jason said. "Don't give up on her."

"I won't. Maybe she'll miss me while I'm gone."

"Have a good trip. We can handle things here."

I checked in with Cindi. She didn't have any concerns.

"Once everybody is set for the night, you can go," she said.

I hustled through the nightly routine, tidying my office space and stashing papers and my personal stuff in a drawer. I said goodbye to Cindi. Jason was outside walking Red. I waved, but he didn't see me.

At home I helped Grams with the chores. Bessie was already part of the pasture gang. I loved looking across the field and seeing the horses grazing. Bessie was a sweet addition to the scene.

I whistled. The horses knew the sound meant snack time. They galloped to the barn for treats. I could see Bessie watch them. She broke into a trot, but as she got farther behind, she switched to a run. The run didn't last long. She trotted for a few yards and returned to walking. Her years on the dairy farm had depleted her stamina. I made the horses wait until Bessie made it to the fence before I doled out the carrots.

"It's nice having a cow on the farm again," Grams said. "They're such gentle animals, but it reminds me of all the cows we had whose fate was slaughter. It's sad. Things will be different for Bessie. She'll be able to keep her baby, and she'll be able to grow old. The majority of cows aren't allowed to live out their natural life."

"She has such a lust for life," I said.

"She does have that," Grams agreed.

We had vegan tacos for dinner. Grams used a ground beef substitute and seasoned it to taste like taco meat. She served it with refried beans, lettuce, tomato and avocado. Delicious.

After dinner, I started packing. My plan was to travel light so I didn't need to check a bag. Cooper called just to chat. Hearing his voice sent shivers throughout my body. He said he was making plans for the week. He had to check in with his parole officer on Monday. After that we were heading north. I couldn't wait.

Just before bed I checked my e-mail. There was a message from Lissa, the woman who offered to find my dog a new home. The name of her rescue was Fur-Ever Homes. I had never heard of it. I debated if I should tell her I had already placed the dog or arrange a meeting with her. I opted for the second. Maybe she would be another resource for placing shelter dogs.

I replied and asked where her shelter was located. I told her I had a busy week ahead but could meet with her the following week. I was mentally and physically exhausted from the day and was asleep as soon as my head hit the pillow.

Chapter Thirteen

Tears filled my eyes as I said goodbye to Grams.

"Dry your eyes. You're only going to be gone a week," Grams said in a no-nonsense voice as she walked me to my car. Instead of romping around the yard, the dogs hung close to us. They knew something was happening. Blue stuck to my legs, making it difficult for me to walk.

"I know, but I wish you were coming with me." I reached down and rubbed Blue's head. "You stay with Grams. I'll be back in a week."

"Blue, come," Grams called. He left me, followed her voice and sat next to her feet.

We hugged goodbye, and I drove off. Once on the road, with the windows down and the music blaring, I regained my composure. Instead of looking back, I looked forward. Forward to Cooper.

My flight was at 1:25 in the afternoon out of the Gerald R Ford International Airport in Grand Rapids. The goal was to arrive two hours early. Southbound traffic was light. Most people were heading north for the weekend. I cruised down U.S. 31 to I-96 and took it east to the airport exit. I parked the car in long-term parking and took a shuttle to the airport. The weather forecast for the entire country was clear and dry so flights were rolling along without delays. The airport was easy to navigate. I had printed my boarding pass at home to save time but still had to stand in the security line for about half an hour. There were plenty of seats at the gate. I brought *World Peace Diet* to read, but I couldn't concentrate—excitement and nerves brought on the jitters. My thoughts flittered from seeing Cooper to dog fighting to leaving Grams alone to sweet Bessie. I could still see the black and white cow trying to keep up with the horses as they ran to me for treats. It made me smile.

The flight to the Minneapolis–St. Paul International Airport took less than two hours. I had a 59-minute layover, but my connecting flight was already boarding when I arrived at the gate. I sighed with relief as I took my seat. The flight to San Francisco took four hours. Before I knew it I was rushing down the Jetway. It was five in the afternoon in San Francisco, but I was still on Michigan time where it was three hours later.

I scanned the crowd for Cooper and didn't recognize him at first. His hairstyle had changed since I'd last seen him. A brush cut replaced his floppy, sun-bleached blond mane. He had gained a few pounds, but his smile was the same. Instead of jeans and a T-shirt, he wore slacks and a buttoned shirt.

His hug felt like a homecoming. I didn't want to let him go.

"I can't believe you're here," he whispered.

"Me neither."

The stampede of people rushing through the corridor jostled our embrace and forced us to separate.

"I bet you're tired," Cooper said.

He stood close enough that I could feel his breath on my cheek. "Tired, but wired."

He took my bag and pointed me in the direction that we needed to go. "We're spending the first two nights at my folks' place. Then we're heading north. I have plans for the week."

The crowd made conversation difficult. It took forever to get through the airport and another forever to hike through the parking garage. He had his dad's BMW. He opened the passenger door for me and put my bag in the back seat. In the privacy of the car, we kissed.

"I still can't believe you're out of jail and I'm here," I said.

"Me, either." We kissed again.

He started the car and held my hand as he drove. From the airport we headed south. Cooper's parents, Bonnie and Richard Malecki, lived in Palo Alto.

"My folks and grandmother are waiting for us. They planned a small welcoming dinner. I told them you'd be tired, but they insisted. We can eat, have a couple of drinks and then be alone."

"I'm tired, but it all sounds good. So this is where you grew up?" I tried to imagine him as a little boy.

"It is. Palo Alto is quite the city. It was named after a 1,000-year-old redwood tree. The tree is still alive and is a California historical landmark. The city is more than a hundred years old. Spanish explorers settled here, but now it's known as the birthplace of the Silicon Valley," Cooper said. "It's known as a leader in cutting-edge technological. My dad is a computer engineer."

"Impressive. I'm not in northern Michigan anymore."

"No, you're not, but you'll feel at home. Nearly a third of the city is open space, and we have more than 30 parks. Bird watching is popular."

The drive went quickly, and soon Cooper pulled into a curved driveway in front of what I would call a mansion. "I know. It's big," Cooper said. "My parents have money, and their home is one of the things they like to spend it on."

I got out and stretched. The air was hot and dry and felt like an oven. The front door opened, and three people came out to greet us. Cooper introduced me to his grandmother first. I felt like I knew her. Grams had told me countless childhood stories of her and Lucia and also shared the highlights of her friend's life that she gleaned from letters. Then there were the notes Grandma Lucia had written to me since Cooper had been in jail.

"We finally meet," she said, giving me a tight hug. "You can call me Grandma Lucia."

"Grams sends her love," I said.

Cooper then introduced me to his parents, Bonnie and Richard Malecki.

"It's a pleasure to meet you, Mrs. Malecki," I said.

"Call us by our first names, dear. Bonnie and Rich," she said. "We're so glad you're here." She, too, hugged me.

"It's good to be here," I said.

His dad gave me a bear hug. "Welcome to our corner of the world," he said. "Come on in and get out of the heat. This is the hottest month and the driest. Don't expect to see any rain."

The coolness of the house welcomed me.

"We've prepared a little dinner. Would you like to freshen up first?" his mom asked.

"I would."

"Cooper, can you take Alison's bag and show her to her room?"

Cooper picked up my bag. "This way." He led me up an open staircase. At the top we walked down a hallway. Near the end he opened a door and stepped aside, allowing me to enter first.

"Wow," I said. A queen-sized bed looked dwarfed in the room. There were double doors with long, sheer curtains leading to a balcony. The walls were a pale yellow and the cream-colored carpeting felt cushiony, like a forest floor of white pine needles. A sitting area with a love seat, coffee table and television occupied one corner. A vase of fresh roses and baby's breath sat on a nightstand by the bed.

"It's beautiful."

"And here's the bathroom," Cooper said, as he walked into another room. "My room is across the hall, but I hope I don't have to stay there."

We hugged and kissed. A kiss that held the passion of time apart. "I wish your parents weren't waiting for us," I said.

"Me too, but they are. We shouldn't keep them waiting."

"I'll take a quick shower ... by myself. Give me 20 minutes and I'll be down."

Cooper kissed me again and left.

The bathroom was elegant and spotless. The moss-green colored walls contrasted with the walnut-brown floor tiles. A folded green and brown striped towel sat on the counter along with a matching hand towel and washcloth. A creamy white whirlpool tub looked inviting. The shower, with walls constructed of the same tile used on the floor, had a glass door. It all called for a slow relaxing shower, but I didn't have that luxury right now. Maybe later. I wished I had brought more clothes.

I slipped into a skirt and blouse and had two choices of footwear. I picked the sandals—it was either that or white walking shoes. I looked in the mirror and felt like a farm girl. To my delight, I realized that's exactly what I was, and I was proud of the fact.

"Would you like a glass of wine?" Cooper's mom asked when I returned downstairs. "It's a bottle we bought when we toured Napa last month, a 2012 Riesling from Goosecross. It's light and fresh."

"I'd love one," I said. It sounded out of my price range but that was okay.

After pouring a glass for me, she pointed out *hors d'oeuvres* on the bar: dried apricots, crackers, hummus, green olives and mixed nuts.

Cooper excused himself to check on dinner.

"You're back to cooking?" I asked.

"It was one of the things I missed. I won't be long."

We each filled a small plate with appetizers. I followed Bonnie, Richard and Grandma Lucia to a counter-height dining table with six high-back stools. The view from the table revealed a wood-fenced yard with a built-in pool.

Bonnie motioned for me to take a seat. "How was the flight?" she asked.

"Uneventful and on time, just the way I like them," I said.

"Have you been to California before," Richard asked.

"No, this is my first visit."

"Cooper has big plans for your time. I offered to fund a week of sightseeing, if he promised to stay out of trouble. I don't want him back in prison."

"That's very kind of you. I'm sure he doesn't want to *go* back. *I* definitely don't want him to go back." Part of me was excited at the prospect of traveling and seeing the sights of California, but the thought of Cooper's dad paying for it didn't feel right. Cooper shouldn't need a bribe from his dad to stay out of trouble. He was an adult and needed to take responsibility for himself.

Cooper announced that dinner was ready. I followed my hosts to a formal dining room. A glass-topped table was set with pale-blue linen placemats and white china. Cooper had prepared my favorite food: spaghetti with homemade marinara sauce, a spinach and romaine salad and garlic bread. Wine glasses were already filled.

"For dessert, chocolate truffle pie," he said. Our eyes locked as he announced the dessert. He knew I loved his truffle pie.

"I've missed your cooking," I said.

Richard sat at the head of the table. Bonnie and Grandma Lucia sat on one side, and Cooper and I sat across from them.

The wine relaxed me. Sharing a meal with Cooper's family was easy, and the food was delicious. When we finished, Bonnie insisted on clearing the table and suggested we take a walk. "It's cooled off by now. Get a little exercise before turning in."

The silence between us was noticeable, making it feel like a first date. Mature trees lined the roads and helped hide the houses from view. No two homes were alike, neither was the landscaping: bricks, rocks, wrought iron, privacy hedges, wood fences, shrubs, ornamental grasses and succulents.

"Drought is a reality here. Most people landscape with native plants that can survive with little water," Cooper said.

"Quite a change from Michigan, but beautiful in its own way," I said.

"That's one of the things I loved about Michigan—the water. Lake Michigan, the little lakes, the rain."

"I like your family, and you haven't lost your knack for cooking," I said.

He took my hand before responding. "They like you too. I knew they would."

His hand was warm. I squeezed it, and he responded with the same. "Your dad mentioned you had plans for the week. What kind of plans?" I thought of mentioning the fact that his dad said he was paying for the trip, but I didn't want to spoil the evening.

"Should I tell you or do you want to be surprised?"

"Tell me. That way I can savor the anticipation."

"After I meet with my probation officer Monday morning, we're off to the Santa Cruz Mountains. I booked us two nights in a treehouse resort."

"A what?"

"It's a resort that specializes in treehouses. I've never been there, but I've always wanted to go."

"Sounds like my kind of place."

"They even have resident cats. It reminded me of you. After that, we're following the coast north to the Wild Horse Sanctuary. They have trail rides up into the mountains where you can see herds of wild horses. We'll spend a night at a bunkhouse and then ride back down."

"Really? I don't know which sounds better."

"I know what sounds best. That's right now. Having you to spend the night with."

"I couldn't be happier."

When we got back to the house, Cooper grabbed a bottle of wine and two glasses. We started our night with a relaxing hour in the whirlpool tub sipping wine. Later, as I listened to him sleep, I thought about home and how much I missed it.

Given the choice of what to do on Sunday—hang out at home or go on a tour of San Francisco—I opted for a morning at home and an afternoon tour.

Richard asked if anyone wanted a mimosa while we waited for Cooper, who was busy in the kitchen. We were sitting around the table overlooking the pool.

"I'm on vacation, so I'll have one," I said.

Bonnie and Grandma Lucia also said yes to the champagne-and-orange-juice cocktail.

The drink was sweet and ticklish. The evening before, I hadn't had the time to take in my surroundings. The night with Cooper relaxed me, and now I could take the time to observe. The pool, with its hourglass shape, dominated the backyard. The water glistened in the morning light. Flagstone paved the area surrounding the pool, and beyond it were boulders and clumps of tall grass. A small waterfall graced the far side of the pool. The gentle rush of water tumbling over stone was soothing. Chaise lounges and a tea table with chairs sat in the shade of a yellow sun umbrella.

"The backyard looks so inviting," I said.

"You're welcome to take a swim," Bonnie said.

It wasn't long before Cooper made an entrance with a pot of coffee. The aroma as he poured the steaming brew wafted through the room. He announced that the entrée was vegan blueberry-oatmeal pancakes and cinnamon applesauce.

"He spoils us with his cooking," Bonnie said. "He sure didn't learn it from me."

"Definitely self-taught," Cooper said with a laugh as he left the room. He returned with plates, silverware and napkins. Grandma Lucia helped set the table.

Ten minutes later he arrived with a platter of the pancakes and a bowl of the applesauce.

"What's on the agenda for the day?" Richard asked as we started to eat.

"Sightseeing in San Francisco," Cooper said.

First stop was the Golden Gate Bridge. The suspension bridge reminded me of the Mackinac Bridge back home. Cooper took me to a small park with a view of the bridge. We took a short walk and then sat on a bench. I found myself talking about work and telling him about Bessie.

"It sounds like congratulations are in order," he said.

"For what?"

"Saving an animal from a factory farm. Remember the Animal Liberation League's Save Five? A take-off on the big game hunters and their Big Five, the five most difficult animals in Africa to hunt."

"What are they?"

"The lion, African elephant, Cape buffalo, leopard, and rhinoceros."

"No, I meant Save Five's five."

"Rescuing an animal from a factory farm, a fur ranch, from hunting, a research lab and entertainment, something like a circus, zoo, and rodeo. So you have two of the five: Kal, the mouse you rescued, and now Bessie."

"It's not a goal."

"I know. So are you keeping Bessie?" he asked.

"I don't know. There's a farm sanctuary down by Detroit that I'm looking into. She'd be with other cows. I feel guilty bringing more animals to Grams' farm."

"Has she said anything?"

"No. She says it's okay, but I still feel guilty. There's a pit bull at the shelter I'd like to bring home too. She needs some TLC, and Grams has a way with dogs."

"Did you talk to her about it?"

"No, but I should."

"You should. Let's get going. We have a lot to see yet."

The afternoon was a blur. We went to Pier 39, where I loved watching the sea lions sunning themselves on the floating docks. Occasionally one would slip into the water and then glide back onto the dock. Cable cars lumbered by as we walked up one of the hills of the city for a view of the Bay. We could see the Golden Gate Bridge and Alcatraz. The sun was going down by the time we got back to Palo Alto.

Chapter Fourteen

Cooper's parents and Grandma Lucia were watching a movie when we came in, so it was easy to say hello and good night and to retreat upstairs.

The soft pillow and sheets felt good. Nestled face-to-face with Cooper felt even better. Our arms and legs intertwined. Peace and comfort settled over me, and I slept.

By the time we got downstairs in the morning, Cooper's parents had already left for work. Grandma Lucia was packed and waiting for a ride.

"My friend Jules is picking me up," she said. "We're going to make a day of it, then she's taking me home."

"I thought you lived here?"

"No, but I'm close. I have a small condo, just ten minutes away. I like my privacy."

Cooper and I had our bags packed and wouldn't be returning until Friday. Grandma Lucia made me promise to see her again before heading back to Michigan.

"I have something for your grandmother that I want to give to you."

"Plan on seeing us Friday night. We'll be back in the afternoon," Cooper said.

Our first stop was to see Cooper's parole officer in San Francisco, which meant another drive over the Golden Gate Bridge. I loved the view of the city from there. Traffic wasn't bad. Cooper parked the car and then took me to a coffee shop where I would wait for him. His meeting lasted less than an hour.

"My PO is a great guy. I told him I was taking a vacation with my girlfriend and would continue to look for work next week. He was good with it."

We continued heading north on US 101. Our destination? Healdsburg, about 70 miles from the city. We had to make one stop and that was for groceries.

"The kitchen is supposed to have the basics—pans, dishes, silverware, sugar, coffee—but we need to bring the main ingredients," Cooper said.

The GPS in Cooper's car made navigation simple. At the resort owners' home, we found an envelope with Cooper's name on it taped to the front door. Inside was a handwritten note apologizing for their absence, and a key and a map showing where we should park. The note instructed us to follow the path from the parking lot and to feed the cat. We'd find cat food in one of the kitchen cupboards.

"Tabitha is the resident cat," Cooper said.

We followed the directions, parked the car, slipped into our backpacks and grabbed the bag of groceries. The woodchip path led us into a forest of redwoods. The majestic giants dwarfed us.

"It's breathtaking," I said. "I've never seen anything like it." I stood next to the trunk of one of the redwoods and ran my hand over the roughness of its bark. I looked up and wasn't sure if I could see the top. "How old are these trees?"

"One, maybe two thousand years."

Soon, a gray tabby cat appeared. I set down my bags and squatted to pet her.

"Hey, baby, are you the welcoming committee?" I asked. She rolled over onto her back so I could rub her belly. Then she jumped up and trotted down the trail. Five minutes later, we saw the treehouse.

"How cool is that?" Cooper said.

The treehouse, about ten feet off the ground, was nestled in a grove of five redwood trees. Its green siding blended into the surroundings, but I could see a deck with table and chairs. A winding staircase disappeared behind one of the trees. We climbed the stairs, thankful for a landing at the mid-point. Pausing, we took in our surroundings. Tabitha, who had followed us up, rubbed against my legs and then hopped up two stairs, turned and stared at us.

"We are so lucky to be staying here for two days," I said.

When we reached the top, we took off our backpacks and walked around the deck. I loved being off the ground and in the canopy of the forest. My neck grew stiff from staring at the spectacular view above us. Finally, I lay down on my back to drink my fill of the majestic redwoods—their trunks, unfalteringly straight, reached for the sun or maybe heaven. "I didn't know trees could grow this tall," I said.

"They're the tallest trees in the world—up to 375 feet. The only place they grow is along the coast from southwestern Oregon to about 150 miles south of San Francisco," Cooper said.

"Were you a Boy Scout?"

"Does it show?"

"You are full of facts."

"I do have a merit badge in forestry."

I rolled onto my stomach and looked down over the edge of the deck. A manicured garden, with a small patch of mowed grass, looked out of place. A woodchip path disappeared down a hill. I got up and continued to investigate.

"Look at this," I said. A covered porch was tucked around the far side of the house and a porch swing hung from the rafters. We sat in the swing and savored the view of the Russian River, which lazed along in the distance. Cooper put his arm around me and gently massaged my shoulder.

"It's magical," I said.

While I loved the place, I worried about the cost and the fact Cooper's dad was paying for it, which bothered me. I couldn't help but compare Cooper to my ex-husband. Rob had put himself through college and prided himself on being self-supportive. He would never ask his parents for a handout.

"Let's look inside," Cooper said, getting up and offering me a hand. I accepted and he pulled me up from the swing.

He unlocked the door and held it open so I could go in first, but Tabitha beat me to it. "Are you hungry, Tabby?" I asked.

The house had an open floor plan. To the right was a dining area with a round wooden table and four chairs. To the left was a sitting area with a couch, coffee table and two chairs. There was a gas fireplace and a television with a DVD player next to a rack with dozens of movies.

Just beyond the dining area, Tabitha sat by an empty food dish on the kitchen floor. "She knows where she's supposed to be fed," Cooper said. He opened cupboards until he found a bag of dry cat food. He poured some into the bowl, and the hungry tabby started crunching.

Next to the kitchen was the bathroom. "Wow, a treehouse with plumbing," I said.

"And electricity," Cooper added.

I marveled at finding a shower and bathtub. I had expected something rustic, like an outhouse.

The bedroom had a queen-sized bed, a small dresser and a closet. Double doors led to the porch, and skylights were installed above the bed. I lay down to get a better view of the giant trunks and the green canopy of needles high above.

"It's all just so perfect," I said, turning to Cooper. We hugged and kissed. His right hand slipped inside my shirt and rubbed my back. I melted with the warmth of his caress. Soon we were naked in the bed. Tabitha sat near our heads purring.

"She sure makes herself right at home," I said.

"We're lucky she can't talk," Cooper said.

"Us and a few dozen other people." We both laughed. Cooper reached out and petted her back while Tabitha rubbed her head against my shoulder. She continued to purr. When Cooper quit petting her, she curled up on my pillow, her body resting against my head. She made getting up difficult.

"What a cuddle bug," Cooper said.

"She is. I'm not used to a cat in the house. At the farm, the cats are in the barn."

After sampling the bed, we dressed and unpacked. Cooper focused on the kitchen. He opened every drawer and cupboard.

"We have everything we need," he announced. "Do you want to go for a walk before dinner?"

"I do!" I replied eagerly.

Below the treehouse we discovered a wooden swing hanging from one of the support beams. I sat in it and held my legs out straight, feeling like a little kid on a playground. Cooper gave me a push.

"This is how we have all the comforts of home," Cooper said, pointing to what looked like a tree trunk, except that it had hinges and a door. "It's fake," Cooper said, opening the door and exposing plumbing pipes and an electrical conduit inside.

"Clever," I said.

We followed the path I had seen from the porch. Tabitha followed us like a dog. The trail meandered through the trees and ended at a pebbly beach by the river. The water level looked low.

"It's our dry season. We don't get rain like you do in Michigan," Cooper said.

I took off my shoes and waded into the water expecting it to be cool but it was warm. "Take off your shoes and join me," I said. He did. At the river's edge on the far side, was a rock formation covered with mosses and vines. We started to walk in that direction, but the water became deeper.

"This would be a good place for a swim," Cooper said.

"I didn't bring a swimsuit," I said.

"Who said anything about swimsuits?" he asked as he took off his shirt and pants and tossed them on the bank. I expected him to leave on his underwear, but he didn't.

"Are you going to stare at me or join me?"

"I think I'll just stare."

After our walk, Cooper busied himself in the kitchen, and I sat on the porch with my book. It wasn't long before he came out with two glasses of wine.

"For you, my lady," he said, holding a glass out to me. When I accepted it, he held his glass in the air. "To us. May we always be together." Our glasses clinked.

"What are you reading?" he asked

I held out the book so he could see it. *World Peace Diet*.

"Oh, I read that."

"I know, that's why I'm reading it."

"What do you think of it?"

"I haven't gotten too far. It's tough reading. The first chapter I read was about dairy, because of Bessie. I've decided to quit drinking milk and eating cheese, but it's hard. I love cheese. I think I'm addicted to it."

"You probably are. Dr. Neal Barnard from the Physicians Committee for Responsible Medicine says cheese is addicting. Cow's milk contains morphine. All milk does. It helps calm a baby. Milk has a drug-like effect on the brain that ensures a baby will bond with its mother and nurse to get the nutrients it needs. Craving milk is a matter of survival."

"Interesting. You sound like an expert."

"I had a hard time quitting cheese. I did a lot of research. The primary protein in milk is casein. When it's digested, casomorphins are produced. They have an opiate-like effect on humans. Because cheese is denser than milk, it has more casein, meaning that eating cheese produces a larger amount of casomorphins. You'll have withdrawal symptoms when you quit eating cheese."

"Like what?"

"Irritability, maybe nausea, difficulty sleeping. Are you having any of those?"

"No, but then I haven't really quit eating cheese yet. I'm easing into it. Starting by cutting down."

"That's a start. I better get back to the kitchen," Cooper said. "Oh, and by the way, there will be no cheese in tonight's meal."

The meal didn't need cheese. Cooper made Spanish rice, spicy refried black beans and guacamole. He served them with soft tortilla wraps, Romaine lettuce, tomato and onion.

Cooper cleaned as he cooked so there wasn't much to do after dinner. As he put leftovers away, I washed dishes. When we finished, we took the wine and sat outside on the porch swing. Cooper had found a candle and brought it out. Its small flame kept away the darkness that had settled in as the sun disappeared.

"Almost like home," I said.

"Almost, but not quite. I really missed you."

"I missed you too. What was it like? Being in prison."

"I missed my privacy. I missed good food. They fed me vegetarian, but it wasn't good. I missed basic freedoms, being able to do what I wanted when I wanted. I missed good conversation. I missed you. I missed being Cooper. I became just another convict, a number. That's what I became: nothing more than a number."

"I'm so sorry. I really am."

"It's not your fault. It was my choice. I knew what I was getting into. I knew there was a possibility that I could get caught."

"I know, but I still feel responsible."

"Don't go there. It's done. We can't change it. How's Blue?"

"He's the same old Blue, other than the fact that he can't bark. The whole debarking thing should be a crime. He settled right in as part of the pack. He gets along with Shadow, but Cody is still his best bud."

"That makes it worth it. He's one lucky dog."

Cooper refilled our glasses with wine. The drink made me chatty. We talked into the night. Tabitha, who wandered off on our walk up from the river, reappeared and jumped on my lap.

"She sure is a friendly cat," I said.

The heat of the day lingered into the night. It felt too hot to consider going to bed. I didn't want to listen to the hum of the air conditioner and hoped it would cool off.

"I know what would cool us off," Cooper said.

"What's that?" I was thinking ice cream but knew that was a *no no* in Cooper's diet.

"A swim."

"I didn't bring a swim suit. Remember?"

"You don't need one."

"Another glass of wine and I'll be game," I said.

Cooper went inside and came back with towels, a blanket, a flashlight and another bottle of wine.

"You take good care of us," I said. He chuckled. I followed him down the stairs and along the path to the river. At the water, he turned off the flashlight. A crescent moon cast a dim glow that grew brighter as my eyes adjusted to the dark.

"Are you sure about this?" I asked.

"The water's warm, and it's not that deep," he said. "Haven't you ever gone skinny dipping?"

"As a matter of fact, I haven't."

"Well, it's about time you did." He spread the blanket on the ground, invited me to have a seat, poured another glass of wine and held it out to me. "Do you need this?"

"I think I do."

He sat down beside me, and we sipped our drinks in silence. The wine made me warm and eased my judgmental mind.

When he emptied his glass, Cooper stood up, leaned over, took my hand and pulled me to my feet. He unbuttoned my blouse and slipped it off my shoulders. He reached behind, unclasped my bra and let it fall to the ground. He unsnapped my shorts and pulled down the zipper. I wiggled and the shorts fell away, my panties following.

The water felt like bathwater—warm and comforting. We waded out and a slight current tugged at our legs. We frolicked in the water, sometimes teasing, sometimes not.

At some point, a cool fog rolled in and shrouded the dim landscape with a misty murkiness. It was our cue to leave. Without the flashlight, I don't know if we would have made it back to the treehouse. A porch light served as a beacon. In its glow, I could see Tabitha waiting for us. She followed us into the house and beat us to the bed.

Chapter Fifteen

We woke to the cat meowing and walking across our pillows—her way of demanding breakfast. Daylight flooded the bedroom, and our nighttime adventure felt like a dream.

"What's on the agenda today?" I asked, as I rolled over on my side with my head resting in one hand. Tabitha had planted herself on Cooper's chest so he couldn't move.

"We can kayak the river or go for a drive, maybe do some wine tasting. This part of California is known for its vineyards."

"Do you have a preference? Can't we do both?"

"We could kayak today and stop at a couple of wineries after we leave tomorrow."

Mike and Jill, owners of the treehouse, owned kayaks and offered them to their lodgers. Cooper called Jill and arranged for transportation upstream so we could paddle to the beach below the house.

While Cooper whipped up a quick breakfast of buckwheat pancakes, I called Grams. I caught her as she was about to leave for her garden club luncheon, so our conversation was short. I checked my voice mail, although a recorded message on my phone told callers I'd be unavailable until Sunday. An auto-reply on my e-mail said the same. I vowed not to let work get in the way of enjoying myself and checked the phone and e-mails only for emergencies.

Once online, I scanned through the sender names and subject lines. The only one that caught my name was from Lissa on Craigslist. She asked if we could meet Sunday afternoon in

Ludington. She gave me her telephone number so I could call to work out the details. I replied saying I'd love to meet and would call Sunday morning.

After breakfast, Mike and Jill picked us up in the parking lot with two kayaks loaded on a trailer. They drove us about five miles upstream. The conversation on the drive was mostly about Tabitha. "She owns the place," Jill said. "She was a stray who never left. We've tried to get her to stay at our place, but she always manages to find her way back to the treehouse. We warn people about her—you better like cats if you're coming here."

I assured her we liked cats. I told her I worked at a county animal shelter and brought home more cats than I should, just to save them from being euthanized. "I live with my grandmother, and we have a barn full of cats. All fixed, of course."

Mike insisted that we take life jackets but didn't care whether we wore them or used them as seat cushions. "The water isn't deep. You can stand up in most places," he said. "The trip will take about two hours if you just float. A little less if you paddle." He steadied the kayak as I got in and then pushed me off. He did the same for Cooper. We waved goodbye.

"Have a good paddle!" Jill shouted.

The sun was already high in the sky and heating up the air. I balanced my paddle on the kayak and took the time to rub sunscreen onto my legs, arms and face.

"Mike was right about the river being shallow," Cooper said.

Looking over the side of the kayak, I could see the river bottom through the shallow water. Turtles, basking in the sun on downed trees, slipped into the water as we approached. A few brave ones stood their ground ready to dive if we made a threatening move. There were herons, ospreys and birds we didn't recognize.

We lazed along, only paddling to steer around trees and rocks. Talk evaporated. We both seemed to appreciate the quiet of the river. At one point when Cooper's kayak was in front, I stared at his back and asked myself, *who is this guy?* I didn't doubt my love for him, but I questioned if we were right for one another. He was a hard-core animal-rights activist. I wasn't.

What did we have in common? We both liked animals. We both liked to drink. We both liked nature. He liked to cook. I liked to eat. Our time together so far had been one adventure after another. Could we be happy in a routine life? Working. Having kids. Did I want another child? I was trying to solve problems without all the parts of the equation. What did Cooper want? What were his plans for the future? I turned my brain off and focused on the water. If I looked hard enough, I could see minnows darting below the surface. Sometimes a large fish would glide by.

"It sure is hot," I said. Whenever there was shade along the shore, I paddled close to the bank and appreciated the brief respite that it offered.

"Let's stop and take a dip. That'll cool you off."

We stopped at the next beach and waded into the river. The water wasn't even waist deep. Cooper splashed me, and I scooped my hand along the water's surface and sprayed him with even more water. The water was warm but refreshing. I floated on my back and then went closer to shore where I could sit on the stony bottom with just my head out of the water.

"This is heaven," Cooper said. He was sitting on a rock on the river's edge. After about a half hour we got back in the kayaks and continued down the river. Not long after we had taken our break, I heard Cooper shout that our place was just ahead. He paddled to shore. I steered the kayak to the beach, and he helped me out.

"That was fun," he said.

"It was," I answered. I doubted if he had been pondering any of the life-altering questions I had been thinking about. "I think I'm ready for a nap. Nothing like heat, exercise and water to tire me out."

"Really? A nap? I thought we'd go into town for lunch."

He was right. I could nap when I got home. I was on vacation. I was in California.

"Sure. I'll perk up with some food. Maybe some coffee."

The town of Healdsburg was an upscale, tourist haven with a mix of historic homes, quaint shops and restaurants. We found a small eatery with a few vegan options. We both had black bean burgers, sweet potato fries and native merlot—we felt obligated since the town was in the heart of wine country. After lunch, we started to explore the town, but we decided we'd rather spend the day lounging with Tabitha.

Instead of driving back the way we came, Cooper looked for a more scenic route. About a half hour into the drive I asked if he knew where we were. I didn't think he did, but he wouldn't admit to being lost. We ended up on River Road, which meandered through the Russian River Valley. He braked when he saw a sign for the Armstrong Redwoods State Natural Reserve.

"This is what I wanted to show you," he said. "I remember my parents bringing me here when I was a kid."

We parked and went into the Welcome Center.

"Let's go see the Colonel Armstrong Tree," I said after scanning a brochure. "Listen to this, it's the oldest tree here, over 1,400 years old. It's named after a lumberman who decided to preserve this portion of the park back in the 1870s."

Cooper was more than willing to take the hike. By the time we finished and made our way back to the treehouse, the sun was low in the western sky. I sat on the porch swing, and Cooper went inside to prepare dinner.

"We sure crammed a lot into one day," I said when he returned with our drinks.

"I dreamed of days like this when I was in prison." He leaned over, gave me a kiss and left again. He returned carrying a chair from the dining room and placed it in front of the swing. "I couldn't find a serving tray," he said. The seat of the chair brimmed with bowls of grapes, almonds, crackers, carrots, guacamole and hummus. "Is this enough or do you want a meal?" he asked.

Laughing at his attentiveness, I told him this would be plenty. Tabitha jumped onto my lap and sniffed the air. "Poor kitty, nothing here worth begging for," I said. Cooper took her in the house for her dinner.

Daylight faded into evening, and the melodic sounds of the forest gave way to nighttime noises—I wasn't sure what insects or critters accounted for the occasional rustling and chirps, but I felt safe in my high perch.

"It was a perfect day," I said. It was followed by a perfect night. One I didn't want to ever end.

Chapter Sixteen

We had to hustle to make the 10 o'clock checkout. Cooper cooked us a quick breakfast. After eating, we packed and loaded the car.

"Goodbye, sweet Tabitha. We're going to miss you," I said as I stroked her back. The tabby sat at the top of the stairs and watched as we readied to leave. I expected her to raise a paw and wave, but she didn't. I took one last look around the place to make sure we weren't forgetting anything. We stopped at the main house to give the key back to Jill and Mike.

"You have a fabulous place," I said. "We loved every second of it.

"Come back again," Jill said.

The Wild Horse Sanctuary, with 5,000 acres and 300 wild mustangs and burros, was 215 miles northeast in the small town of Shingletown. The sanctuary's goal was to protect and preserve America's wild horses. To raise money for their cause, the owners offered two- and three-day rides into the mountains. Cooper signed us up for a two-day trip.

"Have you been there before?" I asked.

"I have. It's where I fell in love with wild horses," Cooper said. "Every year the U.S. Department of Agriculture rounds up horses and makes them available for adoption. There're always more horses than people wanting to adopt, so thousands of horses live in crowded holding areas, sometimes for years. The sanctuary provides a home for as many as they can, but they don't have room for them all."

"Is that how you got involved in the slaughterhouse fire?"

"It is. Now there's a moratorium on killing wild horses."

We found a hotel room for the night in Red Bluff. It was nice but nothing like our treehouse. Cooper spotted an Italian restaurant next door, and we gorged ourselves on spaghetti marinara, even though it wasn't as good as his.

Registration at the sanctuary started at nine o'clock. The itinerary included a horseback ride to base camp, a night in a bunkhouse and an early morning return ride to the ranch.

Sign-in took place in the dining room of the owner's farmhouse. We turned in our backpacks, which were loaded into a pickup truck to be taken to camp.

Since we were early, we had time to explore. We walked to a small pond where a rope hung from a tree. It looked like fun— swinging out and dropping into the water. We strolled to the barn, which had numerous paddocks. A young man worked at saddling eleven horses. Our leader, Nancy, a woman in her middle years, looked lean and tough.

"I want to thank you all for coming," Nancy said. "By taking this ride, you're helping support the work we do here." There were six women, two men and us. Nancy helped each person onto a saddled horse and instructed everyone on how to hold the reins.

"These horses have made this trip dozens of times. Just give them their head. They're going to stay single file and follow the horse in front of them."

About ten minutes after we started, Nancy stopped. She dismounted and checked the cinches on all the saddles to make sure they were still tight. Before we resumed the trip, she gave us some history.

"In 1978, sanctuary co-founder Dianne Nelson and her family rescued 80 wild horses destined to be destroyed and established the Wild Horse Sanctuary. The sanctuary is now home to some 300 wild mustangs and burros, many of which were rescued from federal lands in the Western U.S. At the sanctuary they roam free and live out their natural lives. We have an annual adoption program to manage the herd. In the fall, we adopt out wild colts and fillies that have been weaned from their mothers."

The beginning of the ride was easy, but soon the horses started climbing a rocky, winding path. My horse occasionally stumbled over small rocks, which made for an uncomfortable ride. I tried to focus on the scenery.

We wound through hills covered with pine and oak trees. Nancy stopped occasionally and talked about points of interest, such as outcrops of volcanic rock.

"The wild horses share the range with black bears, mountain lions, deer, bobcats, fox, raccoons, wild turkeys and other small animals. There are bald eagles, owls, hawks, and more than 150 varieties of songbirds," she said.

Nancy pointed, and in the distance I could see a herd of horses.

"This is where they hang out. They like the grasses in the meadow. The stallion will herd the mares into a tight group when he spots us," she said.

I couldn't see the stallion, but soon the herd disappeared from view.

At noon we stopped for lunch. The boxed food packed in the saddlebags consisted of sandwiches, potato chips, and a chocolate chip cookie. We had requested vegetarian and had peanut butter and strawberry jam on white bread.

Nancy continued her narration. "The sanctuary property is rich in Native American and pioneer history. You can see remnants of homesteads. You can also find arrowheads."

After lunch the heat started to get to me. I didn't know what the temperature was, but it was hot. I started checking the time on my watch. Nancy had said we'd make it to camp mid-afternoon. By two o'clock, I wrapped the bridle reins around the saddle horn and simply hung on. My horse could follow the horse in front of him without my guidance. The last hour I was in survival mode, hoping just to stay upright and not tumble to the ground. When we reached base camp, the horses went straight to a watering trough—they knew the routine. Nancy pumped a hand pump to add more water.

"If anyone wants to cool down, come on over," she said.

I could hardly dismount. The heat had gotten the better of me. I wasn't used to the rugged uphill ride. Copper helped me, and I went straight to the trough and splashed water on my face and arms.

"The cabins are all alike. Pick up your bags from the truck and find an empty one," Nancy said. "Dinner will be at 5, and we'll have a campfire afterwards. Keep watch for the wild horses. When their watering holes dry up in late summer, they come here to drink, so it's not uncommon to see them around."

I felt nauseous and lightheaded. Cooper fared better than I did and stayed by my side. The first cabin we came to was empty, so we claimed it. It had a porch with two rocking chairs. Inside was a table and two single beds. "I guess this is frontier-style sleeping," Cooper said. I dropped my stuff on the floor and plopped down on the bed.

"Wake me when it's time for dinner," I said. Cooper came over and rubbed my back. It didn't take me long to recuperate. After feeling better, we took a walk to find the bathroom we'd be sharing with everyone else. At least it had hot water for showers.

Like a couple of characters in a western movie, we hung out on the front porch rocking in our chairs until we were summoned to dinner by the clanging of a bell. The meal, served family-style outside at a long wood table, consisted of steaks and vegetables that had been grilled over an open fire. The cook also served up a pot of baked beans and a plate of biscuits. He cooked us plain old veggie burgers. The meal was a disappointment, but the ambiance couldn't be beat. The heady aroma of burning wood drifted through the air. One woman brought her guitar and, when we settled in around the campfire, played and cajoled the group into singing *Back in the Saddle Again, Happy Trails, Sweet Baby James* and *Home on the Range.*

The fire crackled and burned bright as the sun set behind a mountain to the west. The forthcoming darkness revealed a sky crowded with twinkling stars. Cooper and I were the first to say goodnight. We tried pushing the beds together, but they were bolted to the floor, so we cuddled up close in one bed. Falling asleep in Cooper's arms was comforting.

In the morning, the ringing of the bell signaled us for breakfast. The table had big bowls of scrambled eggs, bacon, potatoes, a plate of toast and a pot of strong coffee. After eating, we hauled our belongings to the pickup and climbed back into our saddles.

Going back down the mountain, we took a different trail that was shorter. The scenery was about the same as on the ride down, except that we didn't see any wild horses. We were back at the ranch by noon. We said our goodbyes, loaded our stuff and hit the road. We stopped in Red Bluff for lunch.

I didn't pay attention to the route we took, but somewhere near Sacramento, Cooper turned off the highway. He had a surprise for me.

It turned out to be a breathtaking view. Acres of sunflowers! Their yellow petals vibrant in the sun. "They're beautiful," I said. I loved that he thought to share them with me.

Traffic was heavy on the trip back. Cooper called his folks and told them we wouldn't make it for dinner. He suggested a family breakfast instead. Grandma Lucia was at the house and said she'd spend the night so we could see her in the morning. We stopped for dinner in San Francisco.

The house was dark when we got back. Cooper grabbed a bottle of wine and two glasses and we went to my room. We stayed up talking and discussing the one thing we had ignored the entire week: I was going to Michigan, and he was staying in California.

"I'd love to be with you, but I can't leave Grams. It's as simple as that," I said. Inside I knew there was more to it. Even if Grams were out of the picture, I didn't know if I could move to the western state. I didn't feel a connection to it like I did to Michigan. Could the lure of Cooper change my mind?

"I know. I know. We'll figure something out. Meanwhile, we'll have e-mails, calls, vacations," Cooper said.

We slept the entire night in each other's arms, not wanting to let go even in sleep. Breakfast with the family was a blur. Grandma Lucia gave me a package for Grams. We ate, said our goodbyes and then Cooper drove me to the airport. My flight was at 9:05. We were stoic in our goodbyes, but my heart was breaking. After my final goodbye, I didn't look back. I went through security, waited for my flight, boarded and slept until we descended in Chicago. The 56 minutes I had to switch planes was again cutting it close, but I made it. I stayed awake for the short flight to Grand Rapids. We rolled up to the gate a little after 6. By 7:30 I was cruising down the highway back to Grams and the farm.

Chapter Seventeen

I wanted to get a chunk of the drive behind me before stopping for dinner, so I decided to stop at Subway at the Coopersville exit of I-96. It didn't take long to get a veggie sub, chips and an iced tea. I ate as I drove. I called Grams and told her I'd be home around 10. I didn't bother to tell her not to wait up for me––I knew she would. Traffic heading north on U.S. 31 was light. The weekenders were already at their destinations—cottages, hotels or campgrounds. I felt safe driving and talking, so I dialed Cooper. I knew he was waiting for my call, and talking made the drive go faster. I already missed him but felt confident that our love could withstand the distance. Our second goodbye for the day came shortly before I got off the expressway at the Ludington exit.

"I love you," I made myself say. Verbally expressing my feelings didn't come naturally.

"I love you, too," he said. "And miss you."

The light was on in the kitchen when I drove up to the farm, as was the backyard light. Grams looked comfortable sitting on the porch swing with Blue next to her and the other four dogs snoozing on the porch. They ran to greet me when they realized who was pulling into the driveway.

"Hey, guys," I said. Cody pushed his head under my hands, his tail wagged so hard he almost lost balance. Shadow was right next to him, as always. Sinatra and Elvis ran circles around us.

A Frank Sinatra tune drifted out from the house through the screen door. Ol' Blue Eyes had captivated Grams as long as I could remember, hence the name of one of her dogs.

Blue and Grams came down the porch steps as I got my backpack out of the backseat. Grams gave me a hug. "Missed you. Welcome home," she said.

"I missed you, too. It's good to be home," I said. It was the truth, but my heart tugged with the pain of missing Cooper. "Looks like the dogs missed me." They crowded around me vying for attention.

"That they did. How was Cooper?"

"He's good. Looking for a job. Still cooking." I set my purse and backpack inside the door and came back outside for some swing time.

"Oh, Grandma Lucia sent a package for you," I said, jumping up to retrieve it from my bag. I handed it to Grams and sat back down on the swing. I picked up Blue, set him next to me and rubbed his head. Grams gingerly peeled away the tape and unwrapped the paper. Inside was a square jeweler's box.

"Oh, what did she do now?" Grams said.

"Open it," I urged.

Grams flipped the lid open. Inside was a necklace with a silver heart-shaped locket. *Friends Forever* was etched on the front. She opened the cover and inside was a tiny photo of Grams and Lucia when they were kids. Grams started to cry.

"We've been through so much together, but I can't even remember the last time I saw her," she said.

I reached over and gave her a hug. "See, you should have come with me. You two would have had a blast hanging out together."

"Next time I will," Grams said. She wiped away the tears and asked me again about Cooper.

"He's good. I liked his parents. I really liked Grandma Lucia. He's living with his folks, so we spent a couple nights there. We drove north of San Francisco to a touristy town and stayed in a treehouse for two nights."

"A treehouse?"

"They called it a treehouse, but it's not what you would think of when you think treehouse. It had electricity and running water, a kitchen, dining room, bedroom and a wrap-around porch. It even had a resident cat."

"Sounds like you."

"It was. From there we went to the Wild Horse Sanctuary and rode in the mountains to a camp where we spent the night. Saw a herd of wild horses."

"So you liked California?"

"It's a fun place to visit, but I wouldn't want to live there. It's hot and too dry. I like water. And no, I'm not moving out there."

"But what about you and Cooper?"

"We'll manage. Other couples have survived living apart. He'll come here when he gets off probation, and I'll be spending all my vacation time there. Next time you'll go, too."

Because of the three-hour time difference between Michigan and California, I wasn't tired. We talked until Grams was incoherent and almost sleeping. After she went to bed, I went to my room, put on my pajamas and started to read, but I couldn't concentrate. I envied the dogs who were sound asleep. I missed Cooper. On a whim I called him again. He answered and we talked until I was ready for sleep.

I didn't wake until 10 o'clock. The dogs weren't on my bed. They weren't even in the room. I went downstairs where they all were hanging with Grams in the living room as she read the Sunday paper.

"Good morning," I said.

"Good morning. Hope you don't mind. I called the dogs when I got up. I figured you'd be sleeping in."

"I don't mind."

Grams already had eaten breakfast, so I made myself a pancake. I really missed Cooper when it came to cooking.

After eating, I called Lissa. Her voice sounded familiar, but I couldn't place it. We agreed to meet at 2 o'clock inside McDonalds in Ludington.

After eating, I took the dogs down to the barn to see the horses and Bessie. It still seemed odd to have a cow among the horses. Grams had already done the morning chores. It made me feel guilty. I needed to be more responsible and timely. I sat with the cats for a while. They never got enough petting.

I decided to take Dappy for a quick ride to the river before meeting Lissa. It was hard to believe it was already September. Monday was Labor Day. I had no plans other than going to the shelter. I had volunteered to work the holiday. The shelter was closed to the public, but the animals still needed care. The quiet would be a good time to get caught up on paper work.

Autumn was in the air—part dry, part fruity, part pollen with hues of yellows. Golden rod bloomed, and the throaty cries of crows dominated.

I rode bareback, loving the feel of Dappy's muscular body between my thighs as he cantered down the lane to the river. Dappy's dependability allowed me the luxury of daydreaming. He never shied at wayward rabbits or squirrels. Fluttering birds didn't faze him. I lost track of time and, when I realized how late it was, had to hustle Dappy back to the barn.

I hurried to the house, changed into clean clothes and said goodbye to Grams. "I'm meeting with a woman from a rescue. Fur-Ever Homes. Have you ever heard of them?" She hadn't.

Lissa described herself as having short blond hair and said she would be wearing jean shorts and a red tank top. She was seated at a booth and stood as I approached. We shook hands. I guessed her to be in her mid-30s. She was thin and her blonde hair looked bleached.

"It's good to meet you," I said.

"Same here. Thanks for coming out."

"I'm going to get something to drink. Do you want anything?" I asked. She had a cup of coffee and there were remnants of a meal on the table, but I asked anyway.

"No, thanks. I got here early and had a burger."

I got an iced tea and returned to the booth. I hadn't told Lissa I worked at the shelter. I wanted to hear her story first.

"So did you find a home for your dog?" she asked once I settled in.

"I did. Just this morning my grandma decided to take her. She's a really good dog."

"Are you sure about your grandmother taking the dog? A lot of times when a relative takes a dog, they don't really want it. They just take it out of a sense of obligation. I'm sure we could find her a good home. It was a cocker spaniel, right?"

"I think my grandmother will give Buffy a good home, but if it doesn't work I'll call." I didn't know why I was continuing with my lie other than the fact that I couldn't find a good way to come clean. That's the problem with lying.

"Where are you moving?"

That question took me by surprise. Then I remembered the ad I posted on Craigslist. I had written I was in a hurry to get rid of the dog because I was moving.

"To California. My boyfriend is out there, and I'm ready for a change," I heard myself saying.

"That's exciting."

"It is. I can't wait. I just went for a visit and loved it. But I have a lot to do before I can go."

"Are you hiring a moving company or doing it yourself?"

"I can't afford to hire anyone. I'm renting a U-Haul and what doesn't fit I'm selling."

"If you have anything you want to donate to a good cause, I'll take it. We have a garage sale once a year to raise money for the rescue. We have a lot of expenses."

"I'll do that. Tell me about your rescue."

"We're based in Ludington and have a network of foster homes. Most of our animals come from the local shelter, but I read Craigslist when I have time. People aren't aware of what can happen to the dogs and cats they give away for free."

"I wasn't aware until you told me. It's scary. What shelter do you work with?"

"The county shelter."

I took a sip of tea to hide my surprise at her answer. Lissa was an excellent liar. If I didn't know better, I would have believed every word she said. She didn't get animals from the shelter, so what else was she lying about? I sipped my tea and tried to act casually. "I heard they put a lot of cats and dogs to sleep there."

"They do. We save as many as we can."

"Do you have a website?"

"Not yet. We can't afford to pay anyone to build one for us. I have a friend who keeps saying he's going to get a site going for us, but he just doesn't get to it. I think I need to find someone else."

"Friends mean well, but actions speak louder than words. How do you find homes for the animals?" I hoped I wasn't asking too many questions.

"We do adopt-a-thons. Mostly down in Muskegon and Grand Haven where there are more people. We list the animals on Petfinder. That's an online site where people go when they're looking for a pet."

"That's awesome. How long have you been in rescue?"

"It seems like forever, but I'm just now starting to get more organized. I did apply for my 501(c) 3 so I can be a non-profit. That way people can get a tax deduction when they donate."

"I'm impressed. Too bad I'm moving or I would volunteer for you." My tea was gone, but I continued to suck on the straw.

"I'm always looking for help," she said as she pulled out her cell phone and looked at the time. "I need to get going."

"I'm really sorry I wasted your time. Like I said, my grandmother just decided this morning to take Buffy."

"Don't worry about it. I needed to get lunch. If grandma changes her mind, give me a call." She handed me a business card. It had a drawing of a cat and dog sitting side-by-side with *Fur-Ever Homes* in bold black letters in the middle of the card. Underneath the name were a phone number and an e-mail address. No physical location or mailing address.

"Great. I'll keep this and be in touch if I need to find a different place for Buffy," I said.

We walked outside together. I watched as she got into a blue van, and I wrote down the number of the Michigan license plate.

Chapter Eighteen

I wondered what kind of scam Lissa was up to. Was she flipping dogs? A flipper is someone who looks for free dogs with resale value. They usually get the dogs from the "free to good home" ads. Flippers then sell the dogs for whatever amount they can get, not caring to whom they sell the dogs.

I didn't have the authorization to run Lissa's license plate number, so I'd have to wait and ask Jason to do it for me.

I spent the rest of the day at home getting caught up on laundry and giving the dogs a bath. One bad thing about living in the country is that dogs always find something stinky to roll in. Grams had a plastic kiddy pool that worked great for giving them baths. I pulled it out of the barn, got the hose hooked up to the warm water faucet in the basement, got the doggie shampoo and then, one-by-one, brought the dogs out of the house and lathered and rinsed each one. Grams helped by holding their leash so they couldn't escape. When bath time was done, they were put in the fenced yard to dry in the sun.

Keeping busy took my mind off Cooper. I knew we would keep in touch via e-mail and telephone, but it wasn't the same. I already missed his touch, the way he would rub my arm when we sat close or caressed my shoulder when he walked near me.

Monday morning was devoted to cleaning dog kennels and cat cages and feeding and watering. It was a daunting task when done alone—Cindi had the day off. I wondered what everyone else was doing on this holiday. After being with Cooper for a week, I felt the loneliness of being by myself creeping into my reality.

Red, the confiscated pit bull in quarantine, was the last dog I needed to care for. I opened the door to her room and talked softly. "Hey, girl. Remember me?" She didn't move, but her eyes were focused on my every move. I needed to move her out of her kennel to clean it.

"Hey, baby, I'm going to open the door and snap a leash on your collar," I said slowly in a low voice. I opened the kennel door a few inches. I reached inside. She trembled as I got closer but didn't retreat.

"It's okay. Jason would be here, but he has the day off. Your life will improve if we could be friends. Why don't you trust me?" I clipped the leash in place, stood up and opened the door the rest of the way.

"Come on, girl, do you want to go for a walk?" She hesitated. I backed away giving her as much space as the leash allowed. "Let's go out." I tugged gently on her collar. She stood and took a step forward. "What a good girl."

Red followed behind me as I led her outside into a fenced-in walking area. I didn't take her off leash, but I did walk her around for about a half hour. She slowly relaxed and started noticing her surroundings. She sniffed the air and watched a blue jay squawk in a nearby oak tree. I tied her to a post while I went back inside and cleaned her kennel. I scrubbed it, put in clean bedding and gave her fresh water and food. When I went back outside, she appeared calm.

"Hey, Red, you enjoying it out here?" I walked over to her like it was an everyday occurrence. I hoped my confidence gave her assurance that she was safe. She watched me but didn't display any signs of aggression. After I untied her, I pulled the leash so she had to walk closer to me. "Come on, girl, we're going in." She walked slowly behind me. Once inside, she went straight to her kennel. I unclipped the lead and, while my hand was close to her, I patted her shoulder. She took a step back.

"That's okay. I think we made some progress today. You're going to be okay," I told her as I closed the door and latched it.

It was close to noon before I finished the shelter chores. I took a break in my office and listened to voice-mails and read e-mails. One from Mary Ellen, the shelter director at Muskegon Animal

Shelter, caught my attention. She thought I'd like to know that two dead pit bulls had been found near the area where the other dogs had been found. She left her cell phone number and invited me to call if I wanted to talk. I dialed her number.

"Mary Ellen, it's Alison. You left me a message," I said after she answered.

"Oh, yeah. Hi. How are you?"

"Fine. Is anyone doing anything about the dead pits?"

"No, that's why I called. I'm not sure what you can do, but you asked me to call if anything else happened."

"I'm not sure what I can do either. Let me think about it and get back to you. Do you have the address where they were found?" I scribbled it down. After a couple minutes of small talk, we said goodbye. I wished I had answers for her.

My growling stomach convinced me to take a lunch break. I shut down the computer, straightened the stacks of paperwork and was heading to the door when I heard a vehicle pull in the driveway. I peeked out the window and saw Jason getting out of his car. I went out to greet him.

"Hey, what are you doing here on a holiday?"

"I came to check on Red. I didn't know if you would be able to handle her," Jason said. He leaned against the front of his car as we talked.

"That was sweet of you to come in on your day off, but I did okay with her. I took my time and got a leash on her. She was nervous but stayed calm. I tied her outside while I cleaned so she's set. I think we're becoming friends."

"Good. She's a sweet dog. I'd hate to have to put her down because she doesn't like women."

"So, it's not just me?"

"No. She doesn't care for Cindi either. I tested her with Carol last week, and it didn't go well. We'll just have to give her time."

"I hope so. I'm sure Grams could win her heart, if Cindi would let us take her. Maybe you could talk to her about it."

"I could. Maybe Grams should come in and see what you're getting her into before we make the decision."

I laughed. "I was just going to grab a bite to eat, do you want to join me?"

"Sure, I've been hungry for Italian. Do you want to go to Luciano's in Ludington?"

"I've never been there, but I'm game to give it a try."

"I'll drive," Jason said. He walked around and opened the car door for me. It made me feel like we were going on a date. He even waited while I got in and then closed the door. On the drive into town, I told him about the meeting with Lissa and asked if he could run her license plate number. He agreed but had questions.

"Tell me again how your meeting with her came about."

Honesty is the best policy so I told him about posting the ad on Craigslist in hopes of finding someone who was masquerading to get animals to use as bait.

"I posted the ad before Sheriff VanBergen told me not to get involved. I removed it after his lecture. The only response I answered was Lissa's, because she was from a rescue. You know me: I'm always on the lookout for rescues to partner with. Then we meet, and she says she pulls dogs from the county shelter. She's lying. I'm thinking she's flipping dogs, but I'd like to keep an eye on her."

"I can run the plate Tuesday," Jason said as he pulled into the restaurant parking lot. I opened my own door, but he opened the door to the restaurant. I felt a twinge of guilt going out to lunch with a man other than Cooper, even though he was just a co-worker.

The hostess led us to a booth and handed us menus. As I scanned the menu, I noticed several dinner entrees that included the choice of chicken or veal. I thought back to the calves at the farm who had been taken away from their mothers. Their innocent faces, their soft cries and innate need for their mother. Milk, their nutritional lifeline, was mechanically sucked from their mothers' teats, bottled and sold for human consumption. The calves' young bodies, valued for its tender meat, were killed and sold as veal. They were a byproduct of the milk industry, but clever marketers made veal a commodity.

I ordered spaghetti with marinara sauce.

"So what's been happening while I've been gone?" I asked.

"Quite a lot, but I don't know if it makes good dinner conversation."

"It's not dinner, it's lunch. So talk."

"We got a call about some dead animals out in the national forest. I went out and found the remains of several cats—couldn't say for sure how many—and five dogs. They didn't even bother to try and bury them this time. Dr. Johnson came out and said it looked like they were killed by dogs. More bait. I scanned them for microchips and took photographs—they're on my computer."

"I thought we scared them off. What did the sheriff say?"

"I don't get it, but he said it's not a priority. He didn't understand why I was talking to him about it. He actually said, 'It's just a bunch of dead animals, and you guys kill animals at the shelter all the time.'"

"He really said that?"

"He did. He doesn't want me to look for owners."

"Did you find any microchips?"

"One, in a cat. I have the owner's name and phone number for you to do a follow-up. I don't dare. It's back in the office."

The food came, and the conversation switched to my trip. I rambled on about my California adventure, leaving details about Cooper out of the conversation. It was a curious position to be in—not long ago I was breaking the law and now I worked hand-and-hand with the police. If anyone took the time to do a thorough investigation into Cooper's stay in Michigan, they'd eventually learn about me. If they investigated me, they'd discover I had two missing dogs who now were both back home.

Although it was Jason's day off, he came into the shelter after lunch and showed me the photos on his computer. I didn't have the stomach to look too closely, but asked him to e-mail them to me so I could have them on file.

"I guess we'll let it ride until something else comes up. The sheriff calls the shots," he said.

"He does for you," I said.

"What does that mean?"

"It means he's not *my* boss."

"I wouldn't piss him off if I were you. He carries a lot of weight, and if he wanted you gone, you'd be gone."

"There's no need for him to know what I do on my own time, is there?"

Jason laughed. He gave me the information about the microchipped cat before he left. Back in my office I read the owner's name—Kevin Palmer. I dialed his number and remembered who he was when I heard his recorded voice message. I left a message asking that he call me on Tuesday. Kevin was the owner of the black and white cat named Groucho, the one I suspected as being the same cat that Linda Levecca had complained about. The same cat her daughter had "taken care of."

Chapter Nineteen

After pondering what to do next, I concluded that one of the best options was to find out who was dropping off dead animals. Surveillance wouldn't work. The drop-offs were too sporadic. At least human surveillance wouldn't work. I called Jason, even though he had just left, and asked what he thought of putting a trail camera near where the animals had been found.

"Did it look like the bodies had been dropped off all at one time, or were there multiple drop-offs?" I asked

"I couldn't say, but there's no way of knowing if they'll come back to the same place."

"Did you look around the area? Maybe their operation is close by. How far would they travel to dump dead dogs?"

"Good questions. I don't have answers. The place is really remote. You could try a trail cam. Couldn't hurt."

"Would you help? I'll go buy one at Meijer right now." It took Jason a few seconds to respond. I could almost hear the debate in his head. His boss said not to investigate it, but he thought the boss was wrong. And here I was coaxing him along.

He concluded that what he did on his own time was his business. "I'll meet you in the store parking lot in an hour."

I bought two trail cameras. The second one was for Muskegon. I spotted Jason's pickup truck parked near my car when I came out of the store.

"Do you want me to drive or do you want to?" I asked.

"Your car wouldn't make it where we're going. That's why I brought my truck. Get in," he said.

I climbed into Jason's pickup, a blue Ford 150. The inside was dusty but clutter free. As he drove I read the camera directions, sometimes out loud. "It has an undetectable flash and 40 feet infrared flash range. During the day it takes color images and video. At night it takes monochrome pictures every 1.2 seconds when it detects movement."

"Have you ever used one of these?" Jason asked.

"No. Have you?"

He hadn't. "It'll be fun to play with. Who knows what we'll come up with," I said.

When I finally paid attention to where Jason was driving, I noticed we were deep in Manistee National Forest. The public land was large enough to get lost in.

"How do you know these woods so well?" I asked.

"I grew up in the area and used to hunt here with my dad when I was a kid."

"I didn't know you were a hunter."

"I'm not. I did it when I was young to please my dad, but hunting isn't my thing. I shot a deer once, and once was enough."

"Is your dad okay with you not following his footsteps?"

"At first he didn't understand, but he's okay with it now."

Jason stopped the truck and pulled out his phone. "It's just a couple hundred feet off the trail," he said. "I saved the coordinates so I'd know for sure."

As we approached the site, I noticed the faint smell of decomposition still lingering. "Do you have the name of the person who found the animals? What was he doing out here?"

"It was a guy out two-tracking with friends. They were curious about the odor and investigated. I wondered if they were involved, but after talking to the guy who called, I don't think so. He seemed traumatized by the whole thing."

"Now that I see the area, I doubt if they'll come back. Why would they? They have hundreds of acres at their disposal. Odds are they couldn't find this place again if they wanted to. It's so remote," I said.

"You're right, but I was thinking of putting the camera on the main trail. There aren't many roads, so we'll get a picture of anyone coming to this area."

So that's what we did. We stood in the back of Jason's truck to get the camera above eye level and strapped it to a tree. We aimed it at the two-track.

"I'll come back after the weekend with my laptop and download the photos," Jason said. The camera had a SD memory card that plugged into a computer to download images.

We went back to the shelter and Jason helped walk the dogs, who were excited to get outside after being penned up for hours. The walks, usually done by volunteers, were time consuming but they were an excellent way to get to know each animal. In the cat room, we scooped litter boxes and made sure each kitty had food, fresh water and a catnip toy.

After Jason left, I called Mary Ellen again. I told her I had a trail cam, and asked if she had the time to go out with me to put it up.

"It won't take long. Maybe an hour."

"It's not the time I'm worried about. Is this really what we want to do?"

"What do we have to lose? It's public property, right?"

"True. I guess we can see what we come up with and decide what to do with it later."

I told her I'd be there in about an hour. It was getting late, but if I hustled, there would be enough daylight to place the camera. The traffic going south was heavy. It was the end of the holiday weekend and everyone was heading back to Grand Rapids or Chicago or someplace in between.

Mary Ellen was waiting for me at the shelter when I arrived. She offered to drive, and I was happy to let her. I brought the stepladder from my shelter and was able to get it into her SUV. I grabbed the camera and we were off.

"How far away is it?"

"Not far. It's near the city's cemetery. The property was bought to expand the cemetery, so for now it's vacant land."

The neighborhood we were going through looked like the low-rent side of town. Potholes riddled the road, and it was hard to tell if the businesses on either side of the four-lane street were closed or just in need of a fresh coat of paint.

"It's not the best area," Mary Ellen said.

"Dog fighting could be happening in anyone of these buildings," I said.

"Wouldn't surprise me."

"Are we stereotyping the type of people involved in dog fighting?" I asked

"Oh, I don't know. Since this area is overrun with pit bulls, I think it's safe to say people who live here could be involved."

She turned down a side road, and the scenery changed from city to country. "It's hard to see because of the hill, but this is the back side of the cemetery," Mary Ellen said. She pulled off the road and parked.

"This is it? This is where they're dropping off dogs?" The area looked like a meadow, serene and peaceful.

"See those trees?" she asked, pointing off to the left. "That's where we found the dogs. You can see where people have been driving through the grass."

"If they're leaving such an obvious trail, why isn't something being done to catch them?"

"That's the million dollar question. I don't know."

I surveyed the field looking for a place for the trail cam. "That tree looks promising," I said. It was away from the area Mary Ellen had pointed out to me, but would give us a direct view. I hauled the ladder over, put the batteries in the camera and then nestled it into the crook of the tree to help hide it. The camera strap fit around one of the branches, holding the camera secure.

We stood back and admired our work. Since the camera was above eye level, it would most likely be invisible to anyone who happened by. "I can drive by on my way to work and make sure it's still there," Mary Ellen said. "If we find any dogs, I'll give you a call."

"Sounds good. I'll come, and we can download the photos and see what we get."

On our drive back to the shelter, I suggested we keep the camera a secret. "You never know who knows who and where the gossip will flow," I said. My real concern was VanBergen finding out I had broken my promise.

Mary Ellen agreed not to tell anyone. It would be our secret.

Chapter Twenty

The sun was setting by the time I got home and, once again, I felt a twinge of guilt for leaving Grams with the evening chores. The dogs greeted me with barks, twirls and wagging tails when I came in the house. I let them out into the fenced portion of the yard. I found Grams sitting in the kitchen reading the newspaper.

"Long day?" she asked.

I hated keeping secrets and decided to confide in Grams. If I couldn't trust her, who could I trust? No one. I poured myself a glass of wine and sat down across from her. I took a long swallow before I started talking.

"Long and crazy. I'm gone a week and come home to two people telling me they found dead pets that look like they've been used in dog fighting."

Grams put down the paper. "I can't stomach it. What's being done about it?" she asked.

"That's what I don't get. Nothing. The sheriff told Jason not to waste time on it, that it was just dead dogs and cats. He actually said that we kill cats and dogs at the shelter all the time so what's the problem?" I took another swig, I needed the numbing effect, and got up and grabbed a bag of pistachios from the cupboard.

"You're kidding. Sheriff VanBergen said that?" Grams asked as she helped herself to a handful of nuts.

"Yup. And the same thing is happening in Muskegon. They find dead and half-dead dogs by a cemetery so often that animal control routinely checks the site, but nothing is being done to catch the people."

"I wonder why."

"'It's only dogs.' They claim they have more important things to deal with, which is crazy."

"What does Cindi say?"

"I'll talk to her tomorrow. I'll tell you what I did do today, but it's a secret."

"Do I want to know?"

"It's up to you."

"I guess you'd better tell me," Grams said as she got up and poured herself a glass of wine and refilled my glass.

She munched on nuts and sipped wine as I told her about installing the trail cameras at the two locations.

"I didn't tell Jason what's going on in Muskegon. I figured the less he knows, the less trouble he'll be in if Sheriff VanBergen finds out."

"What'll you do with the pictures?"

"I don't know. It'll depend on what we get."

"Do you think the two cases are related?" Grams asked.

"I hadn't given it much thought, but maybe. Could there be two separate dog fighting operations 60 miles apart?"

"I doubt it. I'd think they'd at least be aware of each other."

Grams was right. If there were two separate fighting operations, they had to at least know about each other. Or maybe there was just one organizing group with several fight locations. Cody barked, his signal for wanting in, so I got up and let the gang in. They all came into the kitchen and settled in.

"I'm not supposed to be doing what I'm doing, but I feel forced into it, because the cops aren't doing their job," I said.

"Is there anyone with more authority that you could talk to? Someone in the county or city government? The state police?"

"There probably is. I'll talk to Cindi tomorrow," I said, as I put away the pistachios and cleaned the mess we'd made with the shells. Grams rinsed the wine glasses. She went in to watch television, and I went to my room to check e-mails. Cooper sent a sweet note saying how much he missed me. Lissa surprised me by writing again with another offer to take my dog.

Sleep avoided me. I couldn't relax or get comfortable. When I did drift off, visions of men watching dogs fighting plagued my dreams. Deep-throated growls, the sweet scent of blood and the piercing yells of pain were mingled with cheers and taunts.

I scanned the crowd searching the faces for compassion or concern and found none. The men seemed fueled by the blood, the competition and the hope of winning. After I woke, I replayed the scene in my memory for any hint of a location of the fight or any familiar faces.

Chapter Twenty-one

During breakfast I wrote a to-do list: call Linda Levecca again about the cat; talk to Cindi; get hold of Kevin Palmer; and check-in with Mary Ellen.

There was a black car in the shelter's parking lot when I pulled in. Usually an early arriver meant someone looking for a lost pet. As I parked, a man got out of the car and walked in my direction.

"Good morning, may I help you?" I asked.

"Yes, an Alison left me a message yesterday, and I'm assuming it's about my missing cat. I'm hoping she found him."

"I'm Alison. Come to my office and we'll talk." I held out my hand. As we shook hands, he introduced himself as Kevin Palmer. I guessed his age to be around 30. I also guessed he had a gym membership—his legs and arms were tan and muscular. He looked striking in dark blue shorts and a white polo shirt.

I unlocked the door and relocked it once we were inside. "We don't open to the public until noon today," I explained.

"I appreciate you making an exception for me," Kevin said. He followed me to my office.

"No problem. I know you're anxious about your cat." I offered him a seat and then sat down behind my desk. "Unfortunately, the news isn't good." He looked straight at me and asked if his cat was dead.

"I'm so sorry, but he is. The only reason we knew it was Groucho was from the microchip. Without that we wouldn't have been able to identify him."

"What does that mean?" he asked.

140

"Well ... animal control was called to a site in the national forest where some guys found several dead animals. The officer looked for identification. There were no collars, but he also scanned for microchips. He found one. Groucho's."

"How did it happen?" He shifted in the chair.

I didn't want to tell him, but I also didn't want to lie.

"Was it kids? Was he tortured?" he asked, his voice changing from sorrow to anger.

"We don't know the 'who', but he was found with a couple other cats and several dogs. We think there's a dog fighting operation going on in the county, and we think they use small animals to teach their dogs how to fight."

Kevin was silent for a long moment. When he spoke his voice shook. "You're kidding me, right? Dog fighting? Here?"

"I wish I were. We've been seeing signs of it in the past month, but that's all I know."

"What's being done?" He slammed his first down on my desk and stood up.

I couldn't tell him the sheriff wasn't doing a damn thing, so I told him it was an ongoing investigation and I couldn't discuss the details. He asked about Groucho's body, and I told him the remains had been cremated. He wanted to be kept informed of the progress in the investigation.

"I miss him. He was one cool cat. I kept praying he'd come back. I thought the microchip would bring him home. I guess in a way it did. I can quit hoping now."

"I really am sorry," I said. I felt his pain and shared his anger.

As he walked to his car his head hung low. Once in the car, he slumped over the steering wheel. I couldn't watch.

Cindi's car was in the parking lot, and I found her in her office. "Can we talk?" I asked.

"Sure, have a seat. How was California?" She poured us each a cup of coffee.

"It's already history—a day back here will do that."

Cindi laughed. "I'd like to hear about it. Maybe over lunch?"

Our friendship was dissolving into a work relationship. "Lunch sounds good. Let me know when you have time. What I'd like to talk about now is the dog fighting investigation—or the lack of one. Jason came in yesterday and got me caught up on what's been going on while I was gone. He said Sheriff VanBergen told him not to waste time investigating the dead animals found in the national forest. Why isn't something being done?"

"Jason talked to me about it, and I don't understand it either," Cindi said.

"Do we have to have the sheriff's permission to look into it?"

"It's not our job. We're not law officers. Jason is, but he has to do what his boss tells him. I'm new to this job, so I don't know the proper procedure. I'll talk to the sheriff, express our concerns and see what he has to say."

There was a knock at the door. Carol and another volunteer wanted to let us know they were going to start cleaning the cages and walking the dogs.

"Wonderful. I'll be there in a couple minutes to help," I told them. The door closed and I turned back to Cindi. "So you'll talk to the sheriff? Can I be there?"

"I think I'd better handle it alone. I'll call him right now and see if he can come over. I'll let you know what happens," she said.

"Okay," I said, getting up to leave.

"Welcome back. We missed you last week," she said.

"Sorry to say I didn't miss being here. It was good to live in a world without all this," I said, spreading my arms out to encompass the entire shelter, including the kennels with their homeless occupants, "even if it was for just one week."

"Well, don't be having any thoughts of leaving us. I don't know what I'd do without you," Cindi said.

"Thanks. It's good to be appreciated."

It did feel good to be appreciated. The gratefulness kept me powered ... at least for a little while. As we made our way through the morning routine, Carol filled me in on her week. She seemed pleased to say she'd kept the kennel numbers the same. Strays and surrendered pets came in, but she found placements for the same number of cats and dogs.

"That's the way we like it. No euthanasia. Thanks for working so hard. I know it takes effort," I said. We had the dogs outside and were cleaning and disinfecting the kennel floors. Carol had already started washing the bedding.

"It helped having the adopt-a-thon on Saturday at the pet supply store. I wonder if we should do those more than once a month."

"I'd love it if we could. The only thing stopping us is manpower."

"Why don't we advertise for more volunteers?"

"I can post something on our Facebook page and website saying that we need help. Let's see what kind of response we get."

When we finished, Carol was off to set live-traps to catch feral cats in a mobile home park. Carol's first passion was our trap-neuter-return program. Mobile home parks were magnets for homeless cats. Women tended to feed the hungry strays and kids played with the kittens making them friendly, but no one took ownership, and the cats just kept reproducing. The park was a major source of unwanted litters of kittens coming into the shelter. More than we could find homes for.

After Carol left, I went back to my to-do list. Next up, call Linda Levecca. In my mind, the stray cat I briefly saw in her yard had been Groucho. The face markings were too unique to be found on two cats in the same neighborhood. I had Linda's number half dialed when my gut told me to hang up. I had the feeling I'd get more accurate information if I went and talked to her face-to-face. Half an hour later I was knocking on her door. When she answered, I told her I was doing a follow-up on the stray cat and asked if she had any more problems. She stepped outside, and we talked on her porch.

"Didn't you already talk to my daughter about it?" she asked. Linda didn't look old enough to have an adult daughter. A pink sundress complemented her slim figure. Her blondish brown hair, cut in a bob, gave her a stylish appearance.

She was right to question why I was back. If I spent this much time on every call that came into the shelter about a stray, I'd get nothing done. "I did, but I didn't know if the problem was resolved. I thought it was a neighbor's cat and wondered if it was still stalking the birds at your feeder. I know what a nuisance cats can be when you're a bird lover."

"No, I haven't seen it since Missy took care of it."

"Is she home? Could I talk to her?"

"No, she's not. She has her own place, but she's here a lot. She worries about her old mother." Linda placed her hand on the doorknob, indicating that she wanted the conversation to be over. But I wasn't done yet.

"Oh, I thought she lived here."

"No, but she's here so much it sometimes seems like it." She opened the door and started to step inside. "If you'll excuse me, I have something in the oven."

"Sure, thanks for your time. I'm glad everything is okay."

I left, but it still didn't feel right. I made a mental note to track down her daughter.

Jason was at the shelter when I returned. "I have the information on that plate you asked for," he said. As we walked to my office, he handed me a piece of paper with a name and address on it.

"The plate is registered to a Melissa Devine," he said.

"Melissa? She goes by Lissa, must be short for Melissa."

"Must be. She lives south of here. Between Pentwater and Hart, near Pentwater River State Game Area. She has a kennel license and boards dogs."

"Okay, that makes sense. If she boards animals, getting involved in rescue is only a step away. But I still don't know why she lied about getting animals from the shelter."

"She could just be a big talker. Saving dogs from a shelter makes her look like a hero. Who wouldn't like her? Or trust her?"

"True. She did seem to have a big ego."

"She probably *is* flipping dogs. Maybe she has a client looking for a specific breed. Or maybe she just knows which breeds she can sell to make herself a fast buck. She found your ad on Craigslist, so you know she's checking the online sites."

"True. She e-mailed me again offering to take my dog. I'll keep in touch with her just to see what she's up to. Who knows, maybe she'll turn out to be legit and will be able to help us. If nothing else, she could foster dogs if she has extra space."

"Can't hurt."

I told Jason about my conversation with Cindi and her willingness to talk to the sheriff about the need for an investigation

144

into the dead animals. "I think she'll be able to convince him that it needs to be looked at."

After Jason left, I checked my e-mails. One of them surprised me. It was from Rocky Pahn, the man I met with from Friends Not Fighters in Chicago. He asked that I call. He had something confidential he wanted to discuss.

Chapter Twenty-two

Since Rocky wanted to talk confidentially, I thought it best not to call from the shelter phone where I might be interrupted or overheard, so I drove home for a late lunch and called from my cell phone in the privacy of the kitchen.

After the how-are-you small talk, Rocky asked if I was still investigating dog fighting in Michigan.

"Not in all of Michigan, but a little bit in Muskegon and farther north. Why do you ask?"

"We had an opportunity fall in our lap, and we're not sure what to do with it. I thought I'd get your input."

"Sure, what's up?"

"Mike, one of my volunteers, has an uncle—Vic—who lives in Muskegon and breeds and sells pit bulls. He also fights them. Mike used to live with his uncle in Chicago, and when Mike was young his uncle took him to dog fights. Mike never liked going, but he couldn't let on how he really felt. When his uncle moved to Michigan, Mike stayed here. He's been volunteering for me for about a year. His uncle is bragging that he has a champion dog and invited Mike to come visit and see the dog's first fight. Mike is going. He doesn't know where the fight will be, but he asked his uncle if he could bring a buddy and his uncle said yes. Do you know anyone who could go with him?"

Rocky's story surprised me, especially after his warnings about how dangerous it was to investigate the big players. "I thought your policy was not to get involved. That you hand over information to people better equipped to handle it."

"Well, here's the thing. Vic also bragged about the cops being bought off. So I'm leery about calling the police. If I hand over the information to one of the big animal groups, they'll get the local police involved. I don't know what to do. Do you have any suggestions on who I could call?"

I thought about Rocky's question. "From what I've seen and heard, investigating dog fighting isn't a high priority around here. I've never thought about the police being bought off, but I get the impression they wouldn't do anything even if you did call."

"That's what I was afraid of."

"Why do you want someone besides Mike going?"

"It's safer to have two, and someone from the area might recognize people at the fight."

"Really? I doubt if anyone I or my friends know would attend a dog fight."

"I'm not asking *you* to go, and don't be so sure nobody you know isn't into dog fighting. It's not like they'd tell you about it, if they were."

He had a point. Everyone knew where I stood when it came to the treatment of animals. I didn't hide my opinions.

"Let me think about it and see if I can come up with someone who might be interested. Do you have a date for the fight?"

"No, but it could be soon. I'll let you know when I hear anything else."

After we said our good-byes, I sat at the table for several minutes thinking about Rocky's request. Too bad Cooper lived so far away. He'd go. The thought made me chuckle. There was no end to the trouble I could get that man into. I thought about asking Jason, but didn't want him to jeopardize his career.

I didn't want to attend the fight and knew that as a woman, I probably wouldn't blend in with the crowd anyway. I went in the bathroom and pulled my hair back. Could I pass as a guy? No. I'd need some serious makeup. I knew where to turn for help. Google. The best website I found was wikihow.com/Disguise-Yourself-As-a-Boy-or-Girl. The site had several suggestions:

> Appearance: Get a boy-looking hair cut, wear a wig
> or if you have long hair, try to pull it up in a ponytail
> right on top of your head and then stick it under a

cap and pull the ends out. Remove all makeup and earrings. Wear sunglasses. Also, make it a point to not show feminine body things, like shaved legs or pits. Guys do not shave their legs.

Hide your cleavage: If your breasts seem obvious, put on a bra that matches the color of your clothing and tape it tight. Also, it may be necessary to wear something (tight sports bra or try a FTM binder, etc.) to make your chest less noticeable. It may be uncomfortable, but it's a way to keep the dead give-away concealed. (Reminder—Do not use elastic bandages. They can crack ribs and stop fluid flow in your lungs, making passing out a possibility or worse.)

Small Talk: Guys are usually a lot more relaxed than girls; this doesn't open them up too well for many questions. Ease it along slowly, with small talk to set it off.

Wear boyish clothes: Try wearing things like jeans, and T-shirts. Over-sized sweaters are good also. Jeans, however, have their downfalls with being different for each sex. If you can't find baggy jeans, then wear old sweats. Make sure that it won't be creepy though. Wear a baseball cap, and never ever wear pink. The guys will be suspicious of your motives. Wear dirty gym shoes that don't look feminine at all, and walk with a slower shuffle. Slouching shows that you're relaxed. Don't be afraid to get into character.

Produce a new name: For instance, Christina to Christian, Alexa to Alex. If your name does not easily turn masculine, use an easy-to-remember guy name, like a close family member.

I could be Al.

When ready, approach guys, but not ones you know. This is a recipe for disaster. Try not to act funny or goofy around them, but laugh at their jokes and do not talk about girl stuff. This includes purses, dates, makeup, boys.

If by some chance you are injured in the groin area, make sure you act like it hurts. If you want help on your 'disguise', consider asking for aid at transgender or transvestite (cross dresser) forums. They're generally very friendly and have deeply studied the minute details of passing as the opposite sex.

Using the bathroom isn't a big deal but don't pretend to have parts that you don't. It's fine for a guy to sit to pee so take advantage of the stalls and the privacy they afford.

Be careful with makeup. You don't need it to look one sex or the other and messing it up only makes you stand out. If you have a high-pitched voice, try to lower it around other guys.

Interesting stuff. Cutting my hair was not an option. If I wore a hat, I'd be worried it might blow off or someone would ask me to remove it. I'd have to get a wig ... and a skin-colored sports bra. I'd have to practice my guy persona before the big event.

On Amazon.com I found a wig to my liking, dark brown with a short-layered look. The price fit my budget: $7.99. Surprisingly, the wig had pretty good reviews. I also put in my shopping cart a wig cap to cover and hold in my own hair and a chest compression wrap. To complete my persona, I purchased a pair of vintage-style glasses with clear lenses, kind of a Clark Kent look.

Before placing the order, I searched Amazon for tiny cameras. If I went to the fight, I'd want to document what I saw and doubted if they let anyone take photos, let alone someone they didn't know. There were several small cameras, and, after reading the reviews and because of their affordable prices, I decided to order two. For $9.99 I got a Spy Pen, an ink pen that not only writes, but also doubles as a camera and takes photos and video.

For $10.50, I bought a mini camera camcorder that was about the size of my thumb and it, too, could take photos and video. Both stored images that could be downloaded to a computer.

The one-day shipping cost more than the wig, but if this was going to happen, I needed to be practiced and ready. As I placed the order, I wondered ... *When did I decide to attend the fight?* Probably the moment Rocky presented the opportunity.

After the late lunch, I went back to the shelter and settled into routine office work. A couple hours later, it was time to ready the animals for the night. Jason came in to help with Red, although I was comfortable with the pit by myself now. We took her outside into the fenced-in run and let her loose.

"She's filling out and settling down," I said as Red wandered around the area sniffing the ground.

"She's coming along nicely. She's a smart dog." Jason called her name, and Red stopped her investigation and trotted to him. He gave her a treat and told her she was a good dog. He handed me a treat to give to her.

I took a few steps away from him. "Red, come," I said. She looked at me and then at Jason. "Red, come," I said again. She lowered her head and dutifully walked to me. She accepted the treat from my hand and then walked back to Jason and sat by his feet looking up at him.

"She still likes you best," I said. "But I feel safe with her. I don't think she'd hurt me. She needs more time in a safe environment. What does Cindi say about her?"

"She's leaving it up to me." He bent over and stroked Red's back. He told her to go play, and she resumed sniffing the grass.

"So what are your thoughts?"

"Like you said, she needs more time, but I think she's ready for a foster home."

"Do you think she can be placed with other dogs?"

Jason laughed. "I know, you want to take her home to Grams. What does she think of the idea?"

"She'd probably be okay with it, but I better double check with her." I realized I wasn't home as much as I should be, and Grams was doing more than her share of the work. Maybe another dog, especially one with issues, wasn't a good idea.

"So far Red hasn't shown any signs of aggression toward other dogs. With cats, she seems to be curious. I haven't let her loose around a cat so you'd need to be careful. Maybe she needs to start in a place with fewer distractions. I don't want to set her up for failure."

"True, we need to do what's best for her. Maybe you should take her," I said jokingly. I was surprised by Jason's reaction.

"I've been thinking about it. I only have Sheba, and she loves everybody and everything. I can keep them separate in the house while I'm gone and slowly introduce them when I'm home."

Jason's home sounded better for Red than the farm. "Sounds ideal," I said.

Jason called Red and we took her back inside. "Maybe I'll take her home tonight. I don't have anything going on."

While Jason held Red's leash, I gathered her bed, bowls, food, and chew toys and followed as he led Red outside. She hesitated when he encouraged her to jump up into the front seat of his truck. I put her gear behind the driver's seat and stood out of the way while Jason sweet-talked the quivering dog. He climbed into the passenger seat and scooted over to make room for Red. It took a few minutes, but she finally worked up the courage to follow Jason into the truck. I gently closed the door behind her and waved as Jason drove off.

As I was leaving for the night, Cindi stopped me and informed me that she had an appointment the next morning with Sheriff VanBergen at his office.

"Sounds official, meeting on his turf," I said.

"I invited him here, but he said he didn't have time for it, so I offered to make the drive to his office."

"Good luck. I'll be interested to hear what he has to say."

"I'll let you know as soon as I get back." We walked out together and said our goodbyes in the parking lot. After Cindi drove off, I checked my cell phone for messages. There was one from Mary Ellen. Someone had found more dogs out by the cemetery. She wondered when I could come and check the camera. I called her right back.

"I can come tonight. I need to go home and get my laptop. It'll be about an hour and a half. Can you wait for me?"

She said she'd wait for me at the county shelter. I asked about the dogs.

"They must have had something going on over the holiday weekend. Usually there's just one or two dogs. This time there were four. Three were already dead, and one was hurt so bad the vet euthanized it."

"Damn. I hope we caught them."

Grams was home when I got there. I explained the situation. She understood the urgency and said she could take care of the evening chores. Again, I felt guilty. She made me a sandwich for the road while I grabbed the laptop and stepladder. Within ten minutes I was on the road heading to Muskegon.

Chapter Twenty-three

Traffic was light so I made good time. When I pulled into the driveway of the animal shelter, I spotted Mary Ellen sitting on a picnic table in the side yard. She waved and came over to the car.

"You didn't break any speed limits on the way, did you?"

"None that anyone noticed," I said with a smile.

She got in the car, and I made a U-turn in the parking lot.

"I couldn't wait, so I took a drive to see if the camera was still in the tree," she said.

"Was it?"

"It looked like it. Kind of hard to tell from the road. I didn't dare stop. I guess I'm a little paranoid," Mary Ellen said.

"You're funny. You're trying to do what's right, and you're the one who is scared."

"Maybe paranoid isn't the word. Scared. If these people can fight dogs to the death, I don't know what they'd do to us if they caught us snooping around."

"I try not to think about it," I said. She was right to be concerned. I didn't let thoughts about the type of people we were dealing with linger too long in my mind. Thoughts like that could paralyze me with fear. I chose not to be paralyzed.

"Easier said than done," she said. "I feel vulnerable. Maybe because it's happening in my backyard."

"Maybe, but we're being careful. We'll take it slow."

Thankfully, the field was deserted. I drove the car as close to the tree as possible. The camera was right where we had left it. I situated the stepladder next to the tree trunk and, while Mary

Ellen steadied the ladder, I climbed up. I popped out the memory card, leaving the camera in place. Back in the car, I slid the card into the reader of my computer. It took a couple of minutes to download the images.

There were twenty-two photos. The first two photos were of us right after we installed the camera. The daytime lighting made for crisp color photos. Next were photos of deer, then a woodchuck. Next up was a black and white picture of a dark colored van.

The camera was an infrared model. When it took photographs at night no visible light was generated. No flash meant that after dark the quality of the photos deteriorated. The camera switched to black and white mode and the detail and clarity were reduced.

"That has to be them. The van is parked near where the dogs were found," Mary Ellen said.

All we had were grainy images of a van. The dogs must have been unloaded from the side door, which was away from the camera. The driver apparently never got out. In one photo, the van was closer to the road, and I could see they had dropped something off. But I couldn't even say for sure what they had left behind. Next we had photos of animal control. There were several photos of the bodies being picked up, but that happened in daylight so the quality of the photos was better.

The photos were time stamped. The drop-off had been made at 3:03 a.m. Tuesday morning.

"Darn. The angle was wrong and the camera was too far away," I said. "We need to get the camera closer."

We surveyed the area. "The only possibility is that tree partway up the hill. It's closer, but I don't know if the angle will work. We might just get the tops of their heads."

"I don't see any other option, so I say we give it a try," Mary Ellen said.

I climbed the ladder again, this time to remove the camera. I hauled the ladder to the other tree while Mary Ellen followed me with the camera. It took a while to get it situated. We did a walk test to see what the camera would capture. By this time it was twilight. I climbed the ladder again, popped out the memory card and went back to the car where I downloaded the images to my laptop.

"We're definitely closer," I said. "I think the camera needs to be tilted up just a smidgen so we get more of the background. Hopefully we'll get a license number if they come back again." I knew it was just a matter of time before they found a different dumping spot.

I climbed the ladder once more to return the memory card and adjust the tilt of the camera. I felt confident enough not to do another test shot. Maybe I should have, but I was tired.

"I think that will do it. Too bad we didn't get anything incriminating, but now we know they're driving a dark colored van," I said as I climbed down the ladder.

"That's more than we knew before," Mary Ellen said.

We jostled the ladder back into the car and drove Mary Ellen back to the shelter.

"Sorry it was a waste of your time," she said.

"It wasn't. No need to apologize. Next time we'll get something we can use."

After leaving Mary Ellen, I made my way home. It had been a long day. To help keep me awake, I drove with the window open and played the music loud.

Back at the farm, the house was dark except for the stove light in the kitchen. I assumed Grams would be in bed, but I was wrong. She was sitting on the porch swing waiting for me.

"You didn't have to wait up for me," I said, taking a seat next to her. The swing had developed a squeak that seemed amplified by the stillness of the night.

"I didn't have a choice. I was too worried to sleep and couldn't go to bed. Did you get anything?"

"No, the camera was too far away to get details. We saw that it was a van, but that's the only thing we learned. We moved the camera to a closer tree."

Fireflies flickered in the yard. I heard a dog whimper in the house and got up and opened the door. All five of them crowded their way out.

"I hate that you worry. I'm careful," I said, sitting back down.

"I can't help it. I know you're careful, but I also know the type of people you're dealing with. Do you really think they'll drop off more dogs?" Grams asked.

"I hope so, but if they do it's real stupidity on their part. My guess is that some of the dogs aren't dead when they drop them off, and they're hoping they'll get medical care. Maybe their way of easing their guilt."

"You think people who fight dogs have a conscience?"

"No, but why else would they do it? I've been thinking about it and can't come up with another reason," I said.

"Maybe they're too lazy to bury them. Let someone else do the dirty work."

"You're probably right, but they have to know they're running a risk of getting caught."

I debated with myself about telling Grams about the opportunity to attend a dogfight. I knew I had to tell her, even though she would be furious that I was doing it on my own.

"Remember Rocky, the guy I had a meeting with while we were in Chicago?" I asked.

"Is he the one who rescues dogs used for fighting?"

"Yes," I said and then relayed Rocky's story. I told her I was considering going.

"You're crazy! Why you? Do you have any idea what you would be seeing? Isn't there anybody better equipped?"

Her reaction didn't surprise me, but it did irritate me. "You mean somebody like a guy?"

"No! I mean someone with training, like Jason. He'd have backup if he needed it."

"If there were someone I trusted, I'd gladly let him do it. But, besides Jason and Cindi, I don't know who I can trust. Both Cindi and Jason would be putting their jobs on the line if they went, and I won't ask them to risk their jobs."

"And you are?"

"This isn't my dream job, so if I get fired, I think I'll survive."

Grams actually laughed when I told her about ordering a man's hairpiece and my plan to go undercover as a guy.

"You're nuts," she said.

"I'll be more comfortable going as someone else. I can get into character and be a thug without feelings."

"You think?"

"I'll need practice, but, yeah, I think I can do it."

"What about your womanly figure? You should be more worried about that than your hair."

"I ordered a chest-compression wrap, and I'll wear a baggy shirt and a jacket."

"You do keep things interesting around here," she said.

It was time to call it a night, so we called in the dogs and said our goodnights. Once in my room, I checked my e-mails. I could count on an e-mail from Cooper every night. He filled me in on his day and always told me how much he missed and loved me. While I loved the letters, I wondered how long we could survive with only an electronic connection. I craved physical contact. I longed to be kissed, to be held, to cuddle with him as I drifted to sleep.

Knowing e-mails aren't necessarily private, I chose my words gingerly when I wrote back. I shared the every-day happenings and included how much I missed him. My investigative work wasn't divulged. I ended with, "Wish you were here," which was so very true.

Chapter Twenty-four

Jason's truck was in the parking lot when I got to the shelter Wednesday morning. It was unusual for him to beat me to work. Usually he started his day at the sheriff's department. I searched for him in the front offices, then in the kennels. I found him in the cat room. "What's up?" I asked.

"Checking to see how much space you have."

"For what?"

"We got a call last night from a woman who lives on the other side of the state. She'd been trying to reach her brother who wasn't answering his phone. She worried because he had medical issues and wondered if someone could check on him. The dispatcher sent an officer out, and he found the man unconscious on the bed. They got him to the hospital, and he's not expected to make it. The guy has a bunch of cats we need to deal with."

"How many?"

"I don't know. They were too busy dealing with the guy to count, but it sounds like quite a few. Do you have time to go out there with me?"

"I do, but if we bring them here, they'll have to go into quarantine. Good thing you took Red home last night so the room is empty. How's she doing?"

"She was nervous, but I think she'll do okay. I took her for a walk by herself this morning. She's not used to being on a leash but she did fine. I crated her before I left. I'll go home at lunchtime and check on her."

"Glad to hear it. Do I have time to clean and feed before we head out?"

Jason offered to help. Cindi came in when we were almost done and was kind enough to finish.

"We're just doing an assessment," I told her. "We'll come back and decide how we're going to handle it. Hopefully there aren't too many cats."

The house, a dozen or so miles from town, was on a gravel road with the closest neighbor about a half-mile away. As Jason pulled into the driveway, I saw an orange tabby and a calico dodge into the bushes near a dilapidated barn. The grass looked like it hadn't been mowed in a while. Cats sat in every window of the old farmhouse, and one sat on the front porch.

"What did you say this man's name was?" I asked. Seeing the house brought the story into focus. The house and all the cats were his life, and now strangers were snooping.

"Charles River."

"What do you know about him?"

"Not much. He lived alone and had a sister who worried about him. That, and he's probably going to die."

"Well, we also know Charles liked cats," I said. "Do you have a key to the house?"

"I was told it wouldn't be locked. The man's sister gave us permission to check on the cats. She thought he had two."

"I'd say there are definitely more than that. Maybe the *two* weren't fixed. Two cats can multiple into dozens in just a couple of years."

A slight odor of cat greeted us as we stepped from the truck. "This isn't going to be good," Jason said.

Before going inside, we walked around the house. On the back stoop were empty bowls that probably held food and water once. A black cat came up from the barn meowing at us as if to say, "Where's dinner?" He let me stroke his back. He didn't feel as though he had missed too many meals.

"Give us a few minutes, and we'll get you some food," I told him. He sat down next to the dishes, as if he had understood me.

Back at the front of the house, we climbed the three steps to the covered porch. I stood behind Jason as he opened the door.

The smell was offensive, a mix of urine and feces. At least it didn't smell like death.

"Let's get some windows opened," I said.

I took a deep breath of fresh air and held it in my lungs as I dodged inside. Cats scattered as we entered. The floor, covered with dried cat feces, crunched as I walked on it. I noticed a row of litter boxes along one wall. They were so full it was hard to determine if they contained litter or were just overflowing with cat waste.

Three cats—two black and white tuxedo kitties and one gray tabby—sat on the back of a couch watching us. They looked healthy and well-fed. The couch didn't look as good—apparently it doubled as a scratching post.

Luckily the two windows in the front room opened with minimum effort. Jason had similar luck with windows in the kitchen and dining room. After opening the windows, we regrouped outside in the fresh air.

"Thankfully, it's not as bad as dead dogs," Jason said.

"Nothing could be that bad, but it comes in a close second."

"No wonder the guy was sick. Anyone would get sick living in there."

"I can't imagine. If he had health problems, why wasn't someone checking on him?"

"His sister was, but she didn't live close enough," Jason said.

"We need to get a headcount of the cats and make sure they have enough water and food until we can figure out what to do. We'll talk to Cindi, but I think we're going to need help."

I had brought an 18-pound bag of dry cat food, just in case the cats hadn't been fed. We found water bowls in the kitchen and bathroom. After removing dirty dishes from the kitchen sink, I scrubbed the bowls clean, filled them with fresh water and placed them back on the floor. Six cats came up to drink.

Jason handed the filthy food dishes to me to scrub before he went outside to investigate. Cats came running from everywhere when they heard the rustle of dry food being poured.

"Poor babies," I said. Twenty-three hungry kitties squeezed in around the bowls. The sound of them crunching the hard kibbles filled the room. While they ate, I looked through the rest of the house. More cats scattered as I searched the rooms one by one. In one bedroom there was a cardboard box with six brown tabby kittens. I guessed them to be four or five weeks old. I picked one up, and he hissed at me.

"Feisty little guy, aren't you?" I said. The other babies watched but didn't scatter and hide. I opened the two bedroom windows. The smell was still horrendous, but I was getting used to it.

Jason came in with more dirty bowls, which we washed and then filled with water and food. I carried a set to the black cat who still waited out back. He bumped my hand with his head as I placed the food bowl down, spilling a few kibbles, but he didn't mind eating off the floor.

"Some of the guys outside seem friendly like this one," Jason said as he petted the black cat. "I've seen at least a dozen around the barn, but there're probably more hiding."

"Same thing in the house, some friendlier than others. Some scared. Just guessing, but I'd say we've got at least 30 inside, probably more. There is a litter of six kittens. I'm surprised there aren't more litters. I'm betting most of the cats are fixed or we'd be seeing kittens everywhere."

"So we're thinking 40 to 50?" Jason asked.

"That's probably a good guesstimate," I said. "Whatever the number, there are more than we can house at the shelter. So what're our options?"

"For now, they're okay here. If Charles recovers, he'll have some say in what happens to them. We'll have to come out every day to feed and water them and clean the litter boxes," Jason said.

"I noticed two bags of litter and a box of garbage bags in the back room, but we'll need more," I said.

Jason offered to drive back to the shelter for supplies. "You want to stay and start cleaning?" he asked.

"Not really, but I will." I watched as he drove off and then went back inside and started the unpleasant task of cleaning litter boxes. When I finished the first box and filled it with clean litter, a cat walked up, sniffed and started scratching in it. As soon as he finished, I swear the cats started lining up like humans at porta-potties. One-by-one they relieved themselves in the clean litter and then went for more food.

"Mr. River took good care of you at one point," I said to the group. Due to the smell, the cleaning required frequent outside breaks. There was a picnic table that I took advantage of in the backyard. The black cat came up to me, rubbed against my legs and then hopped onto my lap.

"Why are you an outside kitty?" I asked. He head-butted my hand to keep me petting him—he knew the tricks. Other cats began to appear. Two more were eating on the back stoop.

I had all the boxes cleaned and began to get impatient for Jason to return with litter. While I waited, I topped off the food bowls and refilled the water dishes. Finally, I heard the sound of Jason's truck in the driveway. I walked to the front yard to meet him and get some fresh air.

"What took you so long? Waiting to make sure I had all the dirty work done?" I asked jokingly.

"Exactly. Actually, I called the hospital while I was at the shelter. Charles died last night. So I called his sister and told her about the cats. She doesn't want them and gave us permission to do whatever it takes to get rid of them. She wants them gone. She's hiring a crew to come out and clean so she can sell the place."

"Great. Is it our responsibility? Did you talk to Cindi?"

"Briefly. She didn't have any suggestions. I'll tell you what we would've done before she took over the shelter, though."

"What's that?"

"Euthanasia. We would have hired a vet to come out here. Probably would have dug a hole and filled it," Jason said.

"Really?"

"What other options are there? There're too many to take back to the shelter."

"We can't kill them." The black cat had followed me and was once again rubbing on my legs. "Could you?"

"I don't like it, but like I said, what are the options? The shelter is always close to capacity. What are we going to do with 40 to 50 cats?"

"Find them homes," I snapped. Jason's attitude made me mad. If Mr. River had dogs instead of cats, my guess was that Jason would be more inclined to save them.

"Really?" he said.

"Really. Killing them is the easy solution. I won't let that happen. I'll make some calls. Finding them all homes won't be easy, but we'll at least try. From what I can see, most of them are friendly adoptable cats. Some may have to be relocated to barns, but there're a lot of barns in this county." I tried to sound rational and keep my voice calm, but Jason heard the edge in my voice and backed off.

"I'm with you. I'm just saying what would have happened. I'm glad you're willing to try something else. Believe me, I don't want all these cats dead."

"Good." I grabbed a bag of litter from his truck and carried it inside. Jason did likewise. We filled the empty boxes and grabbed the bags of used litter and carried them back to the truck.

First order of business back at the shelter was to get in my car and go home to get cleaned up. Grams wasn't home. A box from Amazon was on the porch. I carried it inside but didn't take the time to open it. I disrobed and put my clothes in the washing machine on the smallest load setting. I took a shower and once again found myself scrubbing a stench from my hair and body. I dressed in a robe, put the clothes in the dryer and made a sandwich for lunch. By the time I was ready to go back to work, the clothes were dry.

On the drive back to the shelter I started thinking of who I could call to help with the cats. First would be Carol. She could help live-trap the wilder ones. I'd go through the list of approved rescues and ask if they could take any of the cats before they were vet-checked.

Jason was talking with Cindi in her office when I came in.

"What's up?" I asked, taking a seat next to Jason.

"Jason's filling me in. Sounds like we have house cats and some who need to go to barns."

"I don't know if any of them are truly feral, but some were outside. I didn't see a cat door. Maybe Mr. River opened the door for them."

"How do you think we should handle it?" Cindi asked.

"I think we should leave the cats where they are until we can find placements for them. I'll start making calls this afternoon.

I'm sure I can find two or three rescues that will help, especially with the mom cat and her kittens and the friendlier adults."

"Any idea how much time we have?" Cindi asked Jason.

"The sister wanted them out of the house before she gets here tomorrow, but I can talk to our attorney and see where we stand legally. Hopefully we can buy some time"

"Do that," Cindi said. "Meanwhile, Alison, you get on the phone and see what you can come up with. A few could come here until we find them homes. We can fit six in the quarantine room. If we had cages, we could set up temporary housing in the garage."

"As I make these calls, I'll see if anyone has cages we can borrow," I said.

Chapter Twenty-five

I spent the afternoon on the phone, e-mailing and Facebooking. One of the things Cindi started when she became director was a Facebook page for the shelter. We used it to post photographs of the cats and dogs that animal control brought to the shelter, as well as animals in need of adoption. The page was also used to notify people of special events. I posted that we'd discovered a hoarding situation and needed rescue groups to take cats and people to adopt or foster them. We also needed cat food and litter.

By the end of the day, I had lined up two women from approved rescues to come in the morning. Jeanine from Reuben's Room Cat Rescue and Sanctuary in Grand Rapids was willing to take the mom cat and her kittens. Diane from Heaven Can Wait in Muskegon had room for adult cats in her adoption program. Two other rescues offered to send someone to assess the cats to determine adoptability. I suggested they come on Friday. Each also had cages we could borrow.

Lissa from Fur-Ever Homes saw my plea on Facebook and messaged saying that she could take some cats. I was sure she didn't realize it was me she was communicating with. As an administrator of the site, my name wasn't associated with it, just the shelter's name. I messaged her back saying she needed to come to the shelter and fill out a rescue approval form, which included references, names of her board members and the name of the group's veterinarian.

Carol said she had three farmers she worked with who would take barn cats. She agreed to meet me at Mr. River's house in the morning to see if we needed to trap cats or just be patient and let them get comfortable with us so we could catch them.

After three hours of networking, I felt we had a good start. We had volunteers for the afternoon shelter work, so I left early to stop at the farm on the way home.

The black cat came trotting out to meet me, meowing all the way. "What a talker you are," I said. I picked him up and held him. His motor rumbled. "You're lonely, aren't you?" I gave him a couple minutes of attention and then set him on the ground. He followed me to the house and walked inside with me. I cleaned litter boxes again; it didn't take long for them to fill with so many cats in the house. I wondered how long Charles had been sick. He must have used his last bit of energy feeding and caring for his cats. I refilled the food and water bowls.

The black cat followed me back to my car. When I got in and closed the door he hopped on the hood, sat down and stared at me. I rolled the window down. "Hey there, you can't be sitting on my car. I need to leave." He ignored me. I had to get out of the car and physically remove him. "You make a beautiful hood ornament, but I don't think you'd like it once I got rolling."

I made the mistake of leaving the car door open when I got out to move him and once his feet landed on the ground, he dashed inside the car. He sat on the passenger seat like he wanted to go for a ride.

"Really, dude? Are you used to riding in a car?" I thought he would panic when I started the engine, but he didn't. I stroked his back, and he began to purr again.

"Okay, I got the message. You want to go home with me." *Why not?* I thought. Once the car was out of the driveway he lay down on the seat and napped.

Grams was weeding the flowers by the back door when I got home. I motioned for her to come to the car.

"What'd you bring home this time?" she asked.

The black cat was standing on the seat, stretching from his nap. I had rolled the window down.

"We got a call on a hoarding case. The owner died last night, and now we have a few dozen cats. This one followed me and then jumped in the car. I didn't have the heart to kick him out."

I felt like a little kid bringing home a stray and begging, "Can we keep it?"

"What's his name?"

"I have no idea. I bet the names all died with the owner."

The cat climbed over me and put his front paws on the edge of the car. Grams petted his head.

"He's a friendly guy," she said.

"What do you think? Is there room for one more at the inn?"

She laughed. "There's always room for one more. At least this one will eat less than the last stray you brought home."

"How is Bessie?" I asked.

"She's getting bigger. You can definitely tell she's with calf."

Grams picked up the cat so I could open the door. "We need to keep him separate from the other cats until a vet can see him."

"Wouldn't hurt. Where are you thinking?" Grams asked.

"Cooper's room?" I remembered how much I enjoyed Tabitha in the tree house and thought maybe this cat could live inside.

"Is he going to be a house cat? What will the gang think?"

"They're used to the cats in the barn. I think they'll do okay. I'm more worried about how he'll do with the dogs. And about you. Are you okay with a house cat?"

"Tom was the one who said, 'no cats in the house.' I don't have a problem with it. It might be kind of nice. I can call Dr. Jack tomorrow and take the cat in for a checkup," Grams said.

"Would you? I'd really appreciate it. Things are kind of hectic at work right now."

We got Black Cat settled in Cooper's room. When Cooper first left, I sometimes slept in his bed to feel closer to him. I took comfort in his belongings still being in his room. I had asked if he wanted me to ship them to him, but he had said no. He planned on returning someday. The dogs didn't understand why I wouldn't let them in Cooper's room, but the newcomer needed time to adjust before being introduced to the rowdy dogs.

"You can meet him tomorrow," I told them.

After dinner, Grams watched TV while I took my laptop to Cooper's room to hang out with Black Cat.

"We're going to have to come up with a better name for you," I told him. As soon as I sat down at the desk, he was on my lap purring. Cooper's nightly letter was similar to those of the past, ramblings about his day and how much he missed me. I wrote him about the hoarding case and my new cat.

After I let the dogs out for their last potty break of the day, I took my three guys to my room. When they settled in, I grabbed my pillow and went back to Cooper's room. Cooper's smell had faded from the sheets, but I still felt closer to him. This time I even had a warm body next to mine. One who purred.

Chapter Twenty-six

Black Cat was still cuddling me when I woke up. He seemed content to continue napping even after I crawled out of bed. The dogs were waiting for me when I returned to my room. They latched onto Black Cat's scent and spent a few seconds sniffing. While the scent intrigued them, they were eager to start the day.

"Are you ready to go out?" I asked as I opened the door. They scampered into the hallway and down the stairs. Grams was already up, so I let the dogs outside to join hers in the fenced yard, then went back upstairs to shower. The Amazon box sat on my dresser. I took the time to open it. The wig looked cheap, which it was. I had my doubts whether it would transform me into a man. The compression wrap made me chuckle. I'd try them on later.

My intention was to meet Carol at Mr. River's farm an hour before anyone else arrived so we could clean and discuss the situation. She was waiting for me in the driveway. We spotted a couple cats sunning themselves by the barn. It was a beautiful autumn morning with a blue sky and crisp air. The leaves on the maples had a hint of color.

"Enjoy the fresh air while you can," I told Carol.

"That bad?"

"The windows were open all night so maybe it's better than yesterday. I was thinking on the drive over that we should look for paperwork on the cats, maybe the name of a vet. I saw a file cabinet in one of the bedrooms. Maybe Charles was organized."

"Can't hurt to look, but I doubt if someone who collects that many cats is organized," Carol said.

We went inside and I noticed that the smell was much better. Still bad, but better.

"Is this your first hoarding case?" I asked.

She nodded yes.

"You'll get used to the smell. Give it a few minutes."

We filled the food and water bowls and cleaned the litter boxes. Next, we went into the bedroom that doubled as an office. Besides a file cabinet, there was a large oak desk piled with papers, plus a computer. Carol started to sift through the papers while I opened the top draw of the cabinet. The folders were filed alphabetically.

"Mr. River was organized," I announced. There was a divider labeled cats, and behind it were several folders. "Look at this. Information on the cats. Let's take it outside."

We took the folders to the picnic table and found a printout of a spreadsheet with the cats listed. There were names, descriptions, birthdays, vaccines and personality traits.

"Wow! I'm impressed," I said.

I went down the list looking for a black cat. There were six. Under the description of one of them, Mr. River had written, "Outgoing, vocal and most likely to find a new home." The cat's name was Ebony. It had to be Black Cat. Mr. River had him pegged. He had, indeed, found a new home.

The folder also contained an envelope that had the name and address of an attorney in the upper left corner. Inside were several pages of legal documents.

"Look at this," I said. "It looks like Mr. River made provisions for the cats in case he died. We better not let anyone take any of the cats until our attorney looks at this stuff." I put the papers back and took the files to my car.

While we waited for the volunteers from the rescues, Carol and I quietly walked around outside and in the barn, counting cats and searching for kittens. We counted 14 adults and didn't find any babies. The cats didn't seem too scared, but most kept their distance. That was normal. We were strangers.

"I think with a little coaxing, we could catch all these guys," Carol said.

By the time we got back to the house a car was pulling into the driveway. It was Jeanine from Reuben's Room.

"Boy, this is way out in the middle of nowhere," she said as she got out of her car.

"A good place to have as many cats as you want," I said. After I introduced her to Carol I told her we had a problem.

"What's that?" Jeanine asked.

"We got here early to feed the cats and took the time to look through a file cabinet. We found information on the cats, including legal documents. I'm no lawyer, but it looks like Charles River made plans for the cats in case something happened to him. We can't release any of the cats until our attorney reviews the papers and gives us the okay."

"That'd be a first."

"What's that?"

"That someone actually included their pets in their estate planning. Usually we get a call saying, 'Grandma died and she had a cat. Can you take it?' The family wants Grandma's money but not her cat."

"I know. We get those calls at the shelter too. It's sad," I said.

Diane showed up as we were about to go in the house. I explained the situation to her.

"Can I at least look at the cats while I'm here?"

"Sure, no problem."

We went in the house and I showed them the kittens first. A gray momma tabby lay in the box and the babies nursed. Jeanine bent over and reached out to the mom cat, who didn't seem to mind the attention.

"She's totally comfortable with our being here," Jeanine said. "What a good mom. I'd have no problem taking her and the babies as long as we got them soon enough to socialize them."

"I hope we know within a day or two," I said.

We went back into the living room where every cat wanted to be petted. "They have a different attitude when they have full bellies," I said.

"It probably helps that they're lonely. If they're used to someone being around all the time, they're starved for attention," Diane said.

After Jeanine and Diane got a good feel for the type of cats at the house, they headed for their cars.

"I apologize that you had to make the trip for nothing. I'll let you know what I hear from the attorneys," I said.

"Oh, don't apologize. It's a beautiful day for a drive, and it renews my faith in people, knowing someone actually made a plan for his pets in case he died," Diane said.

"Nice surprise, isn't it? Hey, we do have a super nice cat with kittens at the shelter you could have, if you want."

"Might as well," Diane said.

Carol left to check traps, Jeanine said goodbye and Diane followed me to the shelter. I introduced her to Cindi and then loaded the cat and kittens into her carrier.

"You don't know how much I appreciate this," I said.

"We'll find them good homes. We do adoptions at Petco and can adopt close to 15 cats every weekend."

"Now that's impressive," I said.

After Diane left, I went to Cindi's office to show her Mr. River's paperwork. She offered me a cup of coffee, which I gladly accepted. "It looks like he made provisions for the cats. I think an attorney needs to look at this," I said as I handed her the envelope.

"Wouldn't that be nice," she said. She glanced at the paperwork, picked up her phone and called the county's attorney.

"Can he look at it today?" I whispered while she was still on the phone. "We need to know if we should start transporting these cats to rescues or if they need to stay put." But I asked too late, she was already hanging up.

"When you drop it off, ask if he can look at it right away. I'm sure if you're insistent, he'll find the time. It can't take much to read through a few documents," she said as she handed the envelope back to me.

I was almost out the door when I remembered she had met with the sheriff. I stopped, turned and asked her about it.

"You might want to be seated for this," she said. I closed the door and took a seat.

"He basically told me to mind my own business. The investigation into the dead dogs was his business and running the shelter was mine."

My pulse quickened. "But from what I hear from Jason, he's not investigating it."

"I know. I know. I'm just telling you what he said. I argued with him, but it went nowhere. He got mad and said it wasn't up for discussion."

"So now what?"

"I don't know. He's the boss, and if he chooses not to make it a priority, I don't know what we can do about it."

"How about some public pressure? We could let someone in the media know about it." I'd love to leak the story.

"Would Jason talk to a reporter? He could lose his job if he did," Cindi asked.

"I don't know, but I'll ask him if he can come in and discuss it in the morning. Does that work for you?" It did.

After meeting with Cindi, I drove to the attorney's office. The office secretary told me he wasn't available and she would give him the documents.

I explained the situation to her and she seemed sympathetic, but I couldn't tell if her words were sincere or simply a platitude.

"I really need an explanation of what these papers mean as soon as possible. There are a few dozen cats sitting in limbo."

She assured me she understood the urgency of the matter. I thanked her and left. I called Jason from my car and filled him in. "When you talked to the sister, did she mention a will?" I asked.

"No, she just acted like she was in charge. From her remarks, I gathered she didn't think too much of her brother and saw the whole thing as a nuisance."

"Well, maybe she'll be relieved of her sisterly duties. I'd love it if the cats could stay where they are."

"When will you find out?"

"I don't know. I just gave the papers to the attorney's secretary. She said she'd stress the importance of the situation to him."

Then I told Jason about my conversation with Cindi and her meeting with the sheriff. "I suggested we go to the media with the story, but she wants the three of us to discuss it first. Can you meet with us tomorrow? Maybe first thing in the morning?"

"I can meet, but I don't know about going behind the sheriff's back to the media."

"Why not? The sheriff isn't doing his job. Do you have any other suggestions on what we should do? We can't just sit here and do nothing."

Jason agreed to meet with us, but I knew Cindi was right. His job was on the line, and he most likely wouldn't agree to go public with the story. I called Cindi, got her voice mail, and left her a message saying Jason could meet in the morning.

Mr. River's cat situation not only left the cats in limbo, it left me dazed. Adrenaline had been surging, and now I no longer needed it. Finding placement for the cats was no longer a life and death matter. Back at the shelter, I called the rescues who planned on coming Friday and asked if they could be on standby. Neither one objected. My cell phone rang, and I was surprised to see it was Rocky.

"Hey, it's Alison. What's up," I answered.

"I just heard the fight is on for Monday night."

"Monday? Why Monday? I didn't expect it so soon."

"Neither did we, but we're not calling the shots."

"I haven't found anyone to go, but I'm seriously thinking about going myself. I bought a wig."

"You what?" Rocky said in a high-pitched voice.

"I'll wear a wig and dress like a man. I think I can pull it off."

"No way! You're not going!" Rocky screamed in my ear.

"Who else you going to get?" I yelled back.

My anger silenced him for a moment. When he resumed talking, he used his normal tone.

"I don't think it's a good idea, but I'll give your number to Mike. He can decide."

"That's fine. Any idea when he'll call?"

"Probably later today."

Rocky's call tipped the basket. I needed a break. It was early for lunch, but I headed home anyway. Grams wasn't there, and Black Cat wasn't in his room, so I assumed she had taken him to the vet. I flopped down on Cooper's bed. A feeling of helplessness consumed me, and I couldn't stop the tears. Missing Cooper, working at the shelter, the buried ache of losing Thomas and the failure of my marriage all of a sudden seemed unbearable. I hated to admit it, but I missed Rob. His no-nonsense approach to life used to keep me balanced. Without him, I felt like a ship without a north star. How had I ended up here?

I heard Grams come home. She came up the steps and into the room with a cat carrier.

"Alison, are you okay?" She put the carrier on the floor and sat down on the bed next to me.

"I don't know. Probably. Work got to me."

"Why? What happened?"

"No one reason. You warned me about taking the job. It's harder than I expected."

"I know. I worry about you."

"I'm sorry. I don't want you to worry. I'm okay. Just had a minute of self-pity. How's Black Cat?"

She leaned over and opened the carrier door. "He's good. Dr. Jack recognized him. His name is Ebony."

Ebony, upon hearing his name, strutted out of the carrier and jumped up on the bed. I stroked his back.

"So you're Ebony," I said. He perked up at the sound of his name. "We found paperwork at the house that listed all the cats and, from the description of one of the black cats on the list, I guessed that this was Ebony. Mr. River had him listed as *most likely to find a new home.*"

"Really? That's uncanny. Dr. Jack was the vet for all of Mr. River's cats, and he has records for each one of them. He said he recommended Mr. River get a Pet Trust. It gives instructions and provides money. He's the trust protector and will oversee their care. The cats are supposed to live out their lives at the farm."

"All of them? Do I have to take Ebony back?" The black cat had curled up next me, purring.

"I asked him that, and he said no. It's in his power to let the cats go to new homes if he thinks they're appropriate. He thought we were appropriate."

"That's good to know."

She handed me a piece of paper with Mr. River's attorney's name written on it.

"That's the best news I've had all day. I'll call Dr. Jack and find out when he can take over the feeding and cleaning."

"I think he planned on going over there when he got out of work today. He hadn't even heard that Mr. River had died."

We left Ebony confined in Cooper's room. Introduction to the dogs would be the entertainment for the evening, but for now I had to get back to work.

Chapter Twenty-seven

Instead of going to the shelter, I drove to Dr. Jack's office. His practice was outside of town with space for a barn and corrals. There was a house on the land, but I didn't know if he lived there, maybe a caretaker did. A herd of sheep grazed in a pasture alongside the driveway.

Patients sat in the waiting room, but I convinced the receptionist to let me talk to the doc for five minutes. She took me to his office and said she'd have him come in as soon as possible. Instead of taking a seat, I wandered about the room. I'd never been in the doc's office before. He usually made house calls. Diplomas hung on the walls, as did photographs of Lake Michigan, whitetail deer and show horses. The desk was clean and organized. A window overlooked the backyard where three bird feeders hung from the lowest branch of a mammoth oak tree. The smorgasbord of seeds attracted finches, a pileated woodpecker, tufted titmice and mourning doves. Squirrels scampered up and down the tree and chipmunks scurried around on the ground.

I was beginning to wonder if I had been forgotten when the door opened and Dr. Jack came in. He greeted me with a hug and then took a seat behind his desk. He motioned for me to sit in a chair across from him, which I did.

"I bet you're here to talk about Charles's cats," he said.

"I am. I was surprised to find out that he'd made arrangements for them. Happily surprised. Actually, I found the paperwork at his house this morning and gave it to the county's attorney before I learned from Grams that you were involved."

"What did the attorney say?"

"I just dropped the papers off. I don't know when I'll hear anything. I thought I'd come here and coordinate the care of the cats with you. We've been cleaning the litter boxes and providing food and water. Mr. River must have been sick a few days because the house is a mess and the grass hasn't been mowed. We have the windows open, but the place smells pretty bad."

"I didn't know Charles had passed until your grandmother told me. I didn't even know he was ill. I'll go there today when I finish with patients."

"I was there this morning, so the cats are good for now."

"Charles loved those cats. I pushed him to do something legally to take care of them in case something happened to him. I was pleased when he did."

"Me, too. I already had rescues lined up to help with the cats, but I didn't know if we could do it in time."

"Time? Time for what?" he asked.

"His sister is coming and said she wants the cats gone."

"Charles didn't get along with her and, as far as I know, she has no legal right to even go on the property."

"Well, someone had better be ready to intercept her."

"I will. I have her name and number and will call her right now," he said.

"Good. I'll plan on you taking over the care of the place. Do you need anything else from me?" I asked.

He assured me he would handle everything and thanked me for what I had done already for the cats. He also said he was glad I had taken Ebony.

"Some cats need people, and he is one of those cats. What I really hope to do is find a caretaker to live at the house. Charles set aside money for all the expenses. I can even afford to pay someone to stay there."

I thanked him profusely before I left. Knowing the cats would be taken care of and wouldn't be uprooted was a relief. I left Dr. Jack's office feeling lighter. I hadn't realized how much the worry of the cats had weighed me down.

When I returned to the shelter, I found a message from the county's attorney saying the cats were part of a trust and would be taken care of by Charles River's estate. That we didn't have to do anything more on the case.

I called the rescues that had been willing to help and gave them the good news. I also updated the shelter's Facebook page with the uplifting turn of events. There already had been donations of food and other supplies brought to the shelter. I wrote that we could use the donated items for the cats at the shelter, but if anyone wanted to reclaim their donations, since we no longer needed them for the hoarding case, to message me. I doubted if anyone would. Carol came in as I was finishing, and I told her about the pet trust.

"That's the best news I've had in a long time. Too bad every pet owner isn't as responsible as that guy was. Maybe you should issue a press release. It'd make a great story. Maybe it would get more people to include their pets in their wills," she said.

I said I'd talk to Cindi about it in the morning.

Grams had dinner waiting when I got home. After we ate, I put the dogs outside and then brought Ebony downstairs. She sniffed around, then came and hopped onto my lap.

"Have you ever seen a dog before?" I asked her. She purred. I picked her up and walked to the window so she could look out and see the dogs. She didn't seem fazed.

"The dogs are used to cats, so I don't think there'll be a problem. Do you?" I asked Grams.

"Why don't you sit with her on the couch while I let the dogs in? If she gets scared I'll put them back outside."

Ebony and I settled on the couch. She seemed content sitting on my lap, at least that's how I read her loud purring. The rumbling quit when the dogs scrambled into the room. When in a pack, nothing the gang did was quiet or slow. Ebony watched every move the dogs made. It took a few minutes before they even noticed she was on my lap. When Cody came over to sniff her, she smacked him on the nose with a front paw. Cody backed off. She didn't use her claws, or Cody would have yelped.

"They won't hurt you," I whispered to Ebony. Grams turned on the television and the dogs settled down. After a few minutes, Ebony ventured to the floor and cautiously approached Cody, who was lying by my feet. He watched Ebony's every move, all the while holding still. She sniffed him and then moved onto Blue. I wondered what Blue sensed. Without sight, he could only hear and smell. His tail thumped on the floor when she got closer. The noise startled Ebony, and she leaped back onto the couch. Blue got up and came over. I patted his head.

"He's a nice doggie. He can't see you, and he's excited about a new smell in the house," I said to Ebony. I hoped the calmness in my voice transferred to her. After an hour of watching television and refereeing, I tired of the game and carried Ebony back to Cooper's room. The dogs stayed with Grams. I went to my room, grabbed the Amazon box and carried it to Cooper's room. Ebony watched as I tucked my hair under the cap. The vinyl head covering felt snug and uncomfortable, but it made putting on the hairpiece a whole lot easier. The wig slipped into place with a few tugs, and I used bobby pins to secure it to the cap. I laughed out loud when I looked in the mirror. *Would anyone fall for this?*

I removed my shirt and bra and wrapped the compression wrap tightly around my chest. It didn't totally hide my breasts, but they were definitely squashed. In the closet, I found a blue-plaid, button-down shirt that Cooper had left. It was large enough to be baggy. He'd also left behind a pair of worn-out faded blue jeans, which were too big for me. I tucked the shirt in and posed before the mirror. I needed a belly. After removing the shirt and wrap, I held two towels on my stomach and included them in the compression. With the shirt back on and tucked in, my profile looked like I had a little paunch, just like guys get when they put on weight. The costume almost looked believable.

Cooper also left behind a Detroit Tigers baseball cap, which made the outfit look a little more realistic. The wig looked phony, but what did I expect for $7.99? For the finishing touch, I donned the vintage glasses.

Grams would be my first test subject. Leaving Ebony snoozing on the bed, I went down the stairs and called out to Grams.

"Don't laugh," I said as I walked into the room.

Although I had warned her, I didn't expect her reaction. She actually jumped when I strutted into the room. Sinatra, who had been sleeping by her feet, sat up and growled.

"It's me," I said. "Sinatra, it's me." When he recognized my voice, the deep-throated growls stopped, but he didn't move and continued to stare.

"Holy cow! You about gave me a heart attack," Grams said.

"Really? I didn't think the getup was that convincing."

"You scared Sinatra," she said, reaching down to assure him everything was okay.

"But he's an old dog and doesn't see that well." I said.

"Old or not, he didn't recognize you. Come over here and let me get a better look."

Grams stood up as I walked over to her. Like a model on a runway, I twirled around so she could see the entire makeover. I pulled off the baseball cap.

"You have to keep the cap on. The hair doesn't look real. What did you do with your boobs?"

"They're wrapped. I ordered a compression wrap from Amazon. I added towels to give me a stomach," I said, grabbing my small belly with two hands. "These are clothes Cooper left here. Luckily, he was a little bigger than me, so they have plenty of room to hide my curves."

"You need to work on your girlie walk. And your voice is a little too high to be convincing."

"I hope I don't have to talk much," I said, lowering my voice a notch or two. "How's that?"

"To me it sounds like you trying to lower your voice. I don't know what someone who doesn't know you would think. Try walking across the room."

I did my best impersonation of Cooper's saunter, which may have been a bit overplayed since Grams burst into laughter. "That bad?" I asked.

"I don't know. You look silly."

"Well, let's go out this weekend and see what happens," I suggested. I knew I needed the practice.

"In public?" Grams asked. The thought of being seen by others left Grams laughing so hard that she had to dab tears from her eyes with a tissue. My cell phone rang, giving me an excuse to leave the room. The caller was Mike, the volunteer Rocky said would call.

"It's on for Monday. Do you have someone who can go?"

"Yeah, me," I said.

"You? I thought you had a guy who could go. I don't think this is the type of thing to bring a date to," he said.

"I'm not a date. I plan on disguising myself as a man. As a matter of fact, I'm trying on my disguise right now."

"Come on. This is serious. It's not just your ass on the line. It's mine, too. We're not playing games," Mike said. His voice sounded angrier than his words.

"Believe me, I know it's not a game. I thought I'd be more accepted as a man than a woman. If I had a guy to send, I'd gladly send him. But I don't. It's me or no one." My voice probably portrayed my annoyance at his attitude.

"You don't sound like a guy," he said.

"I don't plan on talking much. When I do I'll lower my voice," I said using the same voice I had just used on Grams. "Hey, I can chew tobacco, smoke cigarettes or stick a toothpick in my mouth to muffle my voice. Or pretend I have laryngitis or that I don't speak English."

It took a few seconds for Mike to react.

"I'll tell you what. I'll come early and check you out. If I think you can pass, you'll go. If I think you'll jeopardize my safety, you won't. Simple as that."

"Fair enough."

He said we needed to meet his uncle at 9 p.m. in Muskegon. We arranged to meet two hours earlier at a park-and-ride just north of Grand Haven. He gave me his cell number so I could call him in case I decided to back out.

After I hung up, reality came calling and I freaked. *How am I going to keep my composure at a dogfight?* I lay on my back on Cooper's bed. Ebony jumped onto my stomach and stared at me. "Do you feel my fear?" I whispered. She didn't purr.

I needed to talk to someone, and the only person who would understand was Cooper. With the different time zones, I didn't know if he'd be home, but I took a chance and dialed his number. I crossed my fingers hoping he'd answer.

"What a surprise," he said instead of hello.

"A good one, I hope."

"Is there any doubt?"

I lay back on the bed, my head resting on the pillow. "My life is a little chaotic right now, and I'm not sure of anything."

"Well, be sure of this. I love you, and I love it when you call."

"You're so sweet. It feels good to hear you say the words. I love you, too," I said.

"So what's up? I don't usually hear from you during the week. Is everything okay?"

"I've backed myself into a corner and don't know if I can handle it. I wish you were here to help."

"I wish I were there. But I'm not. Tell me about it."

Cooper listened for the next half hour as I poured out the details of what had been happening regarding dog fighting in the area. I ended with the invitation to the fight and my plan to attend it dressed as a guy.

"I'm lying on your bed wearing a man's wig, your old Tigers cap, and your blue-plaid shirt and jeans. I've wrapped my breasts so they don't show and have two towels on my stomach to look like a guy's beer belly."

"Do you have a pair of my socks in your pants?" he asked. His voice was strained and, even though the remark was funny, he wasn't laughing. I didn't appreciate his sarcasm.

"That's all you can say?" I sat up on the side of the bed. Maybe calling him wasn't such a good idea.

"What do you want me to say? That I think it's a grand idea that you're going to a dogfight? Doesn't matter if you're going as a woman or a man, it's a stupid thing to do. You have no idea what you're doing. They'll kill you if they find out who you are. Simple as that. Who is this Mike you're going with? Do you even know if you can trust him?"

"Of course I can trust him. What would be his motive for taking me to a dogfight other than to see if I recognize anyone there? He doesn't even want me to go. He wants a man to go."

"Smart guy."

"I can see it was a mistake to call you," I said. I fought the urge to hang up on him. I needed someone in my corner and was disappointed by his reaction.

"Alison, what do you want from me? You're putting yourself into an extremely dangerous situation, and there's nothing I can do about it. Do you have any idea how much I wish I were there and could go in your place?"

His confession made me pause. "I know it's dangerous. That's why I'm scared. It's why I'm calling you. But I don't see what choice I have. It's a one in a million opportunity. I can't *not* go."

"Who knows you're doing this?"

"Grams."

"That's it?"

"Rocky in Chicago. He's the one who helped arrange it."

"Listen. You need someone besides Grams to know what's going on. Someone you can trust to call for help if you're not back at a certain time."

"Who? If I tell Cindi or Jason, they'll try to stop me. I don't have any friends here close enough to ask."

"How about Sara?" Cooper asked.

I hadn't talked to Sara since my parents' party in Chicago. She was a confidant and the only person who knew the real story behind my relationship with Cooper. She'd met Cooper a couple of times and was instrumental in his not serving more time in prison than he had. She lived in Grand Haven, just a few miles from where I'd be meeting Mike.

"Sara would be perfect. Okay then. I'll call her tomorrow and go see her on Monday before I meet Mike."

"That makes me feel a little better. Do you have any idea where this fight is going to be held?"

"No. It's not something they broadcast ahead of time. All I know is that it's somewhere around Muskegon."

"If you do this, which I'm not recommending you do, you need to take photos, but they aren't going to let you in with a camera or a cell phone."

"I thought of that. When I ordered the wig from Amazon, I ordered two tiny cameras. One is actually an ink pen. I haven't had time to look at them yet"

"Did you talk to Mike about it?"

"No, but I can. He gave me his number."

"You should ask him what safety precautions he has in place."

"Good idea. I'll call him tomorrow."

"Let's talk Sunday. I want to know the details."

I assured him I would call. I also apologized for making him worry. Maybe I shouldn't have called him.

Before going to bed I looked at the cameras. The ink pen, which did actually write, had a pinhole camera in the clip, and the clicker on top of the pen was a multi-function switch. Press it once to take a photo. Press it twice to record. The pen could be clipped in a shirt pocket, and all I had to do was reach over and press the top. I practiced with it by taking photos and videos of Ebony and then downloaded the files to my computer. The quality wasn't the best, but it would do.

The other tiny camera also worked well, but I didn't know how I'd use it without being obvious. Maybe put it in a pack of cigarettes?

Chapter Twenty-eight

By the time I got to the shelter on Friday morning, Jason and Cindi had already taken care of the animals.

"What's up with the early start?" I asked.

"We're not early, you're late," Cindi said as she put a load of dirty towels from the cat cages into the washing machine.

"Late?" Then I remembered the meeting I had set up with the two of them. "Oh, no! I forgot about our meeting. I'm sorry. It totally slipped my mind."

"And here we thought you were just trying to get out of work," Jason said. He was wiping down the counter after washing food and water bowls.

"Me? I would never do that," I said. My gut told me they weren't really upset. I did more than my share of the manual labor around the shelter, and I didn't mind the work. The bending, scrubbing and walking all saved me money on a gym membership.

We each grabbed a cup of coffee and settled into Cindi's office. "I really am sorry," I said, "but I'm glad you both waited for me. What I wanted to talk about is why the sheriff isn't more concerned about the dogs that were found in the national forest, and if there's anything we can do to convince him to do more. Like leaking the story to the media."

Cindi offered her thoughts first. "When I talked to Sheriff VanBergen, he made it clear that the topic wasn't open for discussion, and I can kind of understand his position. He's got a lot on his plate, and the chances of finding out who dumped those dogs is close to zero."

Jason agreed with Cindi, which surprised me. I thought he felt the same as I did; after all, he helped me put up the camera.

"If we had something else to give him, a lead of some sort, I'm sure he'd look into it. But as it stands, it's pretty much at a dead end," Jason said.

"Really? I thought he hadn't done anything and told you not to waste any time on it. You have descriptions of the dogs. Maybe you could try to find their owners? One of the cats had a microchip and we know where he came from. Maybe you could ask the owner some questions and try to figure out how he ended up as bait."

"I thought you talked to the owner?"

"I did, but he was pretty shaken up at the time. Maybe if you did a follow up with him he'd have something else to say."

"I could do that, but really? Cats go missing every day, who knows where they go. We find strays every day. I don't think we'll learn much from a missing cat report," Jason said.

"Not with that attitude."

"Alison," Cindi said, "I think you need to rethink this. Yes, we suspect there's dog-fighting going on in the county, but the leads we have so far are sketchy. If we wait, something more concrete will turn up. What would you tell a reporter? That we found some dead dogs?"

"What about the barn where we got Red? The buried animals we found. You didn't see their bloodied bodies, the ripped flesh. The sight and smell is forever engraved in my head. I think it's beyond, 'we suspect dog fighting.' I think we know damn well that it's going on, and nobody has the balls to do anything about it!"

"You're right," Jason said. "I agree, dog fighting is happening here, but I'm at a loss as to what to do. I understand where VanBergen is coming from when he says he doesn't want to expend any more manpower on it. He's my boss, so I do what he says. Going to the media would make him angry. Do you really want to make him an enemy?"

"Would you talk to a reporter?" I asked, ignoring his last comments. "I don't know what else to do."

Jason took a few seconds to think before answering. "No. I'd be jeopardizing my job, and I'm not willing to do that."

Cindi's position didn't surprise me, but Jason's did. Then I realized my coming in late had given them time to talk, and Cindi probably convinced him he would lose his job if he went public.

"Okay then. We'll wait and see what happens next," I said.

"I think that's best," Cindi said.

Jason nodded in agreement. I got up and went to my office where I could seethe in private. After I'd brought my emotions under control, I turned on my computer and dealt with e-mails and the shelter's social media. On Facebook, SASHA Farm posted they were having an open house Saturday. I made a mental note to ask Grams if she wanted to go. A road trip would take my mind off Monday and give me a chance to try out my wig.

Then I called Sara. She worked nights, and I wasn't sure if she slept when she got home or if she had to unwind first. I had a message ready to recite for her voice-mail so was surprised when she answered. She was just as surprised to hear my voice.

"What have you been up to? I've often wondered if you and Rob have talked since the party."

"Rob? No, we haven't talked. He's crossed my mind a couple times, but nothing serious. So how are you?"

"Fine. Nothing new here. I'm still working, and Ryan is still traveling a lot for his job."

"I'm going to be in Grand Haven Monday afternoon and wondered if you'd be available to help me with a little project."

"Do I dare ask what?"

She knew me too well. "Can I tell you when I get there?"

We agreed to meet at three o'clock. There was a knock at my door, so I had to cut the conversation short.

Carol needed help transporting cats to a store in Ludington where they were holding an adoption event. "Becky was supposed to help, but she called and bailed at the last minute," she said.

To tell the truth, I appreciated the distraction and used it as a reason to get out of the shelter. Neither Jason nor Cindi made an appearance as we loaded the animals and supplies. The weekend adopt-a-thons usually found homes for a handful of cats and a dog or two. People who didn't have the heart to come to the shelter appreciated the off-site opportunity to see the animals available for adoption. I stuck around and helped Carol get set up.

"Are you sure you can handle it alone?" I asked.

"I won't be alone for long. Becky promised she'd be here as soon as she gets out of work," Carol assured me.

"Did you have lunch? Can I grab you a burger or something?"

She turned down my offer for food and told me to go. "I do this twice a month. I can handle it," she said.

So I left. Maybe she didn't want food, but I did. I ordered a veggie wrap at a drive-thru and drove to the public beach on the west end of town. Since it was past Labor Day, most of the tourists were gone and the beaches deserted. I rolled down the windows and ate in my car, listening to the waves and seagulls. A warm breeze drifted through the car. I inhaled the fresh air and closed my eyes. My thoughts wouldn't settle, and I started thinking of questions for Mike. Soon I pulled out paper and pen to write them down. With the concerns fresh in my mind, I decided to call him.

"Mike here," he answered.

"It's Alison. Do you have a few minutes to talk?"

He did. I asked if he had any local backup in case we got in trouble. He didn't. "I don't know anyone up there. Rocky will be on standby, but I don't know what he'll do if we don't check in."

"Will you be allowed to bring in a phone?"

"No. They don't allow phones or cameras. They might have someone frisking people at the door. I've seen that before, but since we'll be with my uncle, they might let us slide."

The image of being frisked lingered with me. "How thorough of a frisk?" I asked.

"I don't know. They'll be looking for phones, cameras, guns. Whatever it takes to find something in your pockets or tucked in your pants or boots. Don't be stupid and try to smuggle anything in. That's the last thing we need."

The tone of his voice kept me from asking about my spy cameras. "Will you have your car there or will we be riding with your uncle?"

"I'm betting we'll be riding with him. They keep traffic to a minimum so as not to draw suspicion."

"I was hoping we could at least have a phone close by," I said.

"I know. I know. But I don't know how it's going to go down."

"I have a friend I trust, and I've been thinking of telling her what I'm doing. If she doesn't hear from me by a specific time she can get together with my grandmother, whom I live with, and go to the police. They'd have Rocky's name and number and yours."

"Might not be a bad idea. But I don't even know for sure if I want you tagging along."

"Maybe instead of going with you, I could follow you and be a backup."

"That's a thought, but who would you call even if you found the location? We don't trust the police."

"That's what Rocky said. Why would you want me to go?"

"I was hoping you would recognize some of the local people."

"But I'm not from Muskegon. I live about forty-five minutes north," I said.

"It's a big thing. People will be coming from all over. I'm not sure what we should do. Let me think on it and I'll get back to you. Are you going to be around this weekend?"

"Probably not Saturday, but I should be Sunday."

"I'll call you Sunday."

The conversation with Mike went much smoother this time.

Work beckoned, so that's where I headed. There was a message from Kevin Palmer asking if we had any new information on Groucho. His call surprised me since he had just received the news about Groucho's death on Tuesday. What did he expect from us in three days? I know what he expected: He expected us to do our job and find out what happened to his cat. Maybe he should be the one going to the media. I waited until the end of the day to return his call. I told him Sheriff VanBergen had called off the investigation due to a lack of leads. If he wanted, he could call the sheriff and talk to him. And if that didn't get him any satisfaction, he could always call the local media and ask them to look into it. Then I went home.

Chapter Twenty-nine

Grams didn't have any plans for Saturday, so she accepted my invitation to go to SASHA Farm.

"But I'm going as Alex, not Alison," I said. "Do you think you can keep a straight face?" I had the ink pen in my shirt pocket while I talked to Grams and casually reached up and pushed the button twice so it would record.

Just the memory of the night before made Grams laugh. "I'll do my best," she said.

"I talked to Cooper last night, and he doesn't want me to go to the fight," I confessed.

"Smart man, but you aren't listening to him, are you?" she said with a twinge of hope in her voice.

"No. I talked to Sara, and I'm meeting her before I go. She'll meet Mike, and we'll set a time for me to call her after I get out. If I don't call, she'll call you and you can call Jason. I'm not sure what he'll do."

"Does Jason know what you're doing?"

"No. He wouldn't let me go. I'm sure everything will be okay, but Cooper insisted I have some sort of plan in place in case something goes wrong."

"Good, but I'll be a wreck waiting for your call. You know that, don't you?"

"I do." I took the ink pen out of my pocket and showed it to Grams. "What do you think of my new pen?" I asked as I handed it to her.

She took it from me and looked at it. "Why do you ask?"

"Because it's also a camera. Did you notice me reach up and turn it on while we were talking?" I reached over and pointed out the button on top.

"I didn't," she said.

"Want to see the recording?"

She did. We took the pen to Cooper's room, where I had my laptop, and downloaded the video. Because the lighting was good in the kitchen, the video turned out quite well.

"That was taken by the ink pen?" Grams asked.

"Pretty amazing," I said. "I can have the pen in my pocket and turn it on and off by pressing the button on top. One click for a photo and two for a video."

My phone rang. It was Cooper. When Grams realized who it was, she asked to talk to him. I handed her the phone. While I only heard Grams' side of the conversation, I knew they were pretty much in agreement on what they thought about my plan.

When Grams handed the phone back to me she said, "You should listen to him."

When I said hello to Cooper again, the first thing he said was that I should listen to Grams.

"I understand where you're coming from. If it were you doing what I'm doing, I'd be telling you not to do it," I said. "But I'm doing it."

Cooper laughed and told me he knew he wouldn't change my mind. "You have a stubborn streak in you. I just pray you won't do anything too stupid and that you'll be safe."

"I don't want anything to happen to me either," I said.

We talked until Grams called up the stairs and said she had dinner ready.

SASHA Farm in southeastern Michigan was a three and a half hour drive. The sanctuary was open to the public once a month, and we were lucky this was the weekend. Included in the $20 admission was a vegan lunch.

When I came downstairs in the morning, I was wearing the getup from Thursday night, including the ink pen camera in my shirt pocket. "Don't laugh," I said when I walked into the kitchen. The warning didn't help. Grams burst into laughter.

"I'm sorry. This whole thing has my nerves on edge. It's either laugh or cry," she said.

"Then go ahead and laugh. Get it out of your system before we get to the sanctuary."

The dogs barked when I went outside. "It's me," I said. My voice shushed them. The horses and Bessie waited for me by the fence. Bessie looked happy, but I still planned on asking someone at SASHA if they would be able to take her.

"We'll miss you," I told her. "But I think a sanctuary would be the perfect home for you."

If my attire got a little dirty with the chores, I figured it would add a bit of realism. Wearing the glasses felt awkward, but I left them in place to get used to them on my face.

Grams had breakfast ready. She didn't say a word about how I looked and there were no more laughs, not even a chuckle. After we ate we hit the road.

Grams asked questions about the sanctuary, and I told her what I remembered from their website.

"It's for farm animals. SASHA is an acronym for Sanctuary And Safe Haven for Animals," I said. "They have about 200 animals: cows, pigs, goats, chickens. I think they have cats and dogs, too."

"Have you talked to them about taking Bessie?"

"Not yet. I hope to today."

"Why don't we just keep her?"

"Keeping her and her calf would be a big responsibility."

"No more than having the horses," Grams said.

"Maybe not, but what about long term?"

"Well, she'll probably outlive me, but when I'm gone the farm will be yours. So if you want to keep her, you can."

Grams questions set me to thinking. What did I want? How did I see my life playing out? Did I want to spend it on a farm? If I didn't, where would I go? California?

"I'm not good at thinking about the future," I finally said. "The sanctuary would be the ideal place for Bessie and her baby. I think we need to let her go, if they'll take her."

The drive flew by while Grams and I chatted. We were more like girlfriends then grandmother and granddaughter. I cherished our relationship.

A hayfield next to the sanctuary had been converted into a temporary parking lot for the open house and was almost full. The number of vehicles surprised me.

"It must be a popular place," I said.

I parked the car. We got out and stretched. During the drive I had become accustomed to my attire, but standing up made me aware of it again. I felt dressed for a Halloween party.

"I'm not feeling very comfortable," I said. My head itched from the tight cap, and I worried that scratching it would look suspicious and get the wig misaligned.

Grams brushed something off my sleeve and looked me in the eyes. "You look fine. Just go with it," she said.

The noonday sun brought the temperatures into the mid-70s; there wasn't a cloud in sight. Cooper's long-sleeved shirt might not have been the best choice for the day. "I'm feeling a little warm," I said.

"Roll up your sleeves," she said. I wasn't going to get any sympathy from her.

The back of the car next to ours was plastered with bumper stickers. We couldn't help but stop and read them: NO I DON'T HAVE ANY SPARE RIBS; YOUR BACON HAD A MOM; CATS NAP, ONLY HUMANS PUT THEM "TO SLEEP" – STERILIZE DON'T EUTHANIZE; STOP ANIMAL TESTING; END FACTORY FARMING.

"Looks like Cooper's kind of crowd," I said, pushing the button on top of the ink pen to take a photo of the bumper stickers. I needed practice reaching up and pushing the camera's button. A pack of cigarettes in the pocket might make the motion seem more casual.

Two women stood under a maple tree near a barbed-wire fence at the far end of the parking area. In the distance I could see a herd of cows. The herd was a mix of breeds. There were a couple of Herefords, an Angus, a few Holsteins and some other breeds I didn't recognize. Grams and I walked down and joined the women.

"Beautiful," one of them said to us.

"What's that?" Grams asked.

"Oh, just the sight of the cows grazing. So peaceful."

What would a guy say in this situation?

"Have you been here before?" the woman asked.

"No," I said in a deeper voice than usual. "My grandmother wanted to come, so I offered to bring her."

"Where're you from?"

The woman's reaction to my answer seemed normal. No hesitation. But then she wasn't looking at me, she was still staring at the cows.

"Near Ludington," Grams said.

"You had quite a drive."

"Alex likes to drive," Grams said, giving me a small jab with her elbow. She continued to make small talk with them and I kept quiet. The women had just arrived so we walked in with them. We stopped at the registration table, paid the entrance fee and a young woman told us we could wander around on our own. I felt her gaze linger on me. Did something give me away?

"A vegan lunch will be served in about 30 minutes under the white canopy," she said pointing to her left.

Rows of tables and chairs were set up and people were already starting to gather. "Thanks," I said in my newfound manly voice. Usually I would have been chatty and asked questions, but I thought that was a feminine trait. Men were more stoic, watchers instead of talkers. I'd let Grams do the talking.

"Enjoy your visit," she said, looking directly at me. "We have T-shirts and other stuff for sale. It all helps support the animals."

I nodded my head. Grams and I stopped at the merchandise table. I found myself looking at the women's shirts. Noting my mistake, I held one up to Grams and told her, in my manly voice, that she should get one. She took it from me and looked it over. Next I looked at the men's T-shirts.

A group of kids stood laughing by a pasture near one of the barns. "Let's go see what's happening over there," Grams said.

"Sure," I said. When we were out of hearing distance from anyone I asked her how I was doing. She looked at me, and I could tell she was trying not to laugh.

"What does that mean?"

"Sorry. You're doing better than I expected. I kept thinking the women in the parking lot would say something. When they didn't ... well, they didn't even give you a second look."

"I thought so, too, but then they were busy looking at the cows," I said.

The kids were watching goats playing on a wooden deck that had ramps. A black goat marched up, butted another goat who, in turn, lost his balance and toppled off. They reminded me of children playing King of the Mountain on snow piles. It was as much fun watching the kids watch the goats, as it was watching the goats. They laughed and pointed and cheered the aggressors on. I pressed the camera button twice, envisioning what was being recorded, but I wasn't sure of the camera's range.

There were more than a dozen goats, all colors and sizes. Several had horns curving back toward their necks. One of the smaller goats came over to the woven-wire fence, and Grams rubbed its head. Two goats stood on their back legs with their front hoofs resting on the fence. They stared at a teenage girl who carried a bucket of fresh greens: chopped lettuce, cabbage and spinach, it looked like. She opened a gate and went into the pasture. The entire herd started *baaing* as they trotted in her direction. She grabbed handfuls of the greens and tossed them on the ground as she walked, leaving a trail of happy goats behind her.

A dozen or so geese joined the feeding. One would grab a chunk of lettuce and run with it, the others giving chase. They were a delight to watch.

We watched the goats and geese until it was time for us to eat. I pushed the ink pen button again to stop the recording. There was no way of knowing whether the camera was working. The pen had tiny indicator LEDs, but I had put black electrical tape over the lights in case anyone took a close look.

The lunch was served buffet style. As we stood in line, I talked to a couple in front of us. They were excited about the variety of vegan food. I pretended I had never eaten vegan before and was concerned about finding something I liked. They assured me that I would find plenty to eat and advised me not to advertise that I was a meat-eater.

"They'll give you grief," the guy said. "When in Rome do as the Romans. When at a farm sanctuary, don't let on that you'd like to eat the residents." His wife kicked him in the shin. We both laughed.

Playing the role of a man became easier with every successful interaction. People looked at the clothes and, since I was dressed as a man, they treated me like one. Having Grams play a supporting role helped. It also helped to have glasses to hide behind.

We sat next to the couple with whom we had stood in line. Grams did most of the talking. I only talked when asked a direct question, and even then she would sometimes answer for me. While she talked, I took more photographs. It felt awkward reaching for the pen in my pocket, but no one seemed to pay attention. Everyone was too busy eating.

The people seated at the tables were a mix of young and old, the majority female. Some dressed casually in jeans and T-shirts, while others looked dressed for a more formal affair. They all were talking, laughing and appearing to love the vegan feast. The food was delicious. Cooper would have been in heaven.

"Did you find enough to eat?"

It took a couple of seconds for me to realize that the question was directed at me. With my man voice, I said that I had. "I thought I'd try a little of everything and found I liked most of it."

"There's hope for you then."

After lunch, Grams and I checked out an enclosure that housed turkeys, chickens and ducks. As with the cows, several breeds were represented. A huge white turkey sauntered around and chickens scratched in the dirt.

There was a pond for the ducks, but none were swimming. I guessed they were a little nervous with the stream of people wandering through their pen.

The sanctuary was also home to a few horses. They stood near the fence and readily accepted attention from visitors. I enjoyed the pigs the most. Two wallowed in a small muddy pond and seemed oblivious to the crowd. A couple others grunted at people, sounding like they were asking for a handout.

As I watched a woman talk with one of the pigs, the pig grunted back as if in conversation with her. I was amazed at how much fun both the people and the animals were having. There was a feeling of tranquility, peace and happiness. The opposite of what I had felt at the dairy farm. I slid my hand to the ink pen and clicked twice to record the scene.

A circular feeder had been filled with hay and the cows crowded side-by-side to get their share. A man stood next to the gate answering questions and telling stories about the animals. He pointed out a pair of reddish-brown cows.

"That's mother and son," he said. "She was rescued from a dairy farm and gave birth to her calf here. It's the only baby she was ever allowed to keep, and she's very protective. He's over a year old and still nursing." The son was nearly as big as his mother, plus he had horns.

"Why does she have a tag in her ear?" someone asked. A yellow plastic tag hung from her right ear. Bessie had a similar tag, as did every cow at the dairy farm I had visited.

"She had it when we got her. It has her identification number on it."

"Why don't you remove it?"

"Our vet said it would be painful for her to have it removed. She probably had it put in as a calf, and the pin holding it in has grown over."

"I think you should still remove it. It's a sorry reminder of where she came from. She's so much more than a number," someone else said.

I asked the guy how they decided which animals to take, and that I knew of a pregnant cow who needed a place to go. He said the sanctuary was near capacity, and they were only able to take animals from desperate situations. After listening to him, I decided I wouldn't even ask him to take Bessie. She had a home with us.

Chapter Thirty

On the drive home, Grams thanked me for taking her to the sanctuary. "I didn't know such places existed. It's the way animals should live. The way they should be treated."

"I bet it's the way most people believe farm animals do live. No one wants to think about factory farms, including me," I said.

"Did you ask them about taking Bessie?"

I confessed my change of heart. While I thought the sanctuary would be an ideal placement, there were too many animals in need. "I think Bessie is fine with us."

"We can have our own sanctuary," Grams said. "It would be a fitting use for the land. Maybe it would atone for all the cows we sent to slaughter."

"At least you gave them a good home until the end. You took good care of them."

"We did our best, but in the end they all went to the slaughterhouse anyway. I remember I tried to ignore it, to keep busy and just not think about it. Tom said I was too softhearted, but I think it bothered him too. Like I said, maybe turning the farm into a sanctuary would make some sort of cosmic amends."

"Then let's do it. Bessie can live out her life there, as can the horses and cats. Actually, I think we've already been running a sanctuary. Look at all the cats and dogs you've taken in and kept until they died of old age. Plus Kal. Remember him?"

Kal was a research mouse that Cooper and I had rescued from a lab. He died four months after we brought him home. We weren't sure what caused his death, but he had a pain-free easy life while he lived with us. We buried him behind the barn in the farm cemetery where a number of cats and dogs had been laid to rest over the years.

"I do. He's the only pet mouse I've ever known."

We reminisced the rest of the way home. About pets, Gramps and even Thomas and how much he loved spending time on the farm. The drive decided my fate. The farm was my home, now and forever. Turning it into a sanctuary meant providing a home for the animals we took in until they died. The decision felt good.

The western sky was streaked with reds and yellows when I pulled into the driveway. The first thing we did was let the dogs out. It had been a long day for them. Then we went to the barn and checked on the cats, horses and Bessie. All was well.

Being Alex for the day left me feeling comfortable in his clothes. As we walked back to the house from the barn, I told Grams I thought I could pull off going to the fight as a man.

"I didn't think you could do it, but I've changed my mind. Not that I want you to. I still think it's foolish," Grams said.

While Grams put together a salad for our dinner, I brought my laptop downstairs and downloaded the photos and videos from the ink pen. The images weren't what I expected. The range was much narrower and only the lower portion of the scenes had been captured.

"I'll have to experiment with it more tomorrow," I said.

After dinner, I went upstairs to see Ebony and call Cooper. "What do you think of moving to Michigan permanently when you're off probation?" I asked. I assumed he would love the idea of turning the farm into a haven for rescued animals and living there with me.

"Like in forever?" he asked. "I'm looking forward to visiting, but I don't know about forever."

His revelation made me catch my breath. I told him about our plans to keep Bessie and turning the farm into a sanctuary. "For some reason, I thought you'd be part of the plan. It seemed natural," I said.

"I loved the time I spent on the farm, but I was only there because I needed to be out of sight. I figured you'd stay there until something happened to Grams and then move here," he said.

"Wow, we're both way off base. I'm going to have to rethink this," I said.

"Maybe we could split our time, be bi-coastal. Lake Michigan is beautiful, much more than I expected, but I love California."

Our disagreement was a sidebar to what was really going on. Rather than argue about my plans to attend the fight, we bickered over our future. Maybe there was a kernel of truth in our disagreement. Truth be told, I felt a slight separation in our trajectory when we vacationed. Rather than dwell on it now, I needed to focus on Monday night.

"I practiced with the ink pen camera, and I think it'll do the job."

"If you get caught with it, you'll be done," Cooper said.

"Come on. Can't you be on my side? I don't need your negativity. If it were you going undercover you'd expect me to support you 100 percent ... and I would."

"You're right, I'd expect you to support me, but I doubt if you would. You're too independent ... no, you're too stubborn."

"It's time to say goodbye," I said.

"For good?"

"Is that what you want?"

"No, but it sounds like that's what you want."

"It's not, but I can't be distracted right now. I'll talk to you later," I said.

Ebony lay on my lap purring. Being with me was enough for her. I picked her up and gave her a hug. Tears welled in my eyes and the ache of being alone crushed down on me as I sobbed. When I had gained control, I rinsed my face with cold water and went downstairs.

"Hey, do you want something to drink?" I asked Grams. She was watching television but had dozed off. My voice startled her.

"What?"

"I was going to have a glass of wine. Can I pour you one?"

She declined and said what she needed was to go to bed. I poured myself a glass and took it and the bottle upstairs. I said goodnight to Ebony in Cooper's room and went back to my room, to my own bed. The dogs were glad to have me back. There were no new e-mails, so I checked Facebook. The fight with Cooper had left me lonely and emotional. I wondered if Rob had a Facebook page. After typing his name in the search box, his name with a headshot popped up at the top of the list. His information was available to the public. I felt like I was invading his privacy, but that didn't stop me. Or should I say it didn't stop the wine from snooping?

I clicked on message and debated if I should send him a quick note. The cursor flashed impatiently at me. Did I really want to reconnect with Rob, or was Cooper's rejection pushing me toward him? I closed the page without contacting him.

Chapter Thirty-one

When my consciousness clawed its way to daylight, I noted that my brain throbbed. The empty wine bottle reminded me of the night before. The bedroom door stood open, and the dogs were missing. What I needed was water to rehydrate my alcohol-ravished body. In the bathroom, I forced myself to drink two glasses. Then I soaked my dried-out skin in a warm shower, moisturizing it with cucumber body scrub. The water brought me back to life.

Downstairs Grams had a pot of coffee brewing. "What happened to you?" she asked.

"Cooper. We had a fight. He doesn't want to live in Michigan." I took a seat at the kitchen table.

"I wondered if that was it. You can change your mind, you know." She poured me a cup of coffee and sat down kitty-corner from me.

"I know, but I don't think I want to. This is home. It feels right. I didn't really fit in California. I tried, but I can't kid myself."

"It'll work itself out. Cooper has to do what's right for him, and you need to do what's right for you."

"It's fine. I'll be fine."

"Do you want to go to church with me this morning?"

Grams found solace in religion. I did until Thomas died. When my prayers for a miracle went unanswered, I became a non-believer and quit going to church.

"No, you go. I'll be okay alone. No more drinking. I swear."

When she left I checked my phone for messages. Mike was supposed to call, but instead there was a message from Rocky. I took the dogs out, sat on the porch swing and called him back. He was worried and wanted to know if I was still going through with it. I filled him in on my disguise and asked his opinion of trying to get photos and video.

"I'm scared of getting caught with the camera, but on the other hand, I need proof. I need to document what I see so it's just not my word against whomever," I said.

He agreed. I asked if I should tell Mike about it or keep it secret from him. "He might be better off not knowing. He's already doubting whether I should go," I said. "He told me he'll decide when he sees me tomorrow if he's going to let me go."

"I know. He called and told me he thinks he'd be better off alone than taking a woman."

I told him about spending Saturday as Alex and how well it went. "I don't think it'll be a problem, but then, he said we might get frisked."

"They'll be looking for cell phones and guns, not feeling you up," Rocky said.

"Right, but will they feel my heart pounding or notice my sweating with fear?"

"I don't know. I hope not. You don't have to go, you know."

"I know, but I shouldn't squander the opportunity. I keep wishing there were someone else who could go, but I'm the one who won't let it go, so I'm the one who should take the risk."

Rocky made me promise to call him as soon as I could after the fight. I gave him Sara's number and told him she was the one who would call out the Mounties if I didn't return on time.

It was unusual to have time on my hands. I wandered to the barn with Cody, Blue and Shadow and took care of the cats and horses. Bessie crowded in next to the horses for her share of the morning feed. She had adapted to life on the farm and felt like part of the family. I couldn't imagine shipping her anywhere, especially in her condition. The farm was her home and mine. If Cooper couldn't find what he needed here, then I had to believe we weren't meant to be.

What I needed was a ride, so I bridled Dappy and slid onto his back. I nudged his sides with my knees and urged him into a canter. I reined him down the lane and to the path along the river. Memories of rides with Cooper crept into my mind. *Damn him for not wanting what I want.* I pushed away the thoughts of him and focused on the perfection of the moment: the warmth of Dappy's back between my legs, the occasional splash of red in the landscape of trees, goldenrod in full bloom, the dogs exploring the sides of the trail, and the reflection of the day in the river water.

Hard as I tried to stay focused on the moment, it eluded me. My thoughts kept returning to Monday night. *Am I doing the right thing?*

Grams was home from church by the time I got back. For lunch we had veggie burgers and salad.

"What are your plans for the afternoon?" Grams asked.

"Nothing except to get ready for tomorrow, and I'm not sure what I should be doing to get ready. I don't even know if Mike is going to let me go."

"With any luck, he won't," Grams said.

Grams put me to work weeding flowerbeds, dead-heading, and digging up iris roots. We rinsed and divided the roots and then replanted them. The physical labor burned off the stress and diverted my attention, although I still waited for Mike's call.

Before I knew it, it was time for dinner. After eating, I gave up on waiting for Mike and called him. I expected voicemail and was surprised when he answered.

"I've been waiting for you to call," I said.

"Call? I thought we were meeting tomorrow night at 7?"

"We are, but we were going to talk about a backup plan. What we're going to do if something goes wrong."

"Oh, yeah. I talked to Rocky, and if he doesn't hear from us by Tuesday morning, he's going to call my uncle."

"That's it?"

"What else do you want?"

"I don't know. I'll see you at 7."

I went to bed early, hoping for a restful night. It didn't happen. I drifted in and out of sleep. Every time I woke, I checked the time, which didn't seem to be advancing. When I did wake up, my head was filled with dream fragments. Nothing solid that I could remember, just shadowy images and unsettling feelings. At one point I was instantly awake and thought someone was sitting on the side of my bed. Fear paralyzed me and all I could do was listen. The only thing I heard was the welcoming sound of the dogs breathing. If the dogs were sleeping, I knew no one was in the room except me.

Chapter Thirty-two

Grams insisted that I have a hearty breakfast of oatmeal with walnuts and fruit, toast and orange juice. The thought of food didn't appeal to me, but I ate what she put in front of me.

I said goodbye to Ebony and reminded Grams to take care of her. She was still staying in Cooper's room to give her time to acclimate to new surroundings. It was just another day for the critters in the barn, but it felt different for me. Emotions welled inside as I rationed the feed. *It's not goodbye*, I reminded myself. I'll be back tomorrow.

After stowing my backpack, which was filled with Cooper's clothes and the other stuff I needed for the night, I kissed all five dogs goodbye and hugged Grams.

"Call me," she said.

I promised I'd call on my drive to Grand Haven and again when it was over. "First Sara, then you, then Rocky, then Cooper," I said trying to lighten the mood for both of us.

Anxiety got the better of me on the drive to the shelter. My stomach felt queasy, my heart raced and I started to sweat. It was so bad that I pulled over to the side of the road. I crossed my arms on the steering wheel and rested my head on my arms, reminding myself to breath slowly and deeply. Control returned and five minutes later I was back on the road.

Jason was sitting in his truck in the parking lot of the shelter when I arrived. I parked next to him; he got out of his truck as I got out of my car.

"What's up?" I asked.

"It's not even eight o'clock, and I've already had my ass kicked," he said.

"By who?"

"I'll give you one guess."

"VanBergen?"

"The one and only."

"For what?"

"Kevin Palmer got hold of him Friday."

"So."

"He told the sheriff that you said his cat was used as bait by someone training their dog to kill, and that there was a dog fighting ring in the county. He wanted to know why no one was investigating it."

"Good question."

"Needless to say, the sheriff's a little pissed. I'd steer clear of him for a while, but he did tell me to look into the disappearance of Palmer's cat. So, what can you tell me about it?"

"Really? Palmer convinced him to do something?"

"I'm not sure why, but yes he did."

Carol was in and already doing the morning cleaning and feeding. She had a new volunteer to train and said she didn't need my help.

Jason fixed a pot of coffee. We sat in my office while I told him about getting the call from Linda Levecca saying there was a stray cat killing the birds at her feeder.

"I went over and saw the cat but couldn't catch it. It was a black and white tuxedo with distinct markings on its face. It looked like it had a mustache. Sort of reminded me of Groucho Marx. I set a live trap and told her to call me when it was caught, but she never called. The next day the trap was sitting outside the shelter with no cat in it. I called and she said her daughter took care of the cat. I talked to the daughter and she said she just shooed the cat away. I don't believe her."

"And you think it was Palmer's cat?"

"He showed me a picture of his cat and it had the same mustache. What are the odds? Plus, he lives fairly close to Linda."

"If he lets the cat run loose, someone may have picked it up after Linda's daughter did whatever it is she did with it."

"But the dates jive. His cat went missing the same day Linda called the shelter. He never saw it again."

"Maybe we should go talk to Linda."

"I did already. She's wondering why I'm asking so many questions about one stray cat. The last time I was there I learned her daughter doesn't live with her. I thought she did."

"Where does she live?"

"I don't know. I always meant to track her down but never got around to it."

"Well, I say we go pay Linda another visit and find out where her daughter lives and go pay her a visit," Jason said.

"I don't have all day, but I could spare a couple hours," I said.

"What do you have going on?"

"I'm going to visit my friend Sara in Grand Haven. She called over the weekend and needs some help. I haven't told Cindi yet." A partial truth was better than a lie—at least the way I looked at it. Someone else might consider it a partial lie or a partial omission. Jason didn't ask anything else.

We took Jason's animal control truck to Linda's, which gave us a look of authority. The last time I talked to Linda she wasn't forthcoming. I felt she knew something she wasn't telling.

I directed Jason to Linda's house. There was a blue van parked in the yard, and it looked familiar.

"That's Lissa's van. I recognize the plate number. She's the one who answered my Craigslist ad and wanted to help me find a home for my dog. She has a rescue, Fur-Ever Homes. Remember the plate number I gave you to run?"

"Oh, yeah. It was registered to Melissa Devine. She lived south of here down by Pentwater. She had a kennel license and boarded dogs. What is Linda's daughter's name?"

"Missy."

"Her last name?"

"I assumed it was Levecca, the same as Linda's."

"Maybe it's not. Maybe it's Devine."

"Let's go find out."

We walked to the back door, and I knocked. Linda came to the door and stepped outside, partially closing the door behind her. I introduced her to Jason.

"Is that your daughter's vehicle?" he asked.

"Why do you ask?"

"I'm doing a follow-up on a missing cat, and I know the owner of the van runs a rescue. Is Melissa Devine your daughter."

Before Linda could answer, the door opened and Lissa came out. "I'm Melissa Devine," she said, holding her hand out to Jason. She wore a red sundress that complemented her blond hair.

"Jason Bentley. Pleased to meet you," Jason said, accepting her hand. "I'm an animal control officer with the sheriff's department, and I'm doing a follow-up on a cat who went missing in the area." He then turned his body slightly towards me and said, "This is Alison Cavera, who works at the county shelter."

Melissa turned and looked at me. "You look familiar," she said. "Have we met?"

If she didn't remember me, I wasn't going to tell her our history. "You look familiar, too," I said. "It's a small town, I'm sure our paths crossed somewhere."

She smiled. "It'll come to me," she said.

Jason took the lead on the questioning. "Your mom called us a couple of weeks ago about a cat killing birds at her feeder. We had a report of a missing cat from this neighborhood. We have reason to believe the cat at your feeder was the missing cat. Your mom said you took care of it. Did you take the cat into your rescue?"

"My rescue?"

"Fur-Ever Homes. Isn't that the rescue you run?"

"Oh, no. I'm just a volunteer. I do fostering. I have a kennel and sometimes board homeless dogs until homes can be found for them."

The mention of Fur-Ever Homes triggered her memory. She turned to me and said, "That's where we met. Didn't you have a dog you needed to place?"

"That's right. My grandmother decided to take it, but then my move to California fell through, so I ended up keeping Buffy."

"I didn't realize you worked for the shelter."

I knew that question was coming. "I didn't mention it. I felt guilty working for a shelter and not keeping my own dog. We always stress that adoptions should be forever, and there I was giving up my dog because my boyfriend didn't like dogs."

"Take it from me, if he doesn't like dogs, you're better off without him," she said.

"I see that now, but you know what love can do to one's thinking," I said with a laugh.

Lissa and her mom both laughed in agreement. "I've been down that road once or twice myself," Lissa said. "And in the end keeping the dog ends up being the better choice. Love me, love my dogs, is what I say now."

"I might have to adopt that philosophy," I said, but I was thinking *love me, love my farm.*

Jason cleared his throat to interrupt our patter. "Back to the cat. It was a black and white cat with moustache-like markings on its face," Jason said.

"Why so much interest in a cat?" Linda asked.

"The owner is still looking for it and has been pestering the sheriff. So the sheriff asked me to look into it. Alison said she loaned you a live trap and saw the cat and, because of its unique markings, she remembered it."

"I do remember that cat," Lissa said. "We did catch it in the trap, but instead of bringing it to the shelter—I know how many cats are euthanized there—I drove around the neighborhood looking for its owner. One of the women I talked to recognized it as her neighbor's cat. She said the neighbor wasn't home so I let the cat out in their yard. Then I dropped the trap off at the shelter. The cat must have wandered somewhere else looking for food."

Her story sounded plausible, but since I had caught her in a lie before, I questioned whether she was telling the truth this time.

"I appreciate your time and patience with us," Jason said. "People shouldn't let their cats roam outside." He shook hands with Lissa and Linda. I did too, and we left.

Neither one of us said anything until we were out of their driveway. "Well, what do you think?" I asked.

"She was convincing. If I didn't know the background, I'd believe her. I don't know how we can prove she's lying, though."

"I don't either. I guess this is where we sit back and see what happens next," I said.

"Just for the heck of it, I'm going to drive by Kevin Palmer's house," Jason said. He turned on a side street and pulled out a piece of paper with an address on it and then pulled off to the side of the road.

"That's it," he said, pointing to a well-kept, one-story brick house. The lawn was mowed, brushes trimmed, and petunias, hollyhock and an array of other annuals and perennials bloomed in flowerbeds.

"Do we want to talk to him?" I asked.

"Maybe we should. At least he'd know we were trying, even though I don't know what else we can do."

Palmer wasn't home, so Jason left his business card in the door. He noticed me glancing at my watch and questioned if I was running out of time.

"I have a few things I need to get done before I leave," I said.

On the way back to the shelter, I asked about Red, but I really wanted to ask about his plans for the evening. If I didn't call Cindi, she would be calling Jason. I wondered what his reaction would be when he heard—if he heard—about my attending a dog fight. He'd recall me anxiously watching the time and probably be mad that I hadn't confided in him. I considered talking to him, but after Cooper's reaction to my plan, I wasn't going to chance it.

"Red's making herself right at home. I don't know how long I'll keep her separate from the other dogs, but for now all is well."

"That's good."

"You're not saying much about Melissa or Lissa. Or is it Missy? Kind of weird to go by three names. So what do you think of her story?" Jason asked.

"I'm still stunned that Lissa is Linda's daughter. I don't know what to make of it. I do know she told me Fur-Ever Homes was her rescue. But then again, she may have been taking ownership in the group as a volunteer. But I've researched the organization and haven't found a website, a Facebook page or any mention of it anywhere. All I've seen is the business card she gave me with her telephone number on it. I figured it was a new group."

"Do you still have the card?"

"It's in my desk. My gut tells me something is wrong. She seemed pretty slick, almost too confident. She had an answer for everything. I can say I wouldn't trust giving her *my* dog."

"Like you said, we'll have to keep an eye on her," Jason said.

Chapter Thirty-three

When we arrived back at the shelter, we went to Cindi's office and filled her in on our morning's activities. She questioned why Kevin Palmer had gone to the sheriff.

"He's been calling me, but I haven't had anything new to tell him. I told him I wasn't on the case, and if he wanted something more to be done, he needed to contact the sheriff. Apparently, he wants something more done," I said.

"You told him that?"

"Was I supposed to lie?"

Cindi looked away, took a deep breath and exhaled slowly.

"It worked," Jason said. "VanBergen was angry, but I got the go-ahead to look into it some more."

"And what exactly are you going to look into?"

"I'm going to go back and review the files from when we found Red. We collected a stack of papers and magazines that had been left behind. Maybe I can spot something we didn't notice before. I'll see if I can connect some of the dead animals to lost pet reports. Look for anything we may have missed."

Cindi's attitude of anger and defiance changed after listening to Jason. She turned to me and said, "I'm sorry I didn't have your back. VanBergen intimidates me. I should have stood up to him."

Her apology took me by surprise. "He does the same to me, and he knows it. He's in a place of authority, and he doesn't let you forget it," I said.

"It's no different for me or anyone else who works under him," Jason said. "He barks, we jump."

I told Cindi something personal had come up, and I needed to go to Grand Haven that afternoon. Jason followed me to my office asking to see the business card Melissa had given me. I made a copy of it before giving it to him.

"Have you checked the camera we put up yet?" I asked.

"No, I've been meaning to. I'll get out there this week. At least now I don't have to sneak around."

With Jason officially investigating our suspicions of a dog-fighting ring in the county, I decided to tell him about Muskegon. "I have a little confession to make," I said.

"Oh yeah?"

"Now that we have permission to investigate what's been going on, I can tell you. I bought a second camera and installed it down in Muskegon. Someone's been dropping dead dogs off in the same place, so the shelter director and I put up a camera. It's close enough to here that it could be related."

"You're kidding me."

He asked for details, so I told him about how Mary Ellen and I installed the camera in the tree and got pictures of dogs being dropped off.

"Where are they? Can I see them?"

"They're on my laptop. They're not good. The camera was too far away. We moved it, but I haven't heard from Mary Ellen since then. I can e-mail the pictures to you but, like I said, they're not very good."

While it felt good to come clean with Jason on the second camera, I still couldn't bring myself to tell him about my plans for the evening. I finished what I needed to get done and left. Since I had my laptop in the car, I stopped for coffee and took the time to e-mail the photos to Jason. I also remembered to buy a pack of cigarettes and a lighter.

Sara was waiting for me and, since we had extra time, we went for a walk on the beach. With most of the tourists gone for the season, we had the sandy shore of Lake Michigan to ourselves. We found a bench where we could talk, and I told her everything. Like Cooper and Grams, she tried to talk me out of it, but she knew me well enough to know she wouldn't change my mind.

"Just promise that this time no one gets shot," she said.

"I hope no one gets shot," I said. "My plan is to keep a low profile and just watch and listen."

Talking with Sara, listening to the waves and watching the seagulls relaxed me. The time sped by and soon we had to head back to her house. I donned my disguise in the bathroom, and before I presented myself to Sara, I asked that she refrain from laughing. When I stepped into her view, I keyed in on her face. She kept her composure and got up and walked around, checking me from every angle.

"If I didn't know it was you, I might fall for it," she said. "I'm not so sure about the glasses. They seem a little too hip for the rest of the outfit."

I took the glasses off and said in a deep voice, "Is this better?"

She stared at me for a moment before answering. "The voice is good. Really good. I don't know about the glasses. Let me see if Ryan has a pair of sunglasses that might work."

Sara disappeared into her bedroom. When she returned she held a pair of glasses. "Here, try these on," she said.

I took them from her and slid them in place. "What do you think?" I asked.

"Better, much better."

I went back into the bathroom for a look-see in the mirror. "They cover up my eyes, which is perfect, but I'll have to take them off when we go inside."

"Once you're inside it won't matter as much. You'll feel more relaxed in a crowd and won't feel the need to hide behind glasses," she said.

I had the ink pen camera and the cigarettes in my shirt pocket. I wore Cooper's blue-jean jacket over the shirt, which hid the pocket. When I came back out of the bathroom, I reached to the pen, moving the jacket aside, and clicked a picture while I was talking. "I bought some cigarettes—thought they added to the disguise. Might give me something to do if it gets to be too much," I said. I pulled the pack from the pocket.

"Did you practice smoking one?"

"No."

"You might want to do that. Let's go outside."

215

We went to the backyard. When I grabbed the pack I fumbled a bit and took another photo. Using the new lighter, I lit a cigarette and inhaled slightly. The taste was as bad as I remembered from when I experimented with smoking in my teen years.

"Here give it to me," Sara said. I handed her the cigarette and she took a puff and blew smoke in my hair and clothes.

"You need to smell the part," she said.

I hated the smell of smoke, and now I reeked of it.

When the cigarette burned down just shy of the filter, I stubbed it out in the dirt.

"Did you notice anything odd about the pack of cigarettes or my pocket?" I handed her the ink pen. "It's a camera. I took your picture twice. Once inside and again out here. You have to press the top," I said, reaching over and showing her how it worked.

"I never would have guessed," she said.

"Hit the button twice and it takes video."

"Really? All that in an ink pen?"

"And it writes. You have to twist it in the middle to get the tip to come out," I said, demonstrating how it worked.

I also showed her the other camera, and said I thought about putting it in the pack of cigarettes, but didn't know if I should.

"Maybe you could hide it in your wig ... reach up, scratch your head and turn it on," she said.

We went back inside, and I took a seat at the kitchen table while she tried fitting the second camera into the wig.

"I think you could hide it in your hair under the cap, but I don't think you're going to get it where it has a clear shot of anything. The hair will be in the way," Sara said.

"Why don't you stuff it under the wig cap? If I need it, I can go to the bathroom and get it out."

"Just remember to go to the men's bathroom," she said.

"That'd be funny if I went to the women's."

Sara asked me what my cover story was going to be, and I felt stupid for not having one. "What are you going to say if someone asks you where you're from? Or where you work? Or how you got started in sporting dogs?"

We brainstormed on my background story, and then she quizzed me until the lies rolled off my lips like the truth.

Although I wasn't hungry, Sara made me eat. She had the fixings for veggie tacos: refried beans, rice, lettuce, tomatoes and avocado. I managed to choke one down.

"It's not the food: it's nerves," I said.

I gave her a piece of paper with telephone numbers on it for Jason, Cooper, Rocky and Grams. "Just in case."

Chapter Thirty-four

Sara insisted on going with me to the park-and-ride. "I'm at least going to meet this guy and see what he's all about." She followed me in her car to the rendezvous. We arrived 15 minutes early. Mike wasn't there yet, so we stood outside talking, waiting for him. When he wasn't there by seven o'clock, I thought he wasn't going to show.

"I should have known he wouldn't come. He didn't want me to go with him," I said.

"You're so impatient. He's not even late yet."

She was right. I took a deep breath and answered her questions. How was Grams? What was work like? How was Cooper?

Ten minutes later a car pulled in, circled around the lot and stopped in front of us. A young guy got out who looked to be in his twenties. He wore a black T-shirt and faded, ripped-in-the-knee jeans that looked too big for him. His shaggy, dark-brown hair covered his ears and, in my opinion, needed to be trimmed.

"Alison?" he asked, looking at Sara.

"Mike?" she said.

He came over and shook her hand. "Who's this?" he asked, looking at me.

"My friend, Alex."

I reached out and shook hands with him. He had a firm grasp. "Nice to meet you," I said in my deep voice.

He looked at Sara and then at me again. "What's goin' on? You bringin' your boyfriend?"

"I'm not her boyfriend. I'm Alex," I said.

He stared at me.

"And I'm his friend, Sara," Sara said.

"Whoa. You're Alison?" he asked, pointing at me.

I nodded yes and then twirled around. "What do you think?"

"You fooled me. So why is she here?" he asked, this time pointing at Sara.

"She's my friend. She wants to know when you'll be bringing me back. If I don't call her by then, she's calling my friend, Jason, who's an animal contol officer."

"And what will he do?"

"I don't know. He doesn't know about any of this, but I'm hoping Sara can give him enough information about you that he'll be able to find us."

Sara walked around to the back of his car and wrote down his plate number. "What did you say your last name was?" she asked.

"Tabor. It's Mike Tabor."

"Can I see your driver's license?"

Her tenacity surprised me. Mike hesitated for a moment then pulled out his wallet and took out his license. She copied down what she needed and thanked him.

"So, why are you doing this?" Sara asked.

He looked around, like he was worried someone might hear what he had to say. "I want 'em shut down. Rocky taught me that dogs deserve better. Rocky lets me stay with the pits, and they don't wanna fight." He sounded sad, almost like he thought it was a hopeless situation.

"I hope you pull the plug on them," Sara said.

"So what's the plan? What are we doing?" I asked.

Mike's voice returned to normal. "We're meetin' Uncle Vic at his place. I don't know if we'll ride with him or follow him. I'm hopin' we can follow."

"Can I bring my cell phone?"

"No, leave it here." I put the phone in the glove box and locked the car doors.

I debated whether I should tell him about the cameras, but decided against it. He probably wouldn't let me take them. And if he did know about them, it'd just be one more thing he'd be worried about.

"What's your uncle's name and where does he live?"

Mike obliged and gave Sara the information.

"What time should I activate Code Yellow?" she asked.

"Code Yellow?" I said.

"It's hospital lingo for missing person."

"A fight can last hours. It's Uncle Vic's show, so we'll be there till the end. How about six o'clock?"

"In the morning?" I asked. "That long?"

"Depends on the pits—they go until one quits or is injured so bad that it can't go on or is dead. I can't say how long that'll take."

I looked at Sara. "Maybe you should call everyone and let them know. I doubt they're expecting it to take that long."

Sara said she would. I hugged her goodbye and apologized for everything. She just hugged me tighter.

"Be safe. Both of you," she said.

I got in Mike's car and waved goodbye to Sara. He headed north toward Muskegon.

"Are you nervous?" I asked him.

"Hell, yes, I'm nervous. I don't like seeing dogs rip each other to pieces. I don't know if my uncle will buy into bringin' you along."

"And if he doesn't?"

"I won't go, and since he wants me to see Diesel's first fight, he'll let you go."

"Diesel is his dog?"

"Yeah. The last time I was up here he was just a pup, a nice little dog, but I bet he ain't that way now."

"What do you know about the training?"

"All of it. I lived with Uncle Vic when he lived on the South side of Chicago. He treated me like a son. I was glad of it. I was proud to help him fight dogs."

"So, what happened?"

"He moved up here. I moved in with a bud and met Rocky. He made me smart."

"I'm sure you were already smart. He just made you aware of it," I said.

"No, I was dumb. I should have figured it out."

Mike got off on Sherman Boulevard. After a couple of turns on side streets, I no longer knew where I was. He parked in front of a tiny white house. The sun had started to set, but in the twilight I could see the house needed a coat of paint and a cracked window that should be replaced. It would take a Dumpster to clear the yard and front porch.

A man with a beer belly stood in the backyard next to a forest-green pickup truck with a cap.

"That's Uncle Vic," Mike said under his breath. He got out, walked over to the guy and greeted him with a handshake. I got out and followed. I held out my hand and he accepted it. I guessed him to be in his fifties. His hairline had receded and what was left of his hair had turned gray. He wore blue jeans, a red-plaid shirt and a leather vest.

"Uncle Vic, this is Alex. He's like a brother to me," Mike said.

Uncle Vic's eyes fixed on mine. It felt like he could read my every thought and knew I was a phony. Thankful for the dim light, I said, "Good to meet you, sir. I've heard a lot about you."

"What did Mike tell you? Only good stuff I hope," he said, followed by a booming laugh.

Mike looked beyond his uncle into the backyard where a chained red and white pit bull stared at us. His stance spoke of power, and his body rippled with muscles. His ears were unevenly cropped, giving him a menacing look. His stub of a tail bobbed back and forth. "Is that Diesel?"

"Looking good, ain't he?" Uncle Vic said.

"He's a topper," Mike said.

"That's two years of work, both him and me," Uncle Vic said. "He's my ticket out."

Mike approached Diesel, and the dog didn't move. He got down on one knee and held out a hand. "Remember me? I knew you when you was a pup."

I don't know if Diesel remember Mike, but he seemed happy to see him. Mike rubbed his hand along the dog's neck, shoulder and a front leg, then his side. "He's solid."

"He's got bloodline. He's a champion. You should've seen him roll; I needed a breaking stick. He would've finished the job if I'd 'a let him. He's ready for the show," Uncle Vic said.

He walked over to Diesel and slapped him hard on the hip. Diesel didn't react. "He likes pain." Then he stood in front of the pit bull, bent down and rubbed a hand on each of Diesel's sides. The dog nuzzled the man's face.

The affection was obvious. How could he send his dog into an arena to fight?

"Let's get loaded," Uncle Vic said as he stood up and unclipped Diesel's chain from his collar. Diesel ran over to an empty water dish and sniffed around.

"No water," Uncle Vic said, turning to me. "He'll bleed less if he ain't filled with water."

I nodded in agreement, once again thankful the lighting was such that he couldn't see my disgust.

"Look at this," he said as he opened Diesel's mouth. "Feel those teeth. Go ahead."

He had noticed my hesitation and urged me on. I felt one of the canine teeth. It felt like the tip of a spear. I quickly pulled my hand back, noting that all the incisors and canines had been filed to a sharp point.

Uncle Vic walked to the back of the truck, opened the cap's door and lowered the tailgate. Diesel jumped into a large kennel that took up close to half the space in the truck bed. Uncle Vic closed the kennel door. There were cardboard boxes of stuff in front of the kennel and a stack of towels and blankets. The windows of the truck cap were painted black. Diesel would be riding in total darkness.

Mike climbed into the cab and I followed, thankful he was between Uncle Vic and me.

It wasn't until we were back on U.S. 31 heading north that I knew where we were. I watched the exits go by: Apple Avenue, North Muskegon, Whitehall. I began to worry about where we were going. Uncle Vic and Mike chatted about family, dogs and Chicago. They left me out of the conversation for a good part of the time, but Uncle Vic realized he was being rude and apologized.

"So, Alex, tell me about yourself," he said.

"I was born and raised on the north side of Chicago. My parents divorced and I moved with my dad to the south side. That's where I met Mike."

"Do you work?"

"I'm between jobs. I'd like to do breeding."

"Maybe you could get one of Diesel's pups."

"We could be partners," Mike said to me.

Once again I became a listener as Mike and his uncle talked bloodlines and the art of breeding fighting dogs.

About 45 minutes after getting on the highway, Uncle Vic finally exited at Pentwater. He headed west and, after driving for a while, he turned left. The street sign passed by so quickly I couldn't make out the name of the road he turned on. A few minutes later, he turned left again. The road curved back and forth, and my sense of direction left me guessing as to which way we were traveling. We were somewhere between Lake Michigan and U.S. 31, in an area unfamiliar to me.

He pulled into the driveway of a farmhouse and followed a two-track drive behind a barn. The drive continued between an open field and a tract of woods. Rounding a curve, I saw several parked vehicles and a pole barn. In the glow of a utility light, I could see a crowd gathered outside. Several in the group turned and watched as Uncle Vic pulled in and parked his pickup. They continued to stare as we got out.

Chapter Thirty-five

"We don't do introductions," Uncle Vic said. "You don't know nobody and if you wanna make a bet, it's green. Let's go in."

We followed Uncle Vic into the pole barn. There was a man collecting money at the door.

"My boys," Uncle Vic said, pointing to us.

The man waved us in. Fluorescent lights hung high from the ceiling. They gave off enough light to give the room some visibility, but not enough to be overpowering. It wasn't Vegas. A couple dozen people milled around, mostly men, but I spotted a few women.

Uncle Vic told us he had business to take care of and said we should just hang out. He slipped Mike a hundred dollar bill and told him to make a bet. "So you can afford one of Diesel's pups," he whispered to us.

The room had a pungent odor, a mix of the stale stink of cigarettes and who knows what else? A whiff of marijuana caught my attention. I pulled the pack of Marlboros from my pocket and fumbled for the lighter. It gave me something to do.

I spotted the fight pit in the center of the room. I guessed it to be about 15 by 20 feet. The plywood walls were about waist high. The floor of the pit was covered in dark carpeting to give the dogs traction and soak up urine and blood.

There was a scaffold next to the pit where a man was setting up a tripod. "Do they videotape the fights?" I whispered to Mike.

He nodded yes. He then nudged me with his elbow and nodded to where a crowd gathered by a card table. I followed him over, and we stood in the line until it was his turn to place a bet. I watched him hand over the cash his uncle had given him. We wandered around. When we were out of hearing range, I whispered, "I'm surprised people have to pay to get in."

"Yeah, it's part of the purse."

"The purse?"

"The dog owners decide on the purse amount and each pays into it. Part of the door is added to it. They sell DVDs, too. It's winner take all."

A commotion at the door caught our attention. The crowd parted as Uncle Vic strutted in with a muzzled Diesel on a short leash. He headed to the pit. Behind him another guy came in with a muscular white dog that strained at its leash in the direction of Diesel. It, too, was muzzled. Its focus on Diesel was uncanny.

We moved closer to the pit. Next to the scaffold the dogs were weighed. The pre-show antics were almost ceremonial. With everyone's attention focused on the dogs, I felt comfortable clicking on the ink pen twice to start the video. With my hand in my coat pocket, I could cover and uncover the camera with my jacket as needed. Each handler washed the opponent's dog with a sponge in the same tub of water. It was to make sure the animal's coat hadn't been covered with poison or any other substance that would kill or hinder a dog's performance. The excess water was toweled off.

I took time to scan the crowd while they fixated on the dogs being readied for the fight. I shifted my body so the camera would film the full crowd. There was a mix of people: mostly men, but some women. All ages. It horrified me to see a handful of young kids, a few so short they could just see over the plywood walls of the fight pit. There were African-Americans, Hispanics and whites.

One of the plywood walls was pulled back so the owners and their dogs could enter the pit. Another guy, the referee, also went in. The crowd shifted to encircle the pit. We were up front, and it was when the white dog's handler came into the ring that I realized it was a woman, not a man. She was slim with her hair tucked under a cap. There was nothing feminine about her clothes, just loose-fitting blue jeans and an untucked red T-shirt.

Uncle Vic took his dog to one corner, and the woman took her dog to the opposite corner. The animals were made to face away from each other. The dogs had to stay behind the scratch line, a painted mark on the carpet, about three-feet out from the corner. The crowd was quiet with anticipation. My own body surged with adrenaline, yet I could hardly breathe.

The referee shouted, "Face your dogs!"

The dogs were turned around so they could see each other. Their eyes locked.

"Let go!" the referee yelled.

The dogs charged each other and met in the middle of the pit. The owners yelled at their dogs urging them on. The woman moved around the pit, and it was when she was right in front of me that I recognized her.

It was Melissa Devine. Linda's daughter. The pieces started to fall into place. I recalled Jason saying her kennel was in Pentwater. My guess was that's where we were.

The camera was still on video, and I made sure it was aimed at her. The dogs were on their back feet, their front legs embraced as they grabbed at each other's face and neck with their teeth. Losing their balance, they slammed to the carpet.

People were shouting, "Git 'im Diesel" or "Go Nitro." Uncle Vic and Melissa egged their dogs on with taunts.

Diesel had struck blood on his opponent's face, and it was turning the white fur red. I was horrified, not only at the viciousness of the fight but also at the crowd's reaction. They were yelling and jeering at the dogs. Everyone had a favorite, so the heckles were a mix of boos and cheers.

I glanced at Mike and saw him grimace. I recalled his affection for Diesel and couldn't imagine how he felt watching the fight. Diesel not only attacked with bloodlust, but he was taking a beating.

Diesel got hold of the side of Nitro's face and his jaws clamped shut. Nitro twisted and turned, yelping in pain but couldn't break the grip. He struggled for several minutes. Blood dripped to the floor and Diesel's fans erupted in cheers.

"You got 'im!" Uncle Vic yelled.

Finally, Nitro was able to free himself.

The referee stepped in and stopped the fight. The owners grabbed their dogs and took them to their respective corners. The referee walked over to a bucket of water and tossed each handler a wet sponge to wipe down their dog and clean away the blood.

Another man with a stopwatch shouted, "Time!" The break was less than a minute. The dogs faced each other again, and this time Nitro was let go first. Since he had shown weakness by backing off, he had to prove himself and attack.

Nitro didn't hesitate. As soon as Melissa let go of the white dog, he exploded across the carpet and, with a viciousness that surprised me, lunged onto Diesel.

"You gotta winner, Mel!" I heard someone shout.

Melissa turned her head and nodded.

I gasped. Mel? I had found the elusive Mel! I had been looking for a man when I should have been looking for a woman! Never in a million years would I have guessed that the Mel the men mentioned when they chased me was a woman. They had been fearful of Mel, and I assumed it was a man. Of course, Mel could be short for Melissa. Just like Lissa had been a spin-off of Melissa.

It didn't seem possible to be any more scared or nervous, but I was. Melissa portrayed herself as a loving daughter, someone who rescued cats and dogs, and here she was, in the pit with her own dog. If she could do this to dogs, I didn't doubt she was somehow involved with the killing of the two men who had been found shot to death.

In the pit, Nitro had Diesel on his back with a hold on his throat. Diesel squirmed, trying to break loose.

Uncle Vic bent down near the dogs, clapped his hands repeatedly and shouted, "Fight, damn it! Diesel! Get up!"

"You got 'im! Hold 'im!" Melissa shouted. She stood just a couple feet away from Uncle Vic.

With renewed effort upon hearing Uncle Vic's voice, Diesel twisted his body to the side throwing Nitro off balance. With the move, Nitro lost his grasp. Diesel rebounded and the two were on their back feet, front legs entwined as they ripped and bit at each other trying to find a place to sink teeth.

Once again, Nitro got a hold, but Diesel was able to wiggle out of it. Nitro was quick, chomping down on Diesel's nose. Diesel winced. He twisted his head back and forth, but his rival hung on. They crashed into the plywood wall. The collision startled Nitro, and he lost his grip.

Diesel turned away, and that was enough for the referee to stop the fight. Uncle Vic and Melissa stepped in and dragged the dogs to their respective corners. Once again they were given sponges to clear away the blood.

"That was bad," Mike whispered to me.

I nodded, noticing the red smear on the plywood and realized the dark stains on the barricade were dried blood. How many dogs had played out this same scenario, and how many had met their death in this very spot?

This time when the break was over, it was Diesel's turn to show he had game. And he did. He charged across the pit and hurled himself at Nitro. Nitro stood his ground, and once again they were on their back feet, entangled with one another, vicious in their thirst for blood. Nitro lost his footing, and they tumbled to the ground. Diesel took the advantage of the moment and got a lock on the side of Nitro's face.

"You got 'im now!" Uncle Vic screamed. "Hold 'im! Hold 'im!" he repeated the phrase, his voice getting harsher.

"Get 'im, Nitro!" Melissa chanted in a warlike shrill.

In the crowd, fists pumped the air as people yelled in support. Their thirst for blood equaled that of the dogs'. One of the young boys whose head stuck up just above the plywood watched in silence. I wondered what thoughts were streaming in his brain.

Nitro squirmed, but Diesel held tight. It was agonizing to watch. Finally Nitro broke the hold and flipped to his feet. Diesel stayed on target and the two were again on their back feet going at each other.

The urgency had disappeared from Diesel's aggression, and he hesitated for just a second. Nitro chomped down hard on his face. Diesel yelped.

"No," I heard Mike whisper.

I turned and looked at him. His face was void of emotion. He had one hand clinched into a fist that he repeatedly slammed into the palm of the other hand. I grabbed his arm, trying to break his trance. "Hey," I said.

"No more!" Mike screamed. "No more!"

The referee, Uncle Vic and Melissa or Mel turned and looked in our direction. I felt as though Melissa looked past Mike and directly at me, and for a second I thought I saw recognition.

"No more!" Mike screamed again. He hurdled over the plywood into the pit. He kicked Nitro to break his hold. The referee called time, and Uncle Vic and Melissa grabbed their dogs. Security men jumped Mike, and I saw Melissa point in my direction.

I turned and walked as fast as I could. The chaos provided cover for my escape. "Bathroom?" I said to the man at the door.

He pointed outside.

Once I was past him, I ran. Down the two-track drive by the house and to the road. I debated about stopping at the house, wondering if there might be a landline inside. That's when I heard a gunshot. Then another.

I didn't stop. I wanted to put as much distance between this hellhole and me as possible.

Chapter Thirty-six

My leg muscles burned, and my lungs felt like they would explode if I ran any farther. Only a few hundred feet down the road past the driveway, my body forced me to stop running. I bent over gasping for air, trying to catch my breath. I listened for sounds of being followed, but the only thing I heard was my own jagged breathing and thumping heart.

I wondered what time it was but couldn't see my watch in the dark. With a flick of my cigarette lighter, I saw it was just after midnight. It would be six hours before Sara made her calls. How long would it take Jason to put together the puzzle? He had all the pieces, but it could be hours before he fitted them together. Waiting for him wasn't much of an option, but what were my choices? Running down the driveway in the dark had been a feat of luck. The night sky was dotted with stars and just a sliver of a moon. For once I wished for the light pollution of Chicago.

The isolation of the kennel made it the perfect spot for illegal activities. From what I remembered by looking at a map, there were acres of national forest in the area. Houses were rare. While my body rested, my brain looked for a way out. The only option was to follow the road and hide in the ditch if a car came.

I kept an eye in the direction of the pole barn, although with the trees I couldn't even see the outside light. All of a sudden headlights appeared on the driveway. Someone in a vehicle had a high-powered light; the kind used for shining whitetail deer, and they were shining it into the trees and fields. Within seconds I could hear the engine.

I sprinted across the road into the forest. As soon as I entered the woods, I knew I was in trouble. The leaves blocked the night sky and the minuscule light the stars provided disappeared. I stumbled over a log, crashed to the ground and landed on my shoulder. It should have hurt, but I didn't feel anything but fear. Instead of getting up, I crawled to the log and tucked my body beside the half-rotted trunk. The rumble of the vehicle got closer. I took the ink pen camera, tucked it into the pack of cigarettes and hid it under the log.

Although I had my head crammed against the ground, I could see a beam of light shining over me. I held my breath and did my best to be invisible.

"There he is," I heard someone shout. I heard a door open and slam shut. Had they really seen me? Should I run? I didn't. There was nowhere to go.

Someone was stumbling through the undergrowth in my direction. "Get up!" a voice commanded from right above me.

A hand grabbed my arm and jerked me to my feet.

"Who are you?" the man asked. I recognized the voice before I did the face. Relief flooded over me. It was Sheriff VanBergen. Before I could answer he yanked me toward the road.

"Do you have her?" It was Melissa.

"It's a *him*. But, yes, I have him."

My thoughts tumbled. *VanBergen and Melissa? She was Mel. How did they know each other?*

VanBergen had a vise-like grip on my arm and dragged me toward the road. Melissa pointed the light in our direction. It wasn't until we reached the vehicle, which turned out to be Melissa's van, that he released me.

"It's a guy," VanBergen said.

"No, it isn't. It's that bitch from the animal shelter," she said. Melissa reached up and yanked off my wig and tossed it on the ground. Then she snatched the cap off my head and my hair tumbled down.

My eyes met VanBergen's, and I saw anger. I wondered what he was up to. *Is he undercover or is he a gamer?*

"No shit," he said. "Now what do we do? We can't let her go. She knows me."

"She knows me, too. Throw her in back. If she tries anything, shoot her. She'll have to disappear."

"Disappear?" VanBergen asked.

"That's what I said. Disappear. Do you have a better idea?"

"No."

VanBergen grabbed my arm again and led me to the back of the van. He opened the door and ordered me to get inside. In the glow of the dome light, I saw a large, wire dog crate.

Melissa ordered me to get into the kennel. "Since you're such a dog lover, you'll feel right at home in there," she said. She tossed VanBergen a padlock.

"No," I said.

She went to the front of the van and returned with a gun. She aimed it at my face. "You want to reconsider that?" she said.

On hands and knees, I crawled into the crate. The bottom was covered with old towels, which at least felt clean and dry, but they smelled of dog. Once in, I twisted myself around so I could face Melissa, but she had disappeared. VanBergen closed the crate door, slid the slide-bolts and clamped the padlock in place.

"I told you to mind your own business. Why couldn't you listen?" he whispered. He slammed the back door of the van closed. The dome light went out, and fear gripped me as darkness settled in. A couple seconds later, the front doors opened. The dome light came back on as Melissa and VanBergen got in.

VanBergen and Melissa spoke in low voices, making it impossible to hear what they were saying. The van started, made a U-turn and drove back into the driveway. By the distance, it felt like they drove all the way to the pole barn. They both got out, and I was left alone in darkness. Using my fingers, I felt along the heavy-gauge steel wire of the crate looking for a weak spot where maybe I could weasel my way out, but it was sturdy. I felt the corners, the hinges and finally the padlock. It was a key lock.

I could hear muffled voices. Soon engines started and vehicles left. I counted fourteen, but I didn't know how many had been there to begin with. I wondered about Mike and the dogs. Had the loser been shot?

The crate was built for an extra-large dog, and I was almost able to straighten out my legs. With my back against the end of the crate, I pushed and kicked with my feet at the other end. Nothing seemed to budge. I felt the door again to see if I had caused any damage. The first time I had checked it, I hadn't felt both slide-bolts. This time I did and was able to slide open the bottom bolt. To my surprise, when I felt the top bolt, I realized the padlock wasn't holding it in place. VanBergen had fastened the lock to the door and not to the slide bolt. *Was it a mistake or intentional?*

I pushed the crate door open and squeezed out. I scrambled to the front of the van and slowly lifted my head high enough between the bucket seats to see out of the windshield. I didn't see anyone so I eased myself into the driver's seat.

I flirted with the idea of hiding by the house or behind the pole barn, but first I checked to see if the keys were in the ignition. They weren't. I felt around on the floor, above the visor, on the dashboard and on the console, which was littered with papers, ink pens, coins, napkins and what felt to be ketchup packets. I found the keys in the cup holder. I fingered them until I found the one that felt like a car key. I stuck it in the ignition and slowly turned, not wanting to start the engine, but wanting to know if it was the right key. It was. I looked around, suspecting a trap. Still I didn't see anyone. I turned the key again, this time wanting the engine to fire. It did.

I jammed the automatic shifter into drive, pressed the gas pedal and sped away. As I bounced along the driveway I glanced in the side-view mirrors. I didn't see any activity behind me. Once on the main road, I pressed the gas pedal to the floor and drove faster than I had ever driven before. When I had a couple miles behind me without being followed, I slowed down.

I didn't know for sure where I was, but when I came to a crossroad I turned either north or east hoping I would find the expressway. I got lucky. When I finally saw the green signs for the on-ramps, I spotted two police cars getting off at the exit. I swerved in front of them. Headlights blinded me as I got out and ran to the driver's side of the first vehicle.

Chapter Thirty-seven

"Help me!" I heard myself scream. "Help! I need help!"

"Alison?"

I recognized Jason's voice coming from inside the cop car. Within seconds he was out of the car rushing to me. I collapsed into his arms.

"Alison, where have you been? What are you doing with Melissa's van?"

Tears of relief poured down my face. I blathered on for several seconds before he put his hand over my mouth. "Slow down. You're not making any sense," he said. "I talked to Sara and know you went to a dog fight. Was it at Melissa's kennel?"

I nodded yes. The other officers got out of their cars and gathered around us.

"Is she still there?"

I nodded again. "VanBergen is with her," I said.

"The sheriff? What's he doing there?"

"I don't know, but he helped me escape," I said. "They have guns. I heard gunshots."

"I'll call for backup," one of the officers said. Another one got in the van and pulled it off to the side of the road.

By then I had calmed down enough to give a rational account of what had happened. A few minutes later, two state police cars arrived. Jason led me to one of the cars.

"You stay here," he said, as he opened the passenger door and ushered me into the front seat. "I'll come back for you after we check out the place."

He ran back to the police car and the cars sped off. The driver introduced himself as Detective Rick Caldwell. He said I could call him Rick, and asked if I needed anything.

"A drink," I said.

"I can't help with that, ma'am," he said.

"I could use a bathroom."

Rick drove me to a McDonalds. In the bathroom, I splashed cold water on my face and tried to straighten out my hair. I looked a wreck.

Rick waited for me outside the bathroom door. "What, you think I'm going to escape?" I asked.

"Not on my watch. No one's going to get you either. Do you want something to drink? Coffee? Water?"

"Coffee. I think it's going to be a long night."

He ordered two coffees to go and then drove us back to the side of the road and parked behind Melissa's van. Neither of us bothered to make small talk. We sipped coffee and waited. The minutes on the car's digital clock couldn't have ticked by any slower.

Sixty-three minutes after the police cars left, one returned. The one with Jason. When I spotted him I got out of the car.

"Well?"

"The place was just as you described. The lights were on in the house so we stopped there first. Found Melissa packing. Took her into custody and then went back to the pole barn. We found three bodies: VanBergen, a young man—I suspect it's your buddy Mike—and an older man, most likely Uncle Vic."

Jason's voice started to sound distant, and I couldn't make sense of what he was saying. My knees buckled.

When I came to, I was on the ground with a blanket covering me from the neck down.

"An ambulance is on its way," Jason said. He hovered over me, his face serious with concern.

"I'm okay. I don't need an ambulance," I said.

He wouldn't listen. He wouldn't let me get up. He wouldn't tell me anymore about what they discovered at the farm.

"Tell me this," I pleaded. "Are the dogs dead?"

That information he shared with me. Neither one was dead. A veterinarian had been called and was on the way.

"Please, don't let them be euthanized," I pleaded. "They deserve a chance at a normal life."

Before the ambulance took me away, I gave Jason my keys and told him where my car was parked. He assured me he'd have someone retrieve my car.

The closest hospital was in Ludington. When they rolled me into the emergency room, Grams was there and greeted me with a hug. "Never again," she said. Her voice quivered as she fought back tears.

Behind her stood Cooper.

"What?" I said.

He gave me a kiss, stoked my hair and held my hand. "I couldn't sit in California once I knew what you were doing. I told my PO I had an emergency to attend to in Michigan. Luckily, he trusted me. He gave me a week. I just got here tonight."

A nurse came and asked them to step back.

In the exam room, she helped me out of my clothes.

"What's this?" she said after she pulled off my T-shirt and found the binding material.

"Long story," I said.

Chapter Thirty-eight

I called Rocky when I got home from the hospital. Breaking the news to him about Mike's death was heart-wrenching.

"At least you caught the bastards," he said. He asked about the dogs, but I didn't have any information for him.

Cindi called Tuesday morning and told Grams she wanted me to take time off until they got things straightened out with the dog-fighting bust. I welcomed the free time, especially since Cooper only had a few days before he had to head back to California.

At the hospital I was given a prescription for something to help me sleep. It worked. I spent most of Tuesday sleeping. I got up for dinner and went right back to bed. I wasn't aware of Cooper sharing my bed until the morning light woke me. It was a pleasant surprise. Ebony lay on my pillow purring. She seemed to like having him there.

The only physical aliment from the ordeal was a bruised shoulder from falling in the woods and that would heal in a few days. The emotional bruises would take longer to mend, if ever.

Watching the savagery of Diesel and Nitro trying to kill each other was etched in my mind. Having Cooper was a comfort.

Sara showed up Wednesday morning. She hadn't seen Cooper since he had been her patient. They hugged, and Cooper thanked her for all she had done.

"I owe you one," he said.

Sara declined a bowl of oatmeal but accepted a cup of coffee. I thanked her for all she had done for me.

"Next time don't ask," she told me.

"And if I do, tell me no," I said. Cooper and Grams both laughed at that.

"You mean you're going to start listening to us?" Grams asked.

"Maybe I should if you all say the same thing."

"Get it in writing," Cooper joked.

Sara was sorry to hear about Mike. "He seemed to be a decent guy," she said. "I don't know why it had to end that way."

"Me either. He went ballistic. He held it in as long as he could, but watching Diesel being attacked was too much. I keep replaying it in my mind. I don't know what I could have done differently."

"Nothing. Even if you hadn't gone with him, his reaction would have been the same."

Sara's reassurance helped, but I still felt responsible.

Cooper prepared lunch for us. It was good to have a personal chef again. Jason stopped by in the afternoon to check on me. We sat on the back porch with Grams, Sara and Cooper.

"You had me scared. I couldn't believe what you were doing," Jason confessed.

"How did you find out? Sara wasn't supposed to call you until the morning."

"I didn't call him. Although I was tempted to," Sara said.

"I called Sara after talking to Grams," he said.

I looked at Grams.

She shrugged. "He asked where you were, and I told him you were with Sara. He asked for her number since you weren't answering your cell, and I gave it to him."

"I still don't get it. Why the concern?" I asked him.

"I checked the camera we installed. There were pictures of a van with the license plate in clear view. It was Melissa's. Then I looked at the photos you e-mailed me. It was the same van. I just wanted to talk to you about it, but when I talked to Grams I could tell she was upset. Lucky she was," Jason said.

I told him about the ink pen camera, and how I had hidden it under the log.

"You're kidding. You're just telling me about it now?"

"I haven't seen you since you insisted I take that ambulance ride. You have her red-handed. I didn't think you'd need photos of the dog fight."

"It can't hurt. The more evidence the better. Do you feel up to going for a ride and getting it?"

We all went with Jason for the drive. He parked in Melissa's driveway, and I pointed in the direction I thought I had ran. "It can't be too far, but it's hard to tell. You wouldn't believe how dark it is out here at night. Just look for a rotten log with a cigarette package under it."

Sara spotted my wig and cap. I forgot Melissa had tossed them into the weeds. From there it was easy to find the log. The pack, with the ink pen safely tucked inside, was where I had left it.

The video from the ink pen was enough to get a confession from Melissa. She had recognized the sheriff at a dogfight earlier in the year and had been blackmailing him. He did what he could do to stifle investigations of dog fighting along the lakeshore. When Melissa realized he had helped me escape, she shot him. She also confessed to shooting Mike, but claimed self-defense in the shooting of Vic Tabor. It didn't really matter. She would be spending the rest of her life in prison.

I questioned how a woman could become so cold-blooded as to be involved in dog fighting. Jason said her only defense was that she was raised in Chicago and saw her first dog fight when she was just a kid. She couldn't remember how young she was when her dad started taking her to fights. Melissa's mother moved to northern Michigan with Melissa to escape the big city violence, but it was years too late for her daughter. Melissa had already become desensitized to the brutality of dog fighting and apparently had little regard for life, be it animal or human.

Against his better judgment, the vet who came out to examine Diesel and Nitro didn't euthanize them. Instead, he took them to his clinic for treatment. When Melissa pled guilty she forfeited her dog.

They also found several pit bulls chained behind Melissa's pole barn. She indeed had a kennel, but it wasn't for boarding or rescue. I called Rocky about the dogs, and he was willing to be part of the team of animal behaviorists and trainers who would evaluate all of the dogs. Nobody in Vic's family came forward to claim Diesel, so he also belonged to the county and would be evaluated.

Red must have belonged to her and now we understood why the dog feared women.

One phone call that I enjoyed making was to Kevin Palmer. He was pleased to hear that his visit to the sheriff had catapulted the investigation, but was saddened to learn of the loss of life. "Hopefully this is the end of dog fighting around here," he said.

I couldn't have agreed with him more.

The night before Cooper had to head back to California, we went for one last horseback ride along the river. We tied the horses up and sat on the riverbank. It reminded me of the summer we first met.

"I forgot how beautiful it is here," he said. The fall colors were almost at their peak with the leaves an eclectic mix of greens, reds, yellows and oranges.

"I know. That's one of the reasons I've decided to stay here."

"And what are the other reasons?"

"To be with Grams. When she's gone, I'll stay. Where could I go with six dogs, I don't know how many cats, three horses and soon to be two cows? And maybe two pit bulls."

"You really want those dogs?"

"I do. I owe it to Mike. He gave his life for those dogs. If it's at all possible, I'd like to see those two dogs become friends."

"You've come a long ways."

"Why do you say that?"

"Look at what you're doing. You saved the life of a pregnant cow and risked your life to find out who was fighting dogs. I'd say you could consider yourself a member of the Animal Liberation League."

"That wasn't my goal."

"I know, but ALL needs people like you. And look, you're real close to being part of the elite membership of Save Five. You have three of five: You've saved dogs who were abused for entertainment; you saved Kal and Blue from research; and you rescued Bessie from a factory farm. All you have left to tackle is the fur industry and hunting."

"Like I said, not my goal. But tell me this: Where do all those rescued animals go? To a farm like this one, maybe? Why aren't you willing to move here and help me start a sanctuary?"

"I am."

I turned to him. "Did I hear you right?"

"You did. I've been a fool. As soon as I'm off probation, I'm here. I hope you'll wait for me."

"You know I will."

More Than a Number is a work of fiction, but a few of the organizations mentioned in the story are real. Following is information from those groups. Also included is information about pet trusts, trap-neuter-return and pit bulls.

SASHA Farm

SASHA Farm is the Midwest's largest farm animal sanctuary. At our shelter, not only do we provide food and water, veterinary care and a roof over their heads, we also give the animal residents affection, social interaction with others of their own species, and a sense of security.

SASHA's founders, Dorothy Davies and Monte Jackson, started saving animals a couple decades ago. Among the first bunch was a nine-month-old pet shop puppy that a family had purchased, but couldn't appropriately care for. A female Border Collie/Spaniel mix with a white tip on the end of her tail, she quickly worked her way into Monte's and Dorothy's hearts. She was the farm dog in charge of it all, keeping tabs on every other animal that came to live at the farm over the years.

Sasha was a wonderful canine companion, a true friend, who lived and loved for 17 years. In honor and in memory of this beloved dog, her caretakers chose to name their sanctuary SASHA Farm. The name SASHA is also an acronym for the animal rescue operation - Sanctuary And Safe Haven for Animals.

The sanctuary currently shelters over 200 animals, each with its own story to tell. Some were dumped and discarded, some left to die. They have come from unhappy circumstances, often mistreated or neglected, but now have a safe, permanent home at SASHA Farm.

As you can see, rescuing and protecting animals has been an important mission for us for many years, and our sanctuary finally became a non-profit 501(c)(3) organization in 2001. Donations made to SASHA Farm are tax deductible, and all donations are used to ensure good quality care for our animals, both now and into the future.

SASHA Farm Animal Sanctuary
PO Box 222, Manchester, MI 48158
www.sashafarm.org
info@sashafarm.org
(734) 428-9617

Michigan Pet Trusts
Are you a pet owner in Michigan?

Do any of your closest friends have feathers, fins or fur? Are you responsible for their room, board and ongoing veterinarian care?

Consider this, if something untoward were to happen to you today what would happen to your feathered, finned or furred friends tomorrow? What arrangements have you made for these friends?

A pet trust may be created under a Last Will and Testament, a revocable living trust or even as a stand-alone revocable or irrevocable trust. Regardless of which trust you ultimately choose, make sure you set aside an appropriate amount of property to fund your pet trust - this will be essential to its success. For example, a horse not only eats like a horse, but has an average life expectancy of 25 to 40 years. By contrast, a cat or dog has a much smaller appetite and a shorter life expectancy. Accordingly, you would want to set aside a larger amount of money from your nest egg to fund the future care of a horse than for a cat or dog. Also, your pet trust should give specific details to your trustee and caretaker about your friend. From favorite daily rituals like walks and feeding, to how your friends seek shelter away from the annual POP POP POP of the neighborhood 4th of July fireworks.

In the end, your pet has been a loyal companion and friend. Unfortunately, if you have no plan, then their future care is simply being left to chance.

We can help you protect everyone you love and everything you have. There are three easy ways to schedule your initial consultation. First, give us a call at 616-682-5574. Second, send us an email. Or third, request a consultation through our online form.

The West Michigan Estate Planning Center
Cottrell & Jacobs PLC
Charles E. Cottrell, Attorney at Law
6739 Fulton E., Suite A-10
Ada, Michigan 49301

616-682-5574 or 888-878-7658
info@cottrelljacobs.com
www.westmichiganestateplanningcenter.com

If you don't live in Michigan, contact an estate-planning attorney in your state who does pet planning.

The Story of Reuben's Room Cat Rescue

Rumor has it that the term 'crazy cat lady' is a direct result of Jeanine Buckner and her crazy love for cats. Jeanine has always been a cat lover, and for years she dreamed of opening her own cat rescue. Finally, after years of encouragement from friends, and some wonderful people who promised to help her and volunteer as often as they could, Reuben's Room Cat Rescue was born.

As a vet assistant, Jeanine saw first hand that the older a cat got, the less likely it would be adopted. Jeanine also noticed how companion cats improved the lives of older people. When Jeanine started Reuben's Room there were no rescues that dealt with re-homing older domesticated cats. There were also no rescues eager to work with senior citizens. Reuben's Room was founded to fill both those needs.

Reuben's Room is an all-volunteer rescue and no-kill sanctuary located in Grand Rapids, Michigan. It is a 501 (c) (3) non-profit organization.

Reuben's Room has cats of all ages residing at the rescue, but there are always several cats who would make a perfect companion for a senior. Jeanine truly enjoys matching the right personality of one of her cats to the personality of a senior who wants to adopt.

Thanks to Reuben's Room's *Worry Free Adoption for Seniors*, Jeanine does not have to consider age when determining an adoption application. In fact, Reuben's Room has placed cats with seniors over 100 years old. When the senior can no longer provide a home for the cat, it comes back to Reuben's Room. Thus, the senior can adopt a cat and not have to worry about what-if. Reuben's Room offers them the security of knowing their cat will always have a loving place to go. Once a Reuben's Room cat, always a Reuben's Room cat. Any cat adopted from the rescue is welcomed back at any time, for any reason.

For years Jeanine Buckner dreamed of starting a cat rescue complete with a sanctuary for cats who are not candidates for adoption. A rescue that would re-home the domesticated cats that other rescues would not accept, and make it possible for a senior citizen to have just the right cat to keep them company. That dream became Reuben's Room Cat Rescue.

Reuben's Room Cat Rescue
P.O. Box 140201
Grand Rapids, MI 49514-0201
www.reubensroom.petfinder.com
Jeanine Buckner, (616) 791-9696

Heaven Can Wait Animal Haven

Founded in 2008, Heaven Can Wait Animal Haven is a non-profit organization dedicated to helping the homeless, abandoned and stray cats of West Michigan. Heaven Can Wait Animal Haven started by providing transport for dogs and cats to a low-cost spay/neuter clinic for pet owners who could not afford to have these services provided by a veterinarian. We knew the root of the overpopulation problem and subsequent euthanasia was due to the lack of access to low-cost spay and neuter, and we were positive we could make an immediate impact with the transport.

Eventually, a low-cost clinic was opened in our area and we shifted our focus to cats and kittens. We are a foster-based rescue and currently adopt between 500-600 cats and kittens each year. Each cat and kitten is spayed or neutered *before* adoption and microchipped, two very important lifesaving procedures.

We are especially proud that we could play a major role in reducing the number of cats in Muskegon County because of our partnership with Pound Buddies Animal Shelter. We communicate on an almost daily basis and help when they are overcrowded.

Our mission has expanded and we have become involved in rescue situations that involve significant numbers of unattended and neglected cats. In October 2013 we were notified by animal control that 25 cats were living in a mobile home in hoarding conditions. It turned out to be 92 cats. We have had several cases with similar numbers since then. We receive much support from other rescues, the public and grants from various sources.

The control of the pet population is a massive task that will not be solved quickly or easily, but every long journey begins one step at a time, and we encourage every pet owner in West Michigan to take advantage of the low-cost spay/ neuter clinics. Only through spay and neuter will we ever solve this problem.

Diane Valk
Stephanie Woods
Lisa Westerburg

Heaven Can Wait
P.O. Box 23, Ferrysburg, MI 49409
(231) 737-5644
heavencanwaitmuskegon@gmail.com
www.petfinder.com/shelters/MI678.html
www.AdoptaPet.com/shelter83069-cats.html

Carol's Ferals

Our Mission: To end feline overpopulation in West Michigan through community education and empowerment.

Our Vision: A future where every cat is valued and cared for.

What We Do: Based in Grand Rapids, Michigan, Carol's Ferals assists community cat caregivers with TNR and support services. Cats are accepted three nights weekly and are spayed/neutered, treated for fleas, parasites and ear-tipped for easy identification. If desired, cats can be vaccinated or tested for infectious feline disease. Sick or injured cats are treated and returned when in the best interest of the cat and feline population. Carol's Ferals also does adoption of friendly cats and kittens obtained through our TNR program. Carol's Ferals is a 501(c)3 organization, run by volunteers and funded by donors.

What is Trap-Neuter-Return (TNR)?

TNR is a non-lethal, three-step method to reduce the number of feral and stray cats both immediately and long term.

Step 1 – Trap: Feral or stray cats are trapped using a humane live-trap.

Step 2 – Neuter: Trapped cats are spayed or neutered by a veterinarian.

Step 3 – Return: Fixed cats are returned to their home.

Benefits to the Community: TNR helps the community by stabilizing the population of the feral colony and, over time, reduces it. Spay/neutered cats cease behaviors that instigate complaints by people. Neutered males have no desire to mark their territory, so they stop spraying. Females never go into heat, so the yowling created by mating no longer occurs. Male cats stop fighting because there are no females in heat to fight over, and neutered males have no desire to mate even if a female in heat is in the area. The practice of TNR enables feral and outdoor cats to live their lives without adding to the overpopulation of homeless cats. The strain on local shelters and rescues is reduced by lowering the number of cats and kittens who flow into their doors. The euthanasia rate for cats at shelters drops when there are fewer ferals because the lack of stray cats and kittens means less competition for spots in adoptive homes.

Benefits to the Cats: Spay/neutered outdoor cats live healthier lives than unaltered cats. Outdoor cats who have been sterilized and live in a colony with a caretaker have longer lifes than unmanaged outdoor cats.

Carol's Ferals
www.carolsferals.org
info@carolsferals.org

Wild Horse Sanctuary

Rather than allow 80 wild horses living on public land to be destroyed, the founders of the Wild Horse Sanctuary made a major life decision to rescue these unwanted horses and create a safe home for them. And just as quickly, they launched a media campaign to bring attention to the plight of these and hundreds of other wild horses across the west that eventually led to a national moratorium on killing un-adoptable wild horses.

Our Mission: To protect and preserve America's wild horses as a "living national treasure" in a publicly accessible and ecologically balanced environment with other wildlife for future generations.

Our Goals: Increase public awareness of the genetic, biological, and social value of America's wild horses through pack trips on the sanctuary, publications, mass media, and public outreach programs. Continue to develop a working, replicable model for the proper and responsible management of wild horses in their natural habitat. Demonstrate that wild horses can co-exist on the open range in ecological balance with many diverse species of wildlife, including black bear, bobcat, mountain lion, wild turkeys, badger, and gray fox. Collaborate with research projects in order to document the intricate and unique social structure, biology, reversible fertility control, and native intelligence of the wild horse.

Our Programs: The Wild Horse Sanctuary is a non-profit, tax-exempt public foundation with a 5,000 acre preserve dedicated to the protection and preservation of America's wild horses. It is currently supported by contributions from individuals and organizations. The Wild Horse Sanctuary conducts pack trips; develops public education programs; sponsors "resistance free" horse training seminars; participates in research projects on ecologically sound wild horse management; consults on related programs in order to help build other wildlife preserves; and cooperates with responsible ecology, animal protection, and educational organizations to further the protection of all species of wildlife, including America's wild horses, and the preservation of our natural environment.

Wild Horse Sanctuary
www.wildhorsesanctuary.org
Physical Address: 5796 Wilson Hill Road, Shingletown, CA 96088
Mailing Address: P.O. Box 30, Shingletown, CA
(530)474-5770

Pit Bull Cruelty

In recent years, pit bulls have gained more than just a foothold in public awareness. Unscrupulous breeding and negative media attention have resulted in many apartment complexes, neighborhoods and even counties imposing bans on pits and pit mixes, citing them as "inherently dangerous" to the public.

Pit bulls can attract the worst kind of dog owners—people who are only interested in these dogs for fighting or protection. While pit bulls were once considered especially non-aggressive to people, their reputation has changed, thanks to unscrupulous breeders and irresponsible owners. And because the pit bull population has increased so rapidly, shelters now struggle to deal with an overflow of image-plagued, hard-to-place dogs.

Pit bulls are descendants of the original English bull-baiting dog—a dog that was bred to bite and hold bulls, bears and other large animals around the face and head. When baiting large animals was banned in the 1800s, people then started to fight their dogs against each other instead. As the "sport" of dog fighting developed, enthusiasts bred a lighter, more athletic canine. These dogs made their way to North America, the ancestors of today's pit bulls. Pit bulls that were not used for fighting were considered ideal family pets—affectionate, loyal and gentle with children. Serious problems started when these dogs gained the attention of people looking for a macho dog—and to meet their demands, unscrupulous and uncaring breeders are producing puppies that were not only aggressive to other dogs, but also to people.

Although a felony offense in all 50 states, organized dog fights still take place in many parts of the country.

Dogs that fight are bred and conditioned to never give up when they are fighting, even if it means that they will be badly hurt or killed. Other animals are victims of dog fights, too—it's not uncommon for trainers to encourage their dogs' aggression by using other dogs and smaller animals such as cats, rabbits and rodents as bait.

Participants and promoters come from every community and all backgrounds, with audiences including lawyers, judges and teachers and other upstanding community leaders.

In recent decades, fights have become informal street corner and playground activities. Many people who participate in these fights lack even a semblance of respect for the animals, often starving and beating them to encourage aggressive behavior.

Source: www.aspca.org